The Chinese Boy

An Orphan Child Raised in a California Gold Rush Town

Kevin Knauss

ISBN: 979-8-9851942-0-3

Library of Congress Control Number: 2024910655

DEDICATION

To mothers and fathers

Contents

Acknowledgments

Imagined and written by Kevin Knauss

Editing assistance provided by Bonnie Osborn

All images from author's collection

1 The Delivery

The only sound to be heard was the irregular swing of the clock pendulum as it struggled to keep time. Ruth Anne focused on the sound as she lay in bed. Her husband had failed to adjust the clock so the pendulum would swing evenly, creating a monotonous tick-tock that fades into the background.

Because the clock could not be set in beat, when it rang 3 o'clock by striking the tiny bell within the case, Ruth Anne knew it was later. The clock ran slow. Even with the odd swing of the pendulum and the chiming of the clock bell, the morning was unusually quiet. Little more than a large shed, their home was what, to most of their neighbors, passed for a house. It was not a house to Ruth Anne. It was a cabin.

The house, or cabin, let in every smell and sound within a mile. Now, the absence of any sound was almost alarming to Ruth Anne. She arose from the bed she shared with her husband to look through the window. Instead of pausing to enjoy the quiet morning, she had to know why there was no sound of trees rustling in the wind or horses stomping over the dirt road. If it was quiet outside, at least that meant no animals or humans were rooting around the town, and that was a good thing.

On this dark winter morning, Ruth Anne spied through the window, trying to figure out why there was no sound. But before she could open the curtain, she noticed a glow seeping around the fabric, almost as if someone had placed a candle outside the window. The light bent around the curtains like smoke from a campfire curling around a person's body.

Pushing the curtain aside, she saw that the landscape was white. Still somewhat drowsy from sleep, Ruth Anne was frightened. Was the white brilliance something foretold in the Book of Revelations? Was some sort of disaster befalling her and her husband? The offbeat swing of the clock pendulum brought her back to reality. The white layer upon the ground and trees must be snow.

In an instant, her demeanor changed from dread of the apocalypse to the joy of a young girl. No one had told her that this small foothill community she and her husband had just moved to could receive snow. Maybe, just maybe, California was not so foreign. Maybe, this little gold mining town was similar to her home in Massachusetts, where it snowed.

She immediately put on her coat and shoes and went outside to experience the snow fall and be a little girl again. Outside the house, the silence was even more complete. The snow absorbed the smallest sounds made by birds, water, or humans. There was no wind. All the storm clouds had quietly vacated the area. The air was still and quiet.

Ruth Anne felt like she had been transported to another world. The new-fallen snow covered all the ugliness of the town. It was the residents who created the unsightly landscape. Half-finished cabins, lean-to sheds, mining scars, and large piles of rocks tossed carelessly aside by men obsessed with finding a few flakes of gold, littered the landscape. All the detritus of human existence, driven by the wild fixation for gold, was now softly covered with snow.

The moon was high in the dark night sky. The air was warm, or it felt warm, with no wind. The only noise was the sound of Ruth Anne's shoes compressing the snow underfoot with crunches and squeaks. All the flimsy, ragtag cabins scattered across the hillside were veiled in the shining snow. For Ruth Anne, it was a pleasant walk, a brief escape from the disappointment of having been brought to this isolated community.

For now, the hot, dusty mining community her husband had moved her to six months earlier disappeared under a more appealing landscape of quiet snow. Ruth Anne walked through the new, snow-frosted town that she knew would not last. She walked down the main road to where the oak groves began. The edge of civilization. She wandered, looking at the trees, at the mounds of mine tailings covered in snow, through towering gray pines, until she came to the meadow. From the meadow, she followed a trail that led down to the river. Even the normal rush of the river was muffled by the snow-covered landscape.

Across the meadow she was met with another visual surprise: a beautiful blue bush. It took Ruth Anne a moment to realize the blue bush was moving. Then it stopped. Ruth Anne stared at a woman with long black hair wearing a blue coat. Another woman awakened by the quiet of the snow, out for a walk exploring the alien landscape, she thought. Ruth Anne tried to suppress a smile at meeting a fellow enchanted wanderer.

As Ruth Anne began to raise her hand in a welcoming motion, the woman with black hair and blue coat bowed her head and kept walking up the trail. Carrolton was a small mining town, and Ruth Anne had thus far found it difficult to make friends or acquaintances among the other women. The woman with black hair and blue coat offered a fleeting chance to make a friend in an otherwise friendless town.

The urge to follow the woman with black hair and blue coat was strong. Ruth Anne remembered being told that beyond the meadow lay uncivilized territory. On the other side of the meadow were Indians and Chinese, a danger to white women. Ruth Anne stopped, straining to see where the woman had disappeared to in the darkness, and then slowly turned around and returned to the cabin.

After a short slumber dreaming of a land she did not live in, Ruth Anne woke up to find Caleb, her husband, rustling around in the dark, trying to light the lamp. Ruth Anne pulled herself out of the small bed and started to go through the motions of getting Caleb's breakfast. With the stove stoked with fresh wood, she went outside to get water to make coffee.

The snow was already beginning to melt. Patches of brown earth were growing as the snow evaporated from the landscape. While the snow was disappearing, the town still seemed quieter than usual. Ruth Anne looked to the south in the early morning glow of the rising sun and saw that Silva's waterwheel was not moving.

The waterwheel, placed in the water ditch that ran above the town, always made a creaking and moaning noise. like someone was slowly dying, over and over again. Ruth Anne found no water in the little well they had dug behind the cabin house, which was fed by the water ditch. She was not surprised, as the ground was so porous that the well water would quickly seep into the sand and gravel of the earth.

Ruth Anne walked up the hill to the water ditch and was about to dip her pot into the canal when she saw that it was empty. No water was flowing. She went back to Caleb and informed him that the ditch was dry.

"Oh, no, not today, not Sunday," Caleb sighed, with an air of resignation and irritation. Caleb was a Water Agent for the Valley Springs Water

Company, which built and maintained the ditch. Even though his primary job was to sell the water and collect the money from customers, when the ditch failed, all the men of the company were called to repair it.

This Sunday was special because the traveling Methodist minister was in town to hold a Sunday church service. The minister visited the town every four or five weeks. The church service was just not a religious event, it was social; it was entertainment for the townsfolk. Most people who were sober enough meandered to the saloon for Sunday services.

Church service was held in the largest building in the town, which happened to be one of the saloons. Regardless of one's brand of Christian religion, atheists included, the social gathering provided a strong attraction to attend a church service. Seated on the wooden benches, chairs, and stools inside the saloon would be Methodists, Episcopalians, Baptists, Quakers, and Roman Catholics, along with anyone else who wanted a little hope instilled in their life.

In addition to the collection of different religions represented, the saloon before the service would sound like the Tower of Babel. Ruth Anne had been surprised to learn that this little town Caleb brought her to was comprised mainly of European and Chinese immigrants. While the Chinese immigrants did not attend the church service, people from France, Germany, Ireland, England, Spain, Portugal, and Scotland were present.

All were speaking in their native tongues or talking in thick dialects as they conversed within their little clans. Ruth Anne found it difficult to understand most of the townspeople when they greeted her and tried to make small talk. Between the broken English, foreign idioms, and the European dialects, Ruth Anne, when spoken to, often replied with a blank look.

For instance, when Mrs. Elliot, a native of Scotland, said her sister had a new bairn, Ruth Anne could not fathom why the woman would have a new barn. What was wrong with her old barn? How was a new barn relevant to Ruth Anne? Was the barn special? Seeing Ruth Anne's blank stare and partially opened mouth, Mrs. Elliot realized that Ruth Anne did not understand. Mrs. Elliot then folded her arms as if holding a baby and swayed back and forth. Ruth Anne immediately figured out that bairn was Scottish for baby.

Caleb always enjoyed the Sunday services. Ruth Anne was less enthusiastic. For her, the gathering was like attending a High Mass Eucharist spoken in Latin: She could follow along with the service, but had no idea what the bells, smoke, and foreign words meant. The Carrolton mass Sunday service was a jumble of noises, smoke, and foreign languages for Ruth Anne.

What she did appreciate, and the irony was not lost on her, were the words of the Methodist minister espousing abstinence from alcohol - while holding a holy service in a saloon. The image almost put a smile on her face. Since arriving in Carrolton, she was struck by the level of alcohol consumption by the populace. The rampant alcohol abuse converted normally content and focused men into wild animals. Fights, stabbings, and the occasional shooting were not unheard of at any one of the town's saloons catering to men growing old and weary with the arduous work of distilling a pinch of gold dust from tons of earth.

Caleb had arrived in the California gold fields late in 1849, when the mining community was younger, and a shared sense of mission and adventure smoothed over many disagreements. Now, the comradery of the old days - only 10 years past - had faded. With a little whisky imbibed, old insults and trespasses were resurrected by the aging men, until only violence could resolve the ancient issues.

After working in the mines for several years, Caleb returned to Massachusetts. He had not struck it rich nor become fabulously wealthy, as had some men who had either struck gold or launched a mercantile business. However, while not having made his fortune, Caleb returned to his North Adams home with more money than he had when he left. A greater treasure for Caleb was the adventure and the wonderous state of California.

Pity the poor soul who was cornered by Caleb and had to listen to his endless stories of gold mining, traversing California, and the state's bright future. One of those people he cornered, at a church social one evening, was Ruth Anne. Caleb was 10 years older than Ruth Anne, and she was intrigued at having the attention of an older man.

Ruth Anne's future was uncertain in North Adams. At 22 years of age and living at the home of her father, it was assumed that Ruth Anne would become her father's permanent caretaker. Her sisters and brothers were still in the western Massachusetts region pursuing their own lives. Ruth Anne had no prospects of a future until the day Caleb Gibbons walked into her life.

Now Caleb put on his leather overcoat and began the trek to discover the source of the water ditch break. He walked along next to the ditch, noting the snow on the bottom, which told him the water had been out for several hours. A mile up the ditch Caleb came to Jonah's cabin. Jonah was the ditch tender, whose responsibility it was to walk the ditch at night looking for weak spots and breaks.

"Jonah," Caleb hollered, but received no response. Caleb pounded on the door to the cabin, which looked like it could collapse with a stiff wind. The door creaked open, and Caleb saw Jonah fast asleep on his straw bed. "Jonah," Caleb hollered again. "Get up, we got a big break on the ditch." Jonah, roused from sleep, haphazardly pulled on his pants, shirt, and overcoat.

As Caleb looked around the shack, he saw a half-empty bottle of whiskey and no food stuffs. This is what Jonah's life had devolved into, by choice, providing him with a level of contentment. Jonah and Caleb had worked in the same mining company back in '51. At the end of the season, the company had mined $14,000 in gold from the river. With 14 members in the company, no one left a rich man.

The mining company then transformed itself into a water company. The company built a dam on the river 15 miles upstream and diverted part of the river flow into the ditch. Caleb, not interested in leaving California with his modest gold earnings at that moment, signed on to the company, buying shares in the new Valley Springs Water Company. His next job was helping dig the ditch.

The plan for the water ditch was to begin it at a dam a couple miles upriver, above Bretton Falls down to the town of Quartz Hill. The water ditch itself was to resemble a trapezoid: 6 to 8 feet across the top, sides of 4 to 5 feet in height, with bottom 3 to 4 wide. Since the ditch mainly ran in the river canyon, one side would be the steep slope of the foothills. The side next to the river would have dirt thrown up and reinforced with rocks. The slope of the ditch was to be approximately 3 to 4 feet of drop per mile.

Of course, there was the design of the water ditch, and there was the reality of an uneven and diverse foothill terrain within a river canyon. To span some of the deep ravines where creeks fed into the river, the company had to build several elevated wooden flumes. Where the slate or granite bedrock intruded into the line of the ditch, alternate designs were employed, such as a narrower, deeper ditch to handle the water flow.

By 1854 the water ditch was finished, and Caleb watched as the water was released into the ditch and flowing all the way down to Quartz Hill. He felt an overwhelming sense of accomplishment. Gold mining was a short, adventurous endeavor. With his participation in this unprecedented water project in the new state of California, Caleb sensed he had left a little scratch on the map and history of California. It was time to return home to North Adams.

Five years later after his return home to Massachusetts, Caleb found himself back in California, walking along a dry ditch, in the middle of winter with an old mining partner, Jonah. While Caleb had taken his gold earnings and invested in the Valley Springs Water Company, Jonah drank and gambled his money away. Jonah could have returned home to his native Pennsylvania. He preferred the freedom of California.

In California, there was no family to answer to. There were no rules or restraints on his behavior or habits. There was no church to cast a disapproving glance upon his lifestyle. There was little government and even less law enforcement in California. For Jonah, who was inclined to a leisurely lifestyle, California seemed to fit him like an old pair of boots.

Jonah, in order to sustain his life of leisure, took up the relatively easy job of ditch tender for the Valley Springs ditch. Most of his time was spent opening and closing the water box connections for customers. He also did some light maintenance. The most important part of Jonah's ditch tender duties was to walk the ditch looking for weak spots and turning out the water when the inevitable break occurred. Caleb couldn't help but wonder if Jonah had been doing his job last night or sleeping off a date with his whisky bottle.

As the two men strode atop the ditch bank searching for the elusive break,

Caleb remembered working on this part of the ditch. It was a difficult patch, as towering granite boulders dotted the hillside, like worn thumbs sticking out of the ground. As the men rounded a corner, they came upon the break in the ditch bank. There was also a gaggle of men frantically trying to rebuild the ditch bank.

One of those granite boulders, 20 feet above the ditch, had broken free, tumbled down the hillside, smashed into the ditch bank and rolled down toward the river. From the moment the boulder landed on the ditch bank, it probably had taken no more than half an hour for the water to slowly seep through the earth and spill toward the river. Shortly after the seepage started, the whole earthen bank had dissolved. There was now a 20-foot opening in the ditch wall, spilling thousands of gallons of water per minute – money and profits rolling down the hillside as they watched.

As Caleb traced the course of the granite boulder from its perch, through the ditch and down to the river, he could see it had smashed through a miner's cabin. A group of Chinese men had formed a mining company and were working the area for gold. Even as some of the Chinese men worked frenetically to stem the flow of water out of the ditch, some of their comrades had taken the opportunity to shovel the dissolved ditch bank into their sluice. An easy opportunity to find some gold, courtesy of the rolling granite boulder.

With no water in the ditch, the Chinese men were carrying buckets of water from the river to wash the dirt in the sluice. As Caleb surveyed the surreal scene of ditch repair and gold mining occupying the same space and time, he heard one of the Chinese men holler, "He's dead, he's dead." The sun had not come up over the hills yet, and Caleb could barely make out a Chinese man pointing to the smashed miner's cabin, yelling, "He's dead."

Caleb and Jonah tumbled down the steep hillside to the smashed cabin, where the giant granite boulder had lost its momentum and ceased to roll any further. They lifted the door to the cabin and peered inside to see a Chinese man lying in a pool of water. It was unclear if the boulder had killed the man, if he had drowned from the ditch's gush of water, or if it had been a combination of the two.

"There is nothing we can do for him now," mumbled Caleb. "Jonah, go up to the waste gate at Rattlesnake Point and turn the water out of the ditch. We can't fix the ditch with this much water flowing." Caleb grew irritated watching Jonah amble up the path with any lack of urgency. He next turned his attention to the circus of Chinese men working to repair the ditch.

Before Caleb could give any instructions, one of the Chinese men rose from moving rocks and declared, "We get paid for this work." Caleb replied, "Sure."

While Caleb paid white men about $1.50 per day, the Chinese men would accept $0.75 per day, and less if it was a gang of men. Since there were no white men within shouting distance of the ditch break, Caleb felt it was expedient and economically beneficial to let the Chinese men repair the break.

When Caleb left California in 1855, the region was just beginning to see the full tidal wave of Chinese immigration. When he returned with Ruth Anne and took the job as a Water Agent, a third of the population in the lower mining region along the river were Chinese men. Another third were European immigrants, and the remainder of the residents had migrated from the East Coast. It was a crazy mix of people from all over the world.

The Chinese miners were working claims that white men had abandoned because of their low yields of gold dust. These new Chinese miners paid for the privilege of working night and day in near-poverty conditions. Not only did they pay the original white claim owners for the right to mine the ground, but they also had to pay a foreign miner's tax collected by the county Sheriff. How the Chinese survived was anybody's guess.

Consequently, the Chinese immigrants were always looking for opportunities to earn a little extra money. There was no denying the Chinese work ethic, even at such low wages. Caleb had hired Chinese men on numerous occasions to clean the ditch, shore up the bank, build rock retaining walls, and, in emergency situations, repair a ditch failure like this one.

While Caleb knew many of the Chinese men by their first names, he really did not understand or relate to them personally. He did not know the man who had perished under the weight of the runaway boulder. The Chinese laborers were economic inputs into the system of managing and maintaining a water system. And yet they were also some of Caleb's best water customers. Rarely were they late paying for their water when he traveled around to collect the payments.

As Caleb traveled along his route selling water and serving as a field manager for the water ditch, the Chinese began calling him the waterman. Along whole sections of the river all the miners were Chinese companies, paying the same rate for the water, $1 a miner's inch, as the white miners. As white men left the mining occupation for steady pay in urban environments, the steady water payment collections from the Chinese miners, combined with the lower wages they received for working on the ditch, was helping the Valley Springs Water Company stay in the black.

Caleb did not know how the Chinese men would handle the dead man's body. His sole focus was getting the break fixed. The repairs would take all day with Caleb and Jonah working next to the Chinese men to rebuild the bank. When their work, which was a temporary patch, looked like it would hold, Caleb told Jonah to go back up to Rattlesnake Point and turn the water back into the ditch. Then Jonah was to return and remain at the break site through the night to watch for any seepage, until Caleb could send up another crew to reinforce the bank with a proper retaining wall of rocks.

Weary, hungry, and tired, Caleb pulled on his coat and turned to walk back home. From a distance he heard a Chinese man calling, "Hey, waterman, waterman, stop." Caleb looked over his shoulder to see the mining camp's cook running toward him holding a large bundle. Quickly, Caleb began to think how he could graciously decline the cook's offering of some odd Chinese meal of vegetables or rice. But before Caleb could speak, the cook said, "Waterman, here, baby cannot stay here."

Suddenly, Caleb was holding a Chinese baby, a gash surrounded by dried blood visible on its forehead. Caleb reached to hand the dead baby back to the cook when the baby cried. Oh, God, it was alive. "Where is the mother?" Caleb asked. The cook shrugged and said, "Maybe dead, too." Caleb wondered if the mother had also been in the destroyed cabin and had somehow stumbled down to the river and drowned. He scanned the water in the fading light of the day but saw no body floating in the shallow water and rapids below the camp.

As Caleb was struggling to communicate with the cook, who was more interested in getting back to his duties, one of the Chinese men, named Ah Kong, spoke up. Ah Kong told Caleb that the baby's mother had left in the night. He pantomimed that Ah Wan, the dead man in the cabin, and the woman had fought, and the woman left some time last night.

The first time Caleb left the East Coast for California, he had to endure a brutal two-month sea voyage to Mexico. Following a disastrous decision to walk from Mexico to the California gold fields, Caleb and other members of his mining company found themselves engulfed in a vast desert with no water. He watched men perish along the trail, killed by lack of water. By some divine intervention, after he had been injured, a Mexican family had let him rest for several weeks with them while he recovered from his near-death experience.

Eventually, Caleb arrived in the gold fields of California in the autumn of 1849, eight months after starting his big adventure. Despite surviving all the perils of sea, land, fever, diarrhea, and injuries, Caleb was lost on what to do with a baby. Possibly because he was so tired, he resigned himself to the bestowed burden of carrying the injured child back home. Surely, Ruth Anne, a woman, would know what to with it.

Caleb fashioned a support for the baby using his suspenders and tightening his leather coat. If carrying a 15-pound baby below his chest and the ensuing enormous ache in the middle of his back, resembled what a woman went through when pregnant, he was happy to be a man. It was a long, slow walk back to the cabin. When he occasionally stumbled over a rock in the dark, the baby emitted a crying sound. He figured by the time he arrived home the child might be dead either from the gash on its head or frozen from the cold night air.

When Caleb stumbled through the door, Ruth Anne thought he had been in a fight the way he was stooped over. "Ruth Anne, help," groaned Caleb. He unbuttoned his jacket, released the improvised baby carrier, and handed the child to Ruth Anne. "Oh, my gosh, this baby is hurt," she said.

As Ruth Anne got some water and a rag to clean the baby's head wound, she turned to Caleb and asked, "What's his name?" Caleb's only response was an expressionless blank stare.

"Name?" Caleb thought to himself. He comes home with an injured baby, and Ruth Anne's first question was what his name was! Who knew what his name was? Did Chinese even name their children? he wondered through his foggy mind.

How did Ruth Anne even know the baby was a boy?

"How do you know it's a boy and not a girl?" he asked her. Ruth Anne returned his blank stare with her own. "You are tired, rest. I'll clean up the child and get you some food."

The young men of 1849, eager to get to California and begin their success stories, could never have contemplated being handed a baby to care for. It was never in Ruth Anne's California vision that she would be handed a Chinese baby boy and asked to mother it. It was not part of the California narrative that orphaned babies represented an opportunity.

2 Massachusetts to California

When Caleb and Ruth Anne first met back in North Adams, it was apparent to Ruth Anne that Caleb was in love with California. He would talk for hours about the clear dry air, the beautiful sunsets, the rushing rivers coming out of the Sierras, and how the land was full of opportunity. California was a blank canvass on which one could paint a life, full of color and depth.

In hindsight, encouraging Caleb to talk about California and how he would build a West Coast life if he returned was probably not the best strategy. But Ruth Anne was so enthralled with a man taking an interest in her she prompted Caleb to relive his California experience and future dreams. Caleb, on the other hand, took Ruth Anne's encouragement to discuss the opportunities of California as evidence of her interest in moving there.

When Caleb asked Ruth Anne to marry him, his proposal came with the caveat that they move to his dreamland of California, site of so many youthful adventures, and of his future family with Ruth Anne. Somewhat stunned at the prospect of leaving North Adams, Ruth Anne also was intrigued by a life not tied to caring for her father. She was not impulsive. By contrast, Caleb was a vortex of energy, an incredible intense weather system when it came to California. Ruth Anne found herself swept up into the stream of Caleb's obsession to return to California.

Ruth Anne was the youngest of five children. The oldest two, more than 15 years older than Ruth Anne, were half-brothers from her father's first marriage. After his first wife died, her father married the young schoolteacher in town and had three more children. Ruth Anne's mother died when she was 10 years old. Her older sisters helped raise her and care for her father until they married, leaving Ruth Anne behind to be the primary housekeeper and cook for her father.

Hers was not an ambitious family. Her father worked in a marble mill processing stone quarried near the town. The family was not rich, but neither were they destitute, simple in their habits and dress.

After an internal struggle that lasted several months, Ruth Anne agreed to marry Caleb. She told her father their sojourn in California would be only for a couple years.

Their wedding, like Ruth Anne, was a simple affair. North Adams was not a town where any wealth was flaunted but a modest community. Because Ruth Anne had never really traveled or lived in any large urban environment, she never had any reason to be self-conscious about her appearance or dress. Everyone in North Adams was a friend. It was not until Ruth Anne and Caleb traveled to Boston to board a steam ship to California that Ruth Anne became aware of her relative plainness.

As Ruth Anne and Caleb prepared to board the steam ship, Ruth Anne saw dozens of women wearing fancy dresses trimmed in lace. The dresses were voluminous, expanded by the crinoline cages supporting the fabric from beneath. As the crowd slowly pressed up the boarding plank, Ruth Anne studied the gloves and hats of the other women, and the soft curls framing their finely featured faces. By contrast, Ruth Anne's hair was pulled back in a bun, and she wore a plain grey dress with matching bonnet. The skin of her face and hands was pale and almost translucent. She wore a thin petticoat, creating a nearly vertical silhouette in her simple dress.

Ruth Anne's only accoutrement that set her apart from the other women onboard was her husband. Caleb was tall, with an irascible mop of blond hair. His blue eyes caught the attention of everyone who met him. When he smiled, which was often, the gleam of his white teeth lit up the room. When Caleb was by Ruth Anne's side, she felt like she was someone, a person, a woman to be noticed. She often wondered what Caleb saw in her, aside from her attentiveness to his California obsession.

Once underway, whenever Ruth Anne was not in her room struggling with seasickness from the constantly rocking ship, she would gravitate to the other simple women on board with whom she felt more at home. She learned that several of the women were, like her, traveling with their husbands to California, Oregon, or Washington. Only occasionally, Ruth Anne would have a conversation with one of the fashionably dressed women.

These elegant-looking women with their lace, gloves, and exquisite hats were not as haughty as Ruth Anne had assumed. Many of the well-dressed women were on their way back to San Francisco after visiting family on the East Coast, where their husbands were bankers, merchants, or worked in shipping. One young woman, who was single, was traveling to San Franciso to live with her aunt. The aunt's husband had committed suicide after his banking house failed, something to do with embezzling money it seemed.

Ruth Anne was impressed and surprised that a young woman would travel alone to a city such as San Franciso, with its reputation for violence, gambling, and corruption. At least, that is what Ruth Anne had read in the newspapers: San Francisco was no place to raise a family, much less live a life in God's truth.

Caleb never got seasick. He was wallowing in the glow of returning to California. If Caleb was not on deck soaking up the wind and sun, he could be found in the salon with the other men, smoking cigars, and swapping stories. Several of the men, like Caleb, were returning to California. The Golden State had an irrational grip on their mind and soul. It was where they belonged, not on the East Coast, so wrapped up in traditions and status.

Often the men would recount their first journeys to California, with all the hardships they had endured. Then they would go on to compare gold mining techniques and experiences. There were tales of the early mining codes to establish order in a chaotic gold rush environment. There were stories of the uneven distribution of justice by the local Alcaldes, and how eventually, they had to take the law into their own hands and dispense justice for an aggrieved party. Vigilante justice was necessary at times in the gold mines.

Caleb was shocked to learn how many Chinese people had immigrated to California. Some of his fellow passengers spoke derisively about the Chinese presence, whose odd dress, unintelligible language, and foreign ways they considered to be a scourge on their small frontier communities. California and its riches were "manifest destiny" for the United States. That destiny, surely ordained by God, was reserved for the white men, not for foreigners.

Those young men traveling to California for the first time were in awe, sitting in rapture as these '49ers recounted their tales. It did not occur to these newcomers that many of the stories were at least modestly embellished to put the storyteller in a more favorable light. The message the young men were left with, after several whiskeys had been consumed, was that California represented unmitigated opportunity to succeed and get rich.

The sun had almost dropped below the horizon of the Pacific Ocean when the steamer began its journey through the mouth of the Golden Gate. Fog was swirling and descending on the bay, and the hills were blanketed with a gauze illuminated orange by the setting sun. To the north was the Point Bonita lighthouse. Directly to their right was the Fort Point lighthouse, with another lighthouse on Alcatraz Island in front of the steamer.

From Point Bonita, the large boom of the 24-pound fog gun was being fired every half-hour. In between the burst of gunfire sounded the six strikes per minute of a 1,500-pound fog bell atop the bluff at Point Bonita. Ruth Anne was most impressed. "Caleb," she said, "you arranged all the lights, fireworks, and music just for our arrival to San Francisco?" Caleb smiled and replied, "Anything for Mrs. Caleb Gibbons."

Ruth Anne stepped off the steamer in San Francisco and went from a world of seasickness and insecurity into a land of coordinated chaos. She had never felt so happy to be on ground that did not move underneath her feet. Whereas the constant motion of the steamer, rocked by the waves, had induced a feeling to purge her last meal over the side of the ship, San Francisco moved with a different sort of motion that almost produced the same reaction.

Across the streets of San Francisco, people, mostly men, were moving in every direction, an impatience and energy in their steps. The speed with which they walked may have been to ward off the cold air of the bay. But all seemed to be going somewhere. They were headed to the wharves to check on cargo that may have arrived or to arrange shipment of goods from California.

Carts and wagons, pulled by mules or horses, were climbing the steep hills of the city. Men were spilling out of hotels and boarding houses on their way to work, eat, drink, or gamble. Every man had some sort of side arm, either a gun, a knife, or both. Mixed among all the men, scurrying around on business and pleasure, were a few women. Although the women moved with the same energy as the men, Ruth Anne did not imagine their destinations were saloons or gambling houses.

Caleb and Ruth Anne spent their first few nights in a hotel on California Street to rest from their long voyage from the East Coast. Each day when Ruth Anne woke, she could not tell if it was morning or afternoon due to the low clouds and fog that enveloped the city. She immediately noticed the concentration of so many smells and aromas wafting from the window into the room.

The smell of the city was most intense when the air was relatively calm. Of course, there was the ammonia smell from the horses and cattle - that was a given in any large city. As the sea air moved from the Bay up the hill, all the odors and aromas of the city were caught up in the draft. Ruth Anne could smell the coal and wood smoke from the steam ships, the cooking steak and sausages, something being fried in lard, alcohol from the saloons, and the ubiquitous smoke of cigars and pipe tobacco.

There was one swirl of aromas that she could not quite identify. They were foreign to her. The smells were not unpleasant, but Ruth Anne could not visualize what was being cooked in order to make the sweet and smoky aroma. As she looked out the window, she saw a sea of men and women walking up, down, and across the sidewalks and muddy street. Where were all those people going? she wondered.

Later in the day, after a light meal, Caleb took Ruth Anne out into the city. Caleb did not particularly like San Francisco, but there was no denying the city glowed with energy, spirit, opportunity. They walked past the Chinese quarter, and Ruth Anne discovered the origins of the sweet foreign aromas she had noticed earlier. Chinese merchants selling a variety of spices, roots, and animals, alive and dead. Chinese restaurants, where chefs cooked with all the food stuffs in the market, the seasonings, citrus, fish, and fowl mixed into exotic-looking plates and bowls of food.

The low clouds and fog had burned off, and in their place were bright sunshine and a fierce north wind. Caleb and Ruth Anne climbed the steep hill, lined on both sides with homes and businesses, until they reached the top. Ruth Anne gazed without words upon the horizon. To the north rose the golden hills of the entrance to the Bay, a golden gate. Below her lay San Francisco Bay, with at least 50 or 100 tall mast ships, steamers, and barges quietly resting in the water.

To the east a bright white line traced the horizon. Caleb pointed out the line and explained to Ruth Anne that the line was the snow of the Sierra Nevada Mountain range. "Is that where we are going?" she asked Caleb. "Not quite," he answered. "Just below the mountains, in the foothills."

"How far away is that?" she asked. Caleb, contemplating the distance in his mind, answered, "The snow is about 150 miles away." Ruth Anne was stunned. "Those mountains are 150 miles away? Oh, my goodness, that is something," she said.

Rarely, if ever, could one look 150 miles across the landscape on the East Coast. In California, with its lack of humidity, wood, or coal smoke, clear sky was the predominant feature. You could see into your future here, thought Ruth Anne. You could see your destination days before you arrived.

That clear air was part of the allure of California for Caleb and for so many other men. The allure was not just the air, it was about the ability to see into the future. In California, the future was not a fixed tree, valley, or snow-covered mountain. The future, the distant landscape, was comprised of opportunities. The sort of opportunities that were not present on the East Coast. Or, if opportunities were present in the East, the air, the people, the culture, the restraints of society, were so clouded and thick one could not see them.

After a few days of rest, Caleb and Ruth Anne boarded a paddle-wheeled steamer to Sacramento. The voyage across the bay and up the river was calm, a stark contrast to their ocean adventure. Once the boat left San Francisco, the rolling hills and plains along the river were barren of human habitation.

Occasionally the passengers could make out a small settlement of buildings and people. Otherwise, the passing landscape was devoid of any industry.

The rolling hills along the river were maturing from a verdant green to a pale yellow as the grasses dried out in the late spring. Covered in dry grasses, the hillsides were simply brilliant as they reflected yellow and green colors capped by the cloudless blue sky. As the boat slowly moved inland, the hills became smaller, and the temperature increased.

Ruth Anne was perfectly content to sit on the deck of the boat, absorb the warm sun and watch the landscape pass by. The air was cool and dry. She could see for miles, the coastal mountains to the west, the Sierras to the east, and the large expanse of the valley beyond the riverbanks. If this incredibly large landscape was California, Ruth Anne could see herself being happy here.

Sacramento was different from San Francisco. It was flat, and so were the people, Ruth Anne thought. While she had been intimidated by the variety of people and their frenetic energy in San Francisco, it had been a spectacle worth watching. Sacramento was quiet compared to San Francisco. It was orderly, mundane, more like an established, staid East Coast town.

If San Francisco was a raucous musical act, Sacramento was a somber Sunday organ hymn. Ruth Anne preferred the simplicity of a hymn sung in unison by the parishioners. Everyone knew the tune and words. Everyone knew when to sing, when to stop, and when to repeat the chorus. Caleb and Ruth Anne did attend one church service in Sacramento before pushing on to their destination.

The Congregational Church service was familiar and comforting to Ruth Anne. The other attendees were pleasant. After the service, some of the ladies asked Ruth Anne where she and Caleb would be making their home. Ruth Anne told them Carrolton along the river. "Oh," said one woman, "I don't think I've ever been there." Ruth Anne quickly realized that most people in Sacramento only had a vague notion of Carrolton, the old gold mining town, and few had visited the little burg.

After the church service, Caleb and Ruth Anne embarked on the last leg of the trip. The journey to Carrolton consisted of several dusty stagecoach rides, as there was no line that made a direct connection between Sacramento and the little town. With each eastward mile, Ruth Anne could feel the heat increase. California, the land of perpetual drought for half of every year.

Caleb's demeanor also had changed with each mile, beginning with the ocean voyage from the East Coast. As he got closer to California, Caleb grew happier. It was not that Caleb was habitually an unhappy a dour fellow, quite the opposite. He was generally congenial and affable with everyone he met. Men that Caleb had never met were subject to his buoyancy, enthusiasm, firm handshake, and friendly slap on the back. Everyone liked Caleb.

However, Ruth Anne noticed distinct changes to his personality as they approached California, steamed up the river, and made their way through the rough stagecoach trip to Carrolton. If Ruth Anne had not known better, she would have figured Caleb was in love with another woman. She was partially correct: Caleb was in the throes of an affair with California. The young state had stolen his heart, and he had vowed his eternal presence to her.

The stagecoach stopped in the town of Quartz Hill, where the Valley Springs Water Company had their offices. Weeks earlier, Caleb had accepted the position of Water Agent for the water company. It was a steady job, albeit unfortunately situated on one of the more remote stations of the company's water ditch.

Caleb had met the superintendent of the water ditch, Theodore Grainger, when he worked on constructing the water canal and the two had become good friends. Their meeting now was tantamount to a school reunion. For hours, Grainger and Caleb talked of the early mining years, the work of digging the water ditch, who had died, who was still alive, the growth of Quartz Hill, and politics. Ruth Anne sat quietly and listened to the confirmation of all the stories Caleb had told her about back in North Adams.

Quartz Hill was slightly reminiscent of San Francisco and markedly different from Sacramento. The small populace of the town moved about with a purposeful randomness. Instead of destinations that promised big money, the residents of Quartz Hill were on a mission of survival. Their energy was directed at cobbling together enough gold dust or coins to put food on their tables.

No ladies in gloves and fancy hats, no bankers, or wealthy merchants, strolled the streets of Quartz Hill. The townspeople seemed more like Ruth Anne, simple. Sacramento had been largely populated by clerks moving from one brick building to the next. The plain men in their dusty suits worked for merchants, hotels, banks, the courts, and a variety of local and state offices.

Quartz Hill was small compared to Sacramento, and but a mere speck of dust in contrast to San Francisco. What Quartz Hill exhibited, a quality somewhat lost on the locals, was a collage of people from all over the world. In this respect, the tiny town reminded Ruth Anne of San Francisco. It was not unusual to hear three or four different languages and dialects while strolling the streets of Quartz Hill. The garb of the people provided easy markers for their countries of origin.

Caleb observed that one could tell how long a man had been in California from his clothing. The immigrants would over time, through necessity, shed their traditional native pantaloons or dresses, for more utilitarian, California climate-friendly dress. Even the Native Americans and Chinese immigrants would adopt more western style clothing. More difficult to discard were one's native language and dialect.

The Cantonese language spoken by the Chinese workers had little in common with either English or the Romantic languages of Europe. Consequently, when two or three Chinese men were having a conversation, their voices pierced the air like the peal of a bell from the local volunteer fire department. Many of the Chinese also held fast to their traditional hair style and clothing. Chinese men working in the gold fields did submit to more suitable and durable pants and shirts.

What Ruth Anne noticed in Quartz Hill, and what made her immediately sit up and look around, was the tangy and sweet smell of Chinese cooking wafting from down the street. She was momentarily lost trying to discern if San Francisco was nearby or if the oriental aromas were really coming from Quartz Hill. Ruth Anne felt oddly comforted that Quartz Hill shared a little piece of San Francisco that she could recognize.

As Caleb and Ruth Anne walked through Quartz Hill, Caleb pointed out some of the water ditches that cut through the town. "That's our water," Caleb said. "Whose water?" Ruth Anne asked. "Valley Springs Water Company's water, from a dam over 20 miles away. These are the ditches that I helped dig. Without this water, Quartz Hill would just be another dusty gold mining ghost town," Caleb proudly explained.

Caleb had a tangible connection to Quartz Hill. Caleb was in the water, in the ditch line; he was part of California. This whole idea that Caleb was part of California partially explained his obsession with the state. As they crossed the town, Caleb showed Ruth Anne how the water was used by the residents, the volunteer fire department, hotels, restaurants, modest farming pursuits, and, of course, gold mining in the outlying areas.

Ruth Anne did not feel as if she could ever have such an intimate attachment to a location. She would never build something and be able to call it hers. There would never be an event, house, church, or garden that people would forever recognize as the legacy of Ruth Anne. But Caleb did have such a connection to the earth, to its history. It made Ruth Anne feel proud that her husband was part of California.

Amid uncertainty whether it would be a historic event or just another fanciful business scheme, there was talk of Quartz Hill getting an extension of the railroad out of Sacramento. The potential coming of the railroad was big news. For all the exponentially grand opportunities that California had become recognized for, mainly promoted in newspapers and local gossip, real progress was hard to see. The grandiose plans of many men silently faded away, as investment in their schemes never materialized.

Regardless, the residents of Quartz Hill were already daydreaming of how the new railroad would boost their flagging prospects. Known as a focal point of placer gold near the river, then later for its hard rock mining with deep tunnels into the earth, Quartz Hill had grown quiet of late, as production of gold had dwindled.

The town was still at a vital juncture of roads leading to other gold mining and lumber producing regions. The marquee of quartz, sandwiched between two granite monoliths, from which the town had taken its name, had been blasted out years prior. The quartz ledge did produce a modest amount of gold, but quickly went dry. Today, gold production continued among the numerous Chinese and European miners there, albeit at the meager rate of some $2 per man per day.

Integral to past, present, and future gold mining was the water owned and provided by the Valley Springs Water Company. The gold production season from spring to autumn also coincided with California's seasonal drought. Most of the streams and creeks dried up by June. It was the water from the Valley Springs company that allowed the miners to keep washing the earth in search of a little bit of color in the bottom of the sluice run. However, as gold production was declining, agriculture was increasing and the demand for water for the crop was growing.

3 Welcome to California

When Caleb and Ruth Anne arrived at Carrolton, like many newlywed couples, they were still floating on the euphoria of marriage, making a home, and absorbing the California climate. Ruth Anne was a prolific author of letters to her friends and family back in North Adams. She struggled to properly convey the excitement of her new home and the beauty of the landscape. It was Ruth Anne's mission to put a woman's touch on the two-room cabin, formerly occupied by the previous Water Agent, who died in an accident on the water ditch.

In addition to the high cost of imported food stuffs, home furnishings also were expensive. The selection of fabric from the local dry goods store that Ruth Anne hoped to use for curtains was meager, limited, and costly.

Nevertheless, Ruth Anne accepted the challenge to transform the creaky cabin into a home for her and Caleb.

While Caleb had slipped into his new job as though he had never left California to begin with, Ruth Anne was beginning to feel the monotony of life in Carrolton. Unlike North Adams, here there was no family to visit. Musical and theatrical events were very few. The few musical acts or theatrical productions that did stop in Carrolton were aimed at entertaining the mining community. The monthly Sunday church service was all the diversion Ruth Anne had to look forward to.

As the excitement of a new life in California slowly waned, so did the production of Ruth Anne's letters back home. She just couldn't find anything interesting to write about that she had not already shared. It got to the point that Ruth Anne would write letters to her family and then never send them. When she reread what she had written, she noticed all she had done was complain or moan about how homesick she had become.

Contrary to published accounts of California, the state does experience seasonal weather, although on a much subtler scale than the East Coast. When the summer months of August and September arrive, the cooling influence of the coastal breeze that floods the valley with cool temperatures subsides. This results in stagnant air and excruciatingly warm temperatures.

It was one of those suffocating August days when Ruth Anne stepped out of the cabin soaked in sweat from the heat of the evening and the wood stove. She looked to the western sky and saw the crescent of the new moon. At that moment she realized it had been more than 30 days since her last period.

In the morning, Ruth Anne woke up, looked out the un-curtained window and took account of her calm body. There were none of the uncomfortable cramps associated with that part of womanhood that plagued so many women, as it did her. She quickly suppressed the urge to be hopeful about her condition. Instead, she went out and worked in the garden.

With the rise of the second new moon, Ruth Anne still had not had her period. Setting about her daily errands, she began to smile as she walked down to the butcher's shop. She greeted the blacksmith with an uncharacteristically wide smile. When the dry goods merchant explained he still could not get any proper curtain fabric, Ruth Anne cheerfully replied, "That is no problem, something will come in next week. Have a wonderful afternoon."

Ruth Anne could no longer contain her newfound happiness at her early pregnancy and at last confided to Caleb. "I knew it," he said. "I could tell something was different about you."

Ruth Anne was both happy and apprehensive. Her sisters were so far away. There was no way they could travel to California and help her. She knew many of the women in town but had not developed the sort of relationship with them to request counsel or assistance for a first-time pregnancy.

For a time, Ruth Anne kept her pregnancy a secret from the locals. This was not hard to do because she rarely conversed with her fellow townspeople beyond mild pleasantries, comments on the weather, or information about the price of goods. As she walked around town, she found herself becoming observant of the families. Which families had toddlers no longer in need of baby essentials. Perhaps those families would part with some of those clothes or little chairs.

By the third month of her pregnancy, Ruth Anne had created a mental map of the town, where all the families with children lived, how many children they had, and which might be done having children and willing to part with baby stuff they no longer needed. Ruth Anne felt a level of guilt for surreptitiously surveying the local families for children's clothes and toys. Exhausted by the pretense of casual conversations about household goods, Ruth Anne decided she would slowly share news of her pregnancy with some of the women in town.

Caleb remained oblivious to Ruth Anne's anxieties about pregnancy, having a child, or being a mother. He told her not to worry about baby clothes or furniture; he had money saved for such necessities. He was just relieved that Ruth Anne was happy and seemed to be adapting to life in Carrolton. He knew the people of Carrolton were good and would help her any way they could.

As the mining and irrigation season was winding down in the autumn, the Valley Springs Water Company decided it was time to rebuild the tall flume over Coyote Ravine. This required the water to be turned out of the water ditch so new timbers could be put in place. Caleb had prepared for the rebuild for some time and had the lumber already staged next to the flume. With luck, they could tear down the original flume and rebuild it in three days, minimizing the time the customers were without water. However, the flume rebuild would require Caleb to be onsite, away from Carrolton, for at least two nights.

Ruth Anne had packed as much food as possible in Caleb's sacks. There were biscuits and jerked beef, along with some local fruits and vegetables. There would be a camp cook onsite, but Ruth Anne still felt she needed to pack something for her husband, the father of her baby. Caleb left early in the morning, and Ruth Anne was left alone to look out the window, view the autumnal colors of the tree leaves, and listen to the faint rushing water of the river below the town.

That evening, low clouds obscured Ruth Anne's view of the sky. She had been tracking her maternal progress by the phases of the moon.

Later in the evening Ruth Anne began to feel cramps in her abdomen. She felt nauseous. It was dark outside, and she did not want to venture out to seek help. She endured the pain, her back hurt, and she was hot and breathing heavily. She saw the bleeding and grabbed some fabric she had thought of using for the curtains.

Ruth Anne's body convulsed painfully, until it expelled her newfound hope for a happy life in California. She sat there in disbelief, too tired to cry. She was alone and did not want to make a sound. She lay on the uneven floorboards of the cabin, in shock, until she fell asleep.

When the hazy morning light began to fill the cabin, Ruth Anne was still lying on the floor. Slowly she rose, not quite understanding what happened in the night. She looked at the bloody mess that had soaked the fabric and was drying beneath her.

What did one do with a miscarriage, the life of her potential child? It seemed sacrilegious to put the remains in the outhouse. It wasn't a baby who died at birth, so there could be no coffin box or attending cross to mark the spot of a life cut short. Ruth Anne resolved to dig a deep hole in the back of the house and mark it with a special rock. The white quartz rock, the one with little crystals on one side that reflected the sunlight, would mark the spot where her future happiness had died and deter the animals from digging it up.

No words were necessary when Caleb returned from the flume rebuild. He could see the truth in her eyes, the way she lay on the bed staring at nothing in particular.

Some would characterize the relationship between Caleb and Ruth Anne as cold, lacking the warmth of an affectionate relationship. That assumption would be wrong. Neither Caleb nor Ruth Anne were adept at expressing affection. Over the year since they were married, they had developed a unique bond, and oftentimes they needed no words to communicate.

4 Mother Ruth Anne

It had been several months since Ruth Anne's brush with motherhood had evaporated, when Caleb entered the cabin with a little baby bundled next to his chest and handed the child to Ruth Anne. She cleaned the baby's head wound, wrapped the boy in clean towels, and tried to spoon feed the baby a little milk. Caleb was exhausted from his travels, and within a short period, everyone had fallen asleep, the baby boy cradled in Ruth Anne's arms. Even the pain of her earlier miscarriage seemed to soften now that she held a baby.

The sleeping inhabitants of the little cabin were awakened with the sounds of a crying baby. For so long Ruth Anne had hoped that a baby's cry would be her morning alarm clock. Now, the baby's presence was a reality, if only for a few days. As she attempted to feed the baby, she was unsure if his fussiness and cries were because he was hungry or injured.

The swelling on the baby's forehead began to subside as the days passed, a nice scab formed, and the wound became less red. The baby was still fussy and crying. News of his arrival had spread through the town, partly through word of mouth and partly because a passersby could hear the child wailing from outside. Ruth Anne dropped her apprehension of talking with the other women and decided to consult with other, more experienced mothers about how to soothe – and feed – a newborn.

To Ruth Anne's surprise, all of the women were sympathetic to her plight and offered a variety of suggestions. Mrs. O'Hara, the blacksmith's wife, suggested she see Doctor Waddle near the edge of town to look at the baby's head injury. Ruth Anne had always avoided Dr. Waddle. He was old and spent more time at one of the saloons than he did caring for patients. Of course, it was probably at the saloons where he found most of his patients.

Overcoming her apprehension, Ruth Anne timidly knocked on the door of Dr. Waddle's cabin. She did not really need to announce herself, as the baby would not stop crying. Doctor Waddle opened the door, his thinning gray hair swirling about his head from the winter wind. "Yes," Dr. Waddle responded, with a hint of resentment at being interrupted from some important task. "Hello Doctor," Ruth Anne quickly blurted out. "I was hoping you could look at my, umm, this baby. He has bumped his head, and he won't stop crying."

"Alright, come in. Sit down, let's have a look," replied the doctor brusquely, as he waived Ruth Anne toward a chair.

Dr. Waddle had come to California in search of gold in 1849. His age and argumentative demeanor did not endear him to any of the mining companies. To supplement his meager income, he ended up panning and sluicing for gold on his own on a little claim he staked below Carrolton.

While the mining companies shunned him as a working member, they were all too eager to visit him for his medical services. Aside from dispensing alcohol or laudanum for pain and injuries, he would occasionally put a splint on a broken arm or leg. Once, much to his disgust, he had to amputate a man's little finger that had been crushed in a steam engine. After the miner's hand had healed, he proudly displayed "Waddle's stub," as he called it. The display of the injury, and its attribution to the doctor, greatly irritated Dr. Waddle.

Dr. Waddle split his days between doing a little mining at his claim on the river, diagnosing the illnesses of Carrolton residents, and drinking in the saloons. Ruth Anne was fortunate to catch him at his cabin, which also doubled as his medical office. She looked around the unkept cabin and wondered if the doctor had ever seen or treated a baby.

Dr. Waddle pulled the blanket over the baby's head and exclaimed, "A China baby! That's interesting. How did you come by this child?"

Not wanting to explain the chain of events, Ruth Anne simply replied, "My husband Caleb was given the baby after the baby's father was killed in an accident." The doctor looked at Ruth Anne and said, "Oh, your husband is Caleb, the water man. The water was out last week, and I could not work my mining claim."

"I think the water is back in the ditch now," mumbled Ruth Anne. With a quick look at the baby's forehead Dr. Waddle proclaimed, "The little scratch is healing nicely; he'll live."

The head injury was not the most important issue for Ruth Anne. "He cries constantly, and I think he is losing weight," she explained. "I keep feeding him milk, but he still cries like he is hungry or something. What can you do for him, doctor?" Ruth Anne spoke hurriedly, as the doctor had risen from his chair and was beginning to motion her out the door.

"There is nothing you or I can do," the doctor replied curtly "The child needs his mother and her milk. That will be one dollar or a pinch of gold dust." No diagnosis, no treatment, just a request for a dollar, was all Ruth Anne received from the doctor, who resembled a broken-down old miner more than a physician.

As Ruth Anne left the doctor's office, she glanced over her shoulder and noticed the doctor making a beeline across the street to the nearest saloon. She went back to Mrs. O'Hara and asked if she knew of any women who were still nursing their children. She agreed with the doctor that the baby probably did need breast milk, but no women in Carrolton were in that state. Mrs. O'Hara told her that she heard of a woman up at Bretton Falls who had a child in the last year. Maybe she could try at that town.

When Ruth Anne got back to the cabin, Caleb had already left on his horse down to Quartz Hill. Bretton Falls was a good 5 miles away. She attempted to get some cow's milk into the baby boy, who continued his colicky crying. She stuffed some biscuits in a sack, tied on a bonnet and shawl, and, with the baby wrapped in a blanket, started off for Bretton Falls. The day was clear and cold. The winter sun warmed her to the point of perspiration as she quickly walked along the road. Under any other circumstances, it would have been a nice day to hike around the countryside.

The road, sometimes little more than a trail, ran above the river and mirrored its twists and turns. The path was used to reach the various mining claims along the river and to access the water ditch for maintenance. Above the road lay the Valley Springs water ditch. Above the water ditch were increasingly tall mountains and cliffs of granite. The main stagecoach road was on the other side of the tall ridge, outside the river canyon. However, traveling by the stagecoach road would have added several miles to Ruth Anne's trek.

Ruth Anne passed several mining camps on the road. She could see and hear the miners at work below her. She wondered if one of those mining camps was where the baby came from. Only the most diligent miners continued to work during the winter. The Chinese men were diligent miners. The river canyon narrowed as she trekked upstream to Bretton Falls. She then came to a part of the river canyon that was nothing more steep rock cliffs.

At this location, the only way to port the ditch water around the craggy rock walls was to run the water into a wooden flume several hundred yards long along the cliff. Ruth Anne looked for another path either above or below the leaky wooden flume. One option was to blaze a trail up the creek gulch to the top of the ridge and then drop down the other side of the sheer canyon wall. As she peered around the granite wall impeding her passage, she could just make out the little buildings of Bretton Falls.

As there was no discernible trail up to the ridge top, requiring an arduous climb of several hundred yards at a minimum, Ruth Anne decided to walk on the flume. The flume was covered with boards evenly spaced apart, but with enough distance between them so she could see the flowing water underfoot. It was a little disorienting for Ruth Anne to walk in the opposite direction of the water flow.

She carefully placed one foot on each board, steadying herself and baby, then took another step. On one side of her was a near vertical cliff of granite. On the other side, a straight 40-foot drop down to the river crashing over the boulders that made up part of the water falls of Bretton Falls.

As Ruth Anne stepped off the flume, her heart was racing. Even though her path was in the shadow of the hills and trees, she found herself sweating profusely from a mixture of work, anxiety, and fear. The baby had been oddly silent during the walk of death over the flume. Maybe the baby had died. She was holding him so tight she was certain she had either smothered or crushed him. She opened the blanket, and the child stared blankly back at her. With a nervous laugh, she said, "You look like Caleb. Maybe he is your papa after all."

Ruth Anne walked into Betton Falls, a small town even more bedraggled than her little town of Carrolton. She saw an old woman in the side yard of a cabin. As Ruth Anne approached, she realized she had misjudged the woman's age. Not much older than Ruth Anne, up close she looked tired, weary, streaks of gray hair, and thick creases in her face.

The Betton Falls woman had finally caught the chicken she had been chasing, threw it across a tree stump, and with one quick blow from the ax in her other hand, severed its head from its body. "Hello," Ruth Anne said meekly uttered. Still holding the chicken, a stream of blood flowing from its neck, the woman responded, "Alo."

Ruth Anne explained that she had a sick child and was wondering if any of the women in town might be nursing. She gave a rambling explanation, telling the women that Dr. Waddle said the baby needed a mother's milk. The woman approached Ruth Anne, looked at the baby in her arms, and said calmly, "You'll save yourself a lot of grief if you just toss that Chinese thing in the river."

Ruth Anne's blank expression belied her disbelief at what she had heard from the chicken-killing woman. Ruth Anne's head was in a whirl. Was this woman attempting some sort of European humor she did not understand? The woman sensed Ruth Anne was too naïve, too new to California, to understand how life played out along the river. Fact was, there were times when it was all one could do to save one's own family from famine. Helping others was a luxury, one most people in Bretton Falls could not afford.

"*Nein,*" said the woman, "no women nursing in town. *Ich* saw an Indian beggar *frau* with babe across the river last week." The chicken-killing woman told Ruth Anne she could try to find the Indian village, where there may be a nursing mother among them. She told Ruth Anne to go over the bridge to the north side of the river, then follow the narrow path to the right to find the Indian beggars' village. Before Ruth Anne started off, the chicken-killer left her with some parting words, warning that Indians were always hungry and might find her Chinese boy to be a nice meal.

Ruth Anne refused to let the disparaging words of the chicken-killing woman shake her faith in humanity. She rationalized that the woman had just had bad experiences with her Chinese and Native American neighbors. Ruth Anne had a difficult experience with Dr. Waddle, but she would not project that experience onto all doctors.

As Ruth Anne approached the bridge crossing the river, she felt God must be testing her. She glanced over her shoulder at the hillside flume she had walked over and turned back to the bridge. "Why?" she asked herself. The flume walk had been an easy test of her resolve compared to the bridge.

It was a fragile looking structure, composed of two wooden A frames on each side of the river. Connecting the A frames were thin wire ropes over the river. From the wire suspension rope, additional cables dropped down to connect to another set of parallel wire ropes across the river. Spanning the bottom wire rope lines were wooden planks in between the vertical cables that connected the wire suspension rope to the bottom rope lines.

The flimsy-looking bridge was no more than 3 feet wide. Except for the thin wire ropes on either side, there were no handrails to grasp. An unsteady woman holding a baby could easily lose her balance and fall into the river 20 feet below. Ruth Anne, feeling the situation called for extreme piety, pulled out the little silver cross she wore around her neck and kissed it. Then, even though she was not a Roman Catholic, she made the sign of the cross, looked up to the sky and said a prayer. Then she slowly climbed the rock ramp up to the bridge's wooden plank deck and began her even slower crossing.

Step by step, as the bridge swayed in the breeze over the cold rushing water, her crossing was the most terrifying event she had ever attempted. At one point, she dropped to her knees, feeling that at any moment she might be tossed off the bridge with the baby clutched to her chest. Rising, she pushed herself to take another step. When she and her bundle finally made it across and dismounted the bridge, she sat down in the dirt, clutching the child to her chest, and cried.

From the north side of the river, Ruth Anne could see the town of Bretton Falls on the south side with the water ditch running below it. A few people walked between cabins and stores. Horses pulled wagons through the town. Smoke rose from the blacksmith building and from many of the homes. She could not hear the people or the hooves of the horses as they pulled their payloads through town.

She saw a man chopping wood. The crack of the axe splitting the wood reached Ruth Anne seconds after she saw the blow fall. The rush of the river water as it tumbled over the rocks buried all the other sounds. She looked up to the ridge of the hills and saw vultures circling over Bretton Falls. She felt detached from that civilization. She was alone with a baby who seemed to be dying.

Ruth Anne found a weathered log next to the river to sit on. She looked up and down the river and saw the piles of round cobble rocks left by the miners in their excavations for gold. She surveyed the hillsides and noted scores of tree stumps. Oak and pine trees had been cut down for lumber. What did the landscape look like before the miners' frenzied activity over the river gold had disrupted it? she wondered.

Alone was the first word that came to Ruth Anne's mind. On the other side of the river, she was isolated. Before her was the cold, flowing water of the river. Underneath her and all around her were the round, gray cobble stones, as cold as the water. The air was cold, but the winter sun warmed her and this dying bundle of a Chinese baby in her arms.

Ruth Anne pulled a tin cup out of her bag and crumbled one of the biscuits she had brought. Then she dipped it in the river to saturate the biscuit, making a runny slurry of dissolved biscuit. She tried to get the baby to accept some of the tasteless biscuit slurry but was unsure if the child swallowed any of it. The Chinese baby was less fussy, but he also seemed less animated. He just gazed at whatever his head was pointed at. He seemed to be sleeping more. Was he dying? Ruth Anne asked herself.

The sun had passed the midpoint of the sky and sat low on the horizon. Ruth Anne had to keep moving, to someplace, to somewhere, to see someone. The Indians were her last hope to save the child, or at least that was her conviction. She gathered herself and baby and trudged up the road, searching for the elusive path to the Indian village. As she climbed up the riverbank, the sound of the rushing river waters grew softer and softer.

The small trail diverging from the main road up to the town of Coleville was barely passable. As Ruth Anne pushed her way through the bushes encroaching on the trail, she glanced occasionally up to the ridge line. Earlier she had seen what she thought was a small wisp of wood smoke rising into the sky. Whether the smoke was from the Indian village or from some forlorn cabin in the woods, she knew not. The smoke trail was her beacon, and she would keep hiking toward it.

After a while, the trail widened into a path, and the buckbrush shrubs retreated. As the vegetation diminished, outcroppings of slate and granite began to dominate the landscape. Ruth Anne had to wind around several massive rocks where she could not see what was around the corner. The tall rocks and boulders and surrounding tall pine trees shrouded the sky. She had lost sight of Bretton Falls as she penetrated deep into the forest land.

The sounds of the river could no longer be heard. There were no birds chirping. There was no wind to rustle the pine needles and make that whooshing sound. All Ruth Anne heard was the crunch of her own shoes on the sandy trail. It was quiet in the wilderness. Ruth Anne felt certain that if she fell and died, no one would find her for months, if ever. Her body would most likely be eaten by scavengers. No trace would be left of her. This path to nowhere would be her final resting spot.

As Ruth Anne walked around one particularly tall and spike-like boulder, she heard some rocks fall from above her. It could have been a squirrel scampering about, a mountain lion stalking her, or, somewhat implausibly, she thought, a man. She continued to walk through the maze of rocks and suddenly found herself in a small clearing of bare earth surrounded by tall granite blocks. The large rectangular boulders seemed to have been placed, one on top of the other, by the hand of God.

The granite blocks were massive. The dark seams between the granite blocks made nearly straight lines vertically and horizontally. Each of the granite blocks was the size of a miner's cabin. Ruth Anne could not help but marvel at the interesting nature of the granite when she rounded another corner and encountered a group of Indians, as surprised to see her as she was relieved to see them.

Even for the Indigenous people, who had seen their native lands overrun by wild-looking white men in search of gold like ants swarming over a dead worm, the sight of a white woman holding a baby appearing before them was perplexing. What could this woman possibly want from them that had not already been taken?

Ruth Anne saw a small group of gaunt Indians, women squatting on the ground as the men stood. The village was a collection of small huts constructed of tree branches, mud, and pine needles. The Indians had also scavenged discarded sawed lumber and canvas from the retreating miners to fortify their shelters. They were dressed similarly in an eclectic mix of native Indian clothing and Western-style pants and hats. For warmth, many of the women wore animal pelts draped over their shoulders, as Ruth Anne wore her wool shawl.

In the center of the clearing, surrounded by the huts, a small fire burned. Ruth Anne's surprise visit stopped all activity. Strewn about the Indian camp were vestiges of civilization from all over the world. There were empty tin cans, scraps of paper, strips of leather and canvas, boards, lanterns, a horse bridle, and wool blankets that looked as if they had been made in Ireland.

Ruth Anne had been told that a man by the name of Sinclair had employed Indians in 1848 to extract over $20,000 in gold from the river. Since the Indian men had no use for the shiny gold nuggets and dust, they were paid for their work in clothing and food. As a result, the original inhabitants of the land did not share in the wealth that the gold accumulation represented. From looking around the forlorn camp, it was evident to Ruth Anne that the lives of the Indians had not been improved by the wealth extraction from their river.

Nothing in California was pure anymore except death. The influx of world cultures to California had adulterated not only the landscape but had changed the Indians' culture as well. The Indians spoke using a collage of foreign words, including English, Spanish, French, and German, to communicate with the white men. The words and expressions they picked up varied from camp to camp, depending on the ethnic makeup of the primary community of miners they were working with. Similarly, the white men absorbed different Indian, Spanish, and European terms as part of their speech.

When an Indian man spoke to Ruth Anne in his native language, she did not flinch. She was used to words and idioms from other languages that she did not understand. The French women in Carrolton would sometimes rattle on to Ruth Anne in long French sentences, their meaning completely lost on Ruth Anne. She would eventually figure out the French woman was requesting sugar or coffee. In lieu of understanding the foreign sounds, she focused on the person's face and body language to glean the meaning.

The Indian man stepped forward and asked what Ruth Anne wanted. For a long moment, no words would come. Even though the Indian man spoke rough English to her, she did not know if her words could be understood. She began to sway back and forth, transferring her weight from one foot to another, a behavior she often exhibited when she became worried or apprehensive.

Ruth Anne finally managed to spit the words out, "Baby, sick," as she pulled the blanket from the baby's head. The Indian man stared at the child, shook his head, lifted his hand, and said, "You leave, go back." Ruth Anne began to stumble over her words, pleading for help, "Oh….but….I can't….he is dying….maybe….I thought…..you could..." Before she could finish her rambling plea, the Indian man said, "Go," and pointed in the direction from which she had come.

Exhaustion and fatigue swept over her. She dropped to her knees, bowed her head, and began to weep. "Oh, dear God, why hath you forsaken me?" she gasped between heaves of breath, tears running down her face. The Indians watched her sobbing as she cradled the baby.

One of the Indian women rose and went over to the Indian man who had confronted Ruth Anne. The Indian woman spoke to the man as she pointed to the baby. When Ruth Anne had dropped to her knees, the Indian women could see that the baby she held was not white, but Chinese.

The Indian woman crept forward to inspect the infant. The Chinese baby's appearance was not too different from the Indians': gaunt, emaciated, tired. The Chinese boy's lips were chapped, and he was lethargic, his eyes focused on nothing. The Indian woman shook her head, as if to say the boy was near death, and began to rise to her feet. In a desperate attempt to communicate her need, Ruth Anne clasped her own right breast and shook her head, saying,

"Nothing…I can't…I can't feed him."

It was apparent to Ruth Anne that she had come knocking on the wrong door for help. She was surrounded by Indians who did not look in much better condition than the Chinese boy. Some of the men stood off to the side, leaning up against the granite and coughing. Ruth Anne figured they were suffering from consumption and likely would not live long. How could Ruth Anne ask these people to help the Chinese boy when they could barely help themselves?

As Ruth Anne sat on the ground, staring at nothing, and wanting to disappear, some of the Indian men were conferring with one of the Indian women in hushed voices. After the conference broke up, the Indian woman came over to Ruth Anne, and without uttering a word, took the Chinese boy from her arms and carried him into one of the small huts. Exhausted and at her wits' end, Ruth Anne leaned back against a log and pondered what to do next. Where had they taken the baby? Should she leave? Should she stay? Would they kill her, the baby, or both?

One question kept repeating in a loop in her brain, "Why am I in California?" She had left a boring and predictable life back in North Adams. There she had a roof over her head, she cooked good food for her father, she went to church. She knew her father would die, and eventually she would die, in the same house, in the same town. Ruth Anne did not know if it was the rapid fire of questions in her head, the repeating al coda, the exhaustion, or the lack of food, but as she looked up to the tall hills surrounding the Indian camp, it all faded out.

Ruth Anne woke up in one of the small huts, covered in an animal pelt. The soft light of the evening glow filtered into the hut. Ruth Anne sat up and saw one of the Indian women braiding some leather strips together. She looked out of the opening of the hut to see some of the Indian women preparing food over the open fire outside. She crawled out, stood up, and looked at the Indian man who seemed to be the leader of this slowly dissipating Indian community.

The Indian man pointed to one of the other huts. She took his gesture to mean that the Chinese boy was in the hut. Ruth Anne walked over to the hut, knelt, and stared inside. There, she saw an Indian woman nursing the Chinese baby, while a second Indian woman cradled an Indian infant. Ruth Anne mustered a smile that could not properly convey her gratitude for this human response to a dying child in need. The Indian nursing the baby motioned that Ruth Anne should leave.

As Ruth Anne stood to go, she was at a loss as to what she should do next. Simply thanking the Indian man seemed inadequate. As she stood there, the evening was at once filled with the sound of crickets and frogs. From this pleasant evening sound, Ruth Anne knew that a water source, maybe a creek, was nearby. She looked around at the hills and realized how sequestered this little spot was. It was the last refuge for the remnant of Indians clinging to life in the hills along this region of the river.

Ruth Anne was offered a little acorn mush that she eagerly consumed, ignoring its bitter taste and odd consistency. The Indian man came over to her and said, "Tomorrow, you go to town. Tonight, sleep." He then motioned over to the hut where she had recuperated from her fainting spell. Inside, Ruth Anne silently said her prayers, prayed for Caleb, prayed for the Chinese baby, prayed for her own speedy return home. How she would navigate her way back home and what Caleb would say to her were trivialities compared to her desire to sleep.

When she woke up the next morning, nothing much had changed in the little Indian camp. The same men languished, coughing, and consumed with what looked like fever. There was a little cooking activity around the fire, while some of the men worked on making arrows or bows, she wasn't sure which. The closed little camp, hidden from the outside world, made the town of Carrolton look like a bustling metropolis.

More aware of the acorn mush taste, Ruth Anne was struggling to swallow the ration one of the Indian women had given her when the Indian man walked over to her and said it was time to go to town. Ruth Anne's task was to get food in Bretton Falls. The Indian led the way down the trail as Ruth Anne struggled to keep up with his pace. The Indian man obviously did not understand how difficult it was for a woman in a dress to climb over fallen trees or hop over puddles of water.

As they approached the bridge, the gaunt Indian stopped, refusing to cross. Ruth Anne knew that Indians had peculiar beliefs and superstitions. Perhaps crossing a floating bridge was against their religion. Ruth Anne attempted to show the Indian that the bridge was perfectly safe by grabbing the wire rope and shaking it. She tried to explain she had already crossed it once without injury to herself or the baby.

Even Ruth Anne herself was unconvinced by her brief assertion of the bridge's safety. Truth be told, she wanted someone to cross this bridge in the sky, high above the rushing river water below, with her. She was frightened. Through stilted sentences, the Indian conveyed to Ruth Anne that the Indians had been warned by the people of Bretton Falls not to cross the bridge and come into their town.

The prohibition from using the bridge had permanently exiled the Indians from their ancestral fishing grounds. Each spring and summer salmon would swim up the river. When the fish reached the series of small waterfalls for which the town was named, the Indians could easily hold out a basket or net and catch the salmon as they leapt over the rocks. With no fish, an important part of the Indian diet was missing. The Indians were malnourished and slowly starving.

As she could not persuade the Indian to cross the bridge with her, she began her crossing. The wind had increased, and the wire rope suspension bridge swayed wildly back and forth over the river. Ruth Anne felt sick, just as she had on the steamer from Panama and then up the coast of California to San Francisco a year earlier.

Ruth Anne suppressed her urge to vomit over the chest-high wire rope. She slowly walked, tightly holding the wire rope and lightly stepping on the boards, which were rotting and uneven. It took Ruth Anne almost half an hour to cross the short span, no more than 100 yards across. When she finally stepped from the bridge, she thought it was her opportunity to continue walking home. She had delivered the sick baby to a woman who could care for it. Her job was done. God would certainly favor her actions with a special place in heaven, she thought.

Ruth Anne walked over a small bridge that crossed the water ditch. She walked up the hill to Bretton Falls. The little town didn't look too different from Carrolton. Perched on a bank above the river, the crude structures trailed up the hillside along Humbug Creek, so named for the lack of gold prospecting miners had assumed should be present.

Like Carrolton, Bretton Falls was struggling to exist. Here were even fewer natural resources for the locals to exploit. The rocky hills did not support any real stands of timber. What few trees existed already had been cut down for firewood, cabins, and lumber to build the flumes of the water ditch. On the flat, the sandy loam soil made an excellent ground for tree and vine crops. Unfortunately, the plain, tucked between the river and hills, was small, limiting any agricultural potential.

Bretton Falls was located on a modestly used road to Coleville, which had several hard rock mines in operation, several miles away on the other side of the river up the hill. A main source of economic activity in Bretton Falls was generated by the men employed by the Valley Springs Water Company. Bretton Falls was situated near the water company's dam on the river. Maintenance on the fragile dam, along with that of the earthen ditch and wooden flumes, created an employment base for the small town. Like Carrolton, Bretton Falls had a diminishing, but dedicated, band of individuals mining for placer gold along the river.

The unexpected outpost of civilization along the river included a few mining camps, primarily operated by Chinese men, butcher, baker, wagon maker, and black smith shops. As Ruth Anne proceeded carefully along the main road through town, one of her first impressions was the noticeable absence of saloons or gambling establishments.

Ruth Anne would learn later the seeming lack of vice was attributable to the religious nature of the town's residents, all of whom seemed to be associated with an obscure Christian denomination, known for its austere lifestyle and strict interpretation of the Bible. The joke in Carrolton was that all the men made regular pilgrimages to Carrolton to get a drink of whiskey. Bretton Falls was alternately known as Temperance Town.

Ruth Anne looked around at the town of Bretton Falls and did not feel welcome. She had come to associate the music of multiple languages swirling in the air along with the diversity of Carrolton's townsfolk as a comfort zone. The populace of Bretton Falls, it became increasingly apparent, was more homogeneous. Other than a few shouts in Chinese, everyone Ruth Anne encountered spoke English or German in a cadence she did not recognize.

Confident that people in town knew she had been accompanied to the bridge by an Indian man, Ruth Anne was fearful of approaching anyone in town. With few options, she set out for the chicken-killing woman's cabin. Ruth Anne tapped on the door of the cabin, but no one answered. She moved to peer around the corner of the cabin and saw the woman working at something in the back of a wagon.

Ruth Anne pushed out her best and most friendly "Hello!" to the woman, who looked up, startled to see Ruth Anne. "*Ja*?" she replied gruffly. Ruth Anne immediately began explaining her mission to find food, without mentioning whose direction she was following.

"I need to buy some supplies, food, for the baby. You remember, we met the other day, the baby is good, we need to get some food, I was hoping you could help…," Ruth Anne sputtered to the woman. Dispensing with any pleasantries, the woman was direct and to the point. "Do you have any *geld*, any money?"

"Money?" Ruth Anne stammered. "No, I just need a few items for the baby, a little flour, make some biscuits, a little meat."

"I can't give food away, I *haben* children to feed," said the woman, standing next to the wagon with her hands on her hips.

Never had Ruth Anne leveraged any personal relationship in order to gain favor. This was most likely because she had never known anyone of any social or business prominence.

But in this instant of dire need, what flashed into Ruth Anne's mind and then came out of her mouth put a chill in her gut. "My husband is Caleb, the Valley Springs Water Company Water Agent. He'll pay you on his next trip up here." She was no longer pleading with the woman; she was telling the woman that she needed food. Ruth Anne had no idea how the information, shaded with a little intimidation, would sound to the chicken-killing woman.

"Oh," the chicken killing woman said, "Caleb, I see." Ruth Anne did not know if the woman would call her bluff and still demand money. Ruth Anne was not a gambler, but she had played parlor games with her sisters as a girl. Now she played the best card she had in her hand. "*Ja*," began the woman's negotiations, "$5 for sack of flour, and $5 for a chicken."

Stunned by the obvious price gouging, Ruth Anne quickly agreed to the terms, without making any counteroffer. The chicken-killing woman then manifested the name Ruth Anne had given her, as she quickly grabbed a chicken from underfoot and lopped off its head with one quick blow of the axe. She handed the chicken to Ruth Anne by the feet, as blood dripped from the neck onto the ground.

"You want the *kopf*, head?" asked the woman. Ruth Anne did not comprehend the question at first, as she held the chicken and tried to take in the sudden turn of events. "Uh, no, thank you," responded Ruth Anne. The woman then went into her cabin and stayed inside a long while. Ruth Anne stood waiting, unsure what she should do. Finally, the woman returned with a large sack of flour.

With the sack of flour in her left hand and a deceased chicken in her right, Ruth Anne nodded at the woman and mumbled a thank you. The chicken-killing woman, a slight scowl on her face, nodded to Ruth Anne and went back to working at the wagon. Ruth Anne turned around and started back toward the perilous bridge crossing.

Within a few steps, Ruth Anne realized how heavy the sack of flour was and how unbalanced and unsteady it made her. As she trudged toward the bridge, the Indian man was nowhere to be seen. Her mind then began to fire off a series of anxiety-ridden questions. Did she get the right food? No one had told her what to get. Where was the Indian man? Had he abandon her? Could she make it across the bridge? Was the Chinese boy even still alive? Was all this effort worth it if the baby was already dead?

Ruth Anne began her crossing over the wire rope suspension bridge. She tried to console herself that this was her third crossing. Her previous trips over the bridge had been successful. Her third attempt should be the same. But on her previous walks over the swaying bridge, she at least had one hand free to grab the wire rope. On this attempt, both her hands were full, holding a chicken and a sack of flour. Her plight was made all the more precarious by the fact that the heavy bag of flour made her tilt to one side.

The task of getting across the bridge without dropping the food consumed Ruth Anne's focus and attention. She let go of all her anxieties related to the Indian man and the baby and concentrated on putting one foot in front of the other on the weather worn boards of the bridge. She was breathing heavily and perspiring from a combination of exertion and fear of the rushing water below.

As she stumbled, sweat-drenched and trembling, onto the rough bridge deck on the north side of the river, Ruth Anne saw the Indian man step out from behind some bushes. He did not offer to carry any of the food, but nodded at her and began leading the way toward the Indian camp.

As they wound their way up the trail, Ruth Anne's left arm became increasingly fatigued from the weight of the flour. She stopped and changed the bag to her right hand. She would repeat the swap several times as she hiked up the trail. The Indian man never slowed down. He never looked back at her. He never offered to help. Ruth Anne began to sense that bearing the burden was part of her payment for caring for the Chinese baby with whom she had no connection.

When Ruth Anne finally arrived at the Indian camp, flagging several hundred yards behind the Indian man, several women awaited their arrival. One of the women was holding the Chinese baby, who had a poultice of crushed roots and plants on his forehead where he had been injured. Briefly the thought flashed through Ruth Anne's mind that the Indians might accept the Chinese baby, as they seemed to be caring for him as if he was one of their own. Maybe they would keep this baby, and she could go back to her previous life, however bereft that life was, in Carrolton.

The Indian woman approached Ruth Anne and relieved her of her load of flour and chicken. The other women immediately went to work skinning the chicken and mixing the flour into small, round cakes. One of the Indian men who had appeared sick earlier had evidently died while Ruth Anne was bargaining for food in Bretton Falls. Several Indian men were preparing the dead man's body for the departing ceremony. Ruth Anne, exhausted from her trek, lay down in one of the huts and fell fast asleep.

After a nap, Ruth Anne woke up and was aware of the silence in the camp. Most of the Indian men were gone, along with the dead man's body. Ruth Anne walked through the camp and saw one of the Indian women in a hut, nursing both her own young child and the Chinese baby, one at each breast. Not knowing quite what to do, Ruth Anne entered, sat down, and smiled at the nursing woman. The Indian woman returned a nod, a faint acknowledgement of Ruth Anne's approval.

It was not until the next morning that the rest of the small group of Indian men returned to camp. Ruth Anne was hoping some sort of meal would be the next task, as she had begun to feel incredibly hungry and faint. One of the women handed Ruth Anne a tightly woven basket and motioned her to follow another Indian woman, who was carrying a similar basket and a wooden bucket. The Indian woman led the way down to the creek, where they filled the baskets and bucket with water.

The rough peaks towering over the ravine that held the creek blocked most of the bright blue sky above. Ruth Anne was in a perpetual shadow of some hill. She did not know where the sun was in the sky. She glanced up at the creek to see the steep sides of the ravine near the ridge line were covered in snow. No, she thought, that could not be snow; the air was too warm. The sun had peeked over the hills and was lighting up the ravine near the head waters of the creek.

The reflecting white light could not be coming from the snow, Ruth Anne thought. She focused on the craggy rocks that only supported small shrubs. Near the summit of the ravine, she could make out a dark spot. While Ruth Anne was trying to comprehend this strange environment, she saw two figures crawl out of the dark spot. The dark spot was a cave. The two figures, she realized were two men. Their silhouettes were outlined by the same white powder that dusted the landscape down the ravine.

The Indian woman said something to Ruth Anne that jolted her from of her observations. She interpreted the command as "let's go." Ruth Anne obediently followed the Indian woman up the steep trail back to the camp. When they reached camp, Ruth Anne carefully counted the men to see if any were missing.

Ruth Anne quickly realized she wasn't sure how many men resided at the camp, so her tally was inconclusive. What she did notice was that some of the men had white dust or clay on their knees, hands, and moccasins. She concluded that the two figures she had seen emerging from the cave were Indian men from this camp. "What were they doing up there?" she thought to herself. Perhaps, she concluded, that is where they placed the body of the Indian man who had died.

Ruth Anne wasn't sure how many days she had been at the Indian camp. As the days passed, the construct of time was beginning to slip away from Ruth Anne. She knew only daylight and darkness, with no concept of morning or afternoon or those activities that indicated a specific time of day. She would rise in the morning and stand at the ready to receive direction or orders from one of the Indian women. She busied herself fetching water from the creek, gathering wood, tidying up the huts, or helping one of the dying Indian men try to drink some water or eat a little mush.

During all that time, Ruth Anne never felt that she was accepted by the Indian camp members. Her presence was tolerated while the Chinese baby regained his strength, and she could be of use in gathering food and water. At one point Ruth Anne did feel courageous enough to ask the lead Indian man about the white cave that had captivated her imagination. She pointed toward cave location and asked, "Is the white cave your burial ground?"

The Indian man at first looked perplexed; while he understood English well enough, the combination of the words "burial" and "cave" made no sense to him. The light from the fire flickered across his face in the evening light. Ruth Anne watched as his face reflected his transition from confusion to understanding. In a stern voice he addressed her, "No, that is the…." He paused as he searched for the correct or best suited English term to convey his meaning. "That is the creator's cave, home. No white people allowed. Never go there," he explained to her.

Ruth Anne slowly nodded her head to show that she understood his admonition: The cave was off limits to white people. She then went back to helping the other women. As Ruth Anne crushed some roots in a portable mortar and pestle carved from native rock, she remembered hearing some of the men in Carrolton talking about the Indians' 'Devil Den' somewhere up in the hills. The myth they told was that Indian men would kidnap white men and women, take them to Devil's Den and sacrifice them to their Gods in a hole in the mountain. The men had no proof this rural legend was true, other than some men and women had disappeared over the years, never to be found.

To Ruth Anne, a Devil's Den did not comport with a Creator's Cave. How could an evil act ever be associated with a location that housed the native people's creator or God? When Ruth Anne saw a church, even if it was not of her faith, she assumed good people gathered under the roof. A church was thought to be the house of God, Lord, creator of heaven and earth. It was not possible that the Creator's Cave could also be the Devil's Den. Men, especially when plied with a little alcohol, could be silly and tell tall tales that had no basis in reality, Ruth Anne thought to herself.

One morning the rhythm of life that Ruth Anne had established at the Indian camp was abruptly interrupted. As Ruth Anne emerged from her sleeping hut, she saw that several of the Indian men and women were standing in a line waiting for her. In the middle was the Indian woman who had been nursing the Chinese baby. The Indian woman stepped forward and presented Ruth Anne with an alert, bright-eyed Chinese baby, wrapped tightly in cloth and animal skins.

The lead Indian man spoke. "The baby now good. Time for you to leave." Ruth Anne was speechless. She looked at the Chinese baby who had been returned to health. He was gurgling and almost smiling. The Chinese baby looked at Ruth Anne; she looked at the boy. Ruth Anne looked to the line of Indian men and women as, with tears beginning to fill her eyes, she bowed her head and gave a small curtsy. She did not know what else to do.

As awkwardly as she had arrived in the Indian camp, she turned around and started down the path to the river. The bundled baby felt heavier in her arms than when they had arrived. His weight was quickly fatiguing her arms. As she tried to figure out how to carry the baby more easily, she noticed that some of the animal skin strips were loose on both sides of the bundle. Suddenly understanding, she slipped each arm through the loops on either side, so that the weight of the child was on her shoulders.

Now the Chinese baby was hanging across her chest, positioned so he could look over her shoulder. Ruth Anne was certain that she was carrying the child incorrectly, but her arms were free of the weight of the bundle. Once she had the baby bundle situated, and she could increase her gait for the long trek back home, all she could do was cry as she walked.

The walk down the trail, over logs, around boulders, under fallen trees, and through overgrown brush was a blur in Ruth Anne's mind. After several hours of maneuvering over the trail, she emerged on the road down to the river. She looked down at her dress, torn and covered in dirt and stray leaves, and figured people would think she was crazy. Those people were partly correct, in that Ruth Anne, too, felt she had become slightly crazy.

Unbeknownst to her, Caleb sat on his horse scanning the river in search of his wife's body, either floating down stream or snagged on a log. In Bretton Falls he asked everyone he passed if they had seen a woman carrying a baby. When Caleb finally called on the chicken-killing woman, she immediately demanded payment for the flour and chicken she had sold to the woman with the Chinese baby. Caleb paid the woman. Sadly, she could not give him much information, other than she thought Ruth Anne had crossed over the river.

From Caleb's perspective, Ruth Anne was not a pioneer woman. She was a little too meek, mild, and fragile to have crossed the plains in a covered wagon. She was not a chicken-killing woman who could quickly kill a bird, or a man, and then go back to making biscuits. Ruth Anne, for all her beauty in Caleb's eyes, was naïve and not meant to settle the new frontier of the West Coast.

He didn't believe it had been a mistake to marry Ruth Anne, the woman who had become infatuated with him and his stories of California. But it had been a mistake to bring her to California... and now he had lost her forever. How was Caleb going to explain to Ruth Anne's family that he had given her an injured Chinese baby, and the responsibility for caring for the infant had driven her out into the wilderness to perish. Her death lay squarely on his shoulders.

Just then, in the fading light of the afternoon, Caleb saw an odd figure starting across the wire rope suspension bridge over the river. His first thought was he had never seen such a bedraggled miner returning empty-handed from unsuccessfully prospecting one of the numerous creeks that drained into the river. From the odd clothing the person was wearing, Caleb thought it must be a Chinese miner. As the figure continued crossing the bridge, he could make out a bundle strapped to its chest. Then he realized the figure was not a Chinese miner, but Ruth Anne, carefully crossing the bridge with her fragile burden.

Caleb rode up to the foot of the bridge and leapt from his horse, just as Ruth Anne was descending with the bundled baby. She finally recognized Caleb, fell to her knees, and wept. Caleb gingerly removed the bundled baby from Ruth Anne's shoulders and quietly said to both of them, "You're alive." Caleb helped Ruth Anne up onto the horse, handed the baby up to her, and they started up Humbug Creek to pick up the road to Carrolton. Not a word passed between them. The only sounds were the clomping of the old mare's feet on the ground and the gurgling and cooing vocalizations of a revitalized Chinese baby.

5 Bonding

Ruth Anne had little chance for rest when she returned home to Carrolton. Her next task was to find a way to feed the baby, as it continued to reject small spoons full of cow's milk. She found an old powder horn that had been discarded, as flint lock rifles were no longer in use. After thoroughly cleaning the powder horn of any gun powder residue, she fashioned a nipple from some cloth and secured it to the tip with some small twine for the baby to suck on. The powder horn feeding apparatus worked, but the baby still swallowed too much air, leading to long periods of colicky crying.

Mr. Hoxie, whose place lay just down the road from Caleb and Ruth Anne, kept a milk cow that supplied milk to various families in Carrolton. Ruth Anne had become acquainted with Mr. Hoxie when she would stop by his place to buy milk. He was a nice man. He kept his milk cow, named Roxie, in a barn behind the little house he, his wife, and five children shared. Mr. Hoxie's family consumed most of the milk Roxie produced.

It had been a particularly bad morning for Ruth Anne. The Chinese baby was crying and not taking any of the milk from the spoons or other delivery systems she devised. Ruth Anne knew the baby needed some kind of nipple in order to take in nourishment; that is what had brought him back to life at the Indian camp. She bundled up the baby and walked down to Mr. Hoxie's house. He was in the barn milking Roxie.

"Good morning, Mr. Hoxie," greeted Ruth Anne. Mr. Hoxie turned, smiled, and, before he could return the greeting, Ruth Anne continued in a rush of words. "Do you think I could let the baby suck on one of Roxie's udders? He has been fussy all morning, and I don't know what to do." Ruth Anne was usually very reserved and quiet when it came to interactions with other people. Then there were those times when the situation demanded that she just spill out her desires or complaints in a manner that often left the listener slightly dumbfounded.

"Oh sure," said Mr. Hoxie. "Martha used to let our youngest nurse on Roxie, more for amusement than for milk. We can give it a try." Ruth Anne stepped closer to the cow and started to sit on the milking stool when Roxie shifted her hooves and let out a bellow. Clutching the baby, Ruth Anne gasped sharply and ran for the barn wall. She just was not comfortable around large animals. Mr. Hoxie covered his mouth with his hand and worked hard to suppress a laugh.

"Here, I tell you what," began Mr. Hoxie as he moved the milking stool away from Roxie, "you sit over here." Ruth Anne did as she was instructed, not knowing if Mr. Hoxie was going to move the cow to them or how the baby would get the udder. Mr. Hoxie got down on one knee, grabbed one of Roxie's udders, pointed it at the baby and began to squirt milk at him. Ruth Anne, believing this was a new method of feeding the baby, held the boy in position so the stream of milk would reach his mouth.

Ruth Anne soon concluded this was a most inefficient method of feeding a baby. The Chinese boy, on the other hand, thought it was great fun. He squealed with joy as he tried to catch the milk in his mouth. Ruth Anne did not know who was laughing harder or louder, Mr. Hoxie or the baby. Mr. Hoxie finally took the baby from Ruth Anne and fed one of Roxie's udders to him, where the boy happily nursed for 10 minutes.

The walk back to the house felt a little colder, as both the baby and Ruth Anne were covered in Roxie's milk. Ruth Anne had a smile on her face and worked to avoid laughing out loud as she replayed cow's milk scene in her head. The baby seemed content as well. He looked around town, up at the trees, pointed at the river, and patted Ruth Anne's head as they walked down the road.

Ruth Anne sent Caleb into Quartz Hill and Sacramento in search of bottles, tea pots, or any spouted instrument that could be altered into a feeding device for the Chinese boy. Over weeks and months Ruth Anne became an expert on how to feed a fussy baby, and local women began calling on her for advice for their own infant feeding problems.

To the women of Carrolton, the oddity of a white woman raising a Chinese baby was balanced by Ruth Anne's maternal, pioneering resolve to meet any challenge laid upon her in this new frontier. Ruth Anne did not take much notice of local gossip or of how she was viewed in the community. Her sole purpose in life, at that point, was to ensure the life of this infant boy. It was a purpose she needed, as California life had not unfolded as she had dreamed.

Other than the daily stagecoach, Carrolton did not get many visitors. The layout of the town most resembled a cul-de-sac. The road into Carrolton was fairly level and easy to travel. To exit Carrolton in the direction of the river was a difficult proposition, as the road to the top of the ridge was steep -- an 800-foot climb in less than a mile up to the top. Consequently, most visitors to Carrolton turned around at the end of town and headed back to the easier roads to Flagston, the county seat.

When Ruth Anne spied a horse and buggy driving into town as she worked in the garden, she thought to herself that she would shortly see it heading back in the direction it came from. Instead, the buggy stopped in front of the house, and when Ruth Anne looked up, she saw Caleb holding the reins attached to their old mare. "How do you like it?" asked Caleb. Before she could answer, he added, "I bought it from Grainger, as he got a new buggy a couple of weeks ago."

Theodore Grainger, superintendent of the Valley Springs Water Company and Caleb's long-time friend, lived in Quartz Hill, a solid 15 miles to the south of Carrolton, depending on which roads you took. Ruth Anne did not take in who it was Caleb had bought the buggy from; she was just excited to see the new transportation vehicle. They had been using the old wagon they kept behind the house to travel into Quartz Hill. One trip in the wagon and Ruth Anne's butt was always sore for a week.

The buggy, while several years old, featured metal leaf springs to cushion the ride. There was a canopy of oil cloth that could be raised to shelter passengers from the sun or rain. The buggy was not as heavy as the wagon, which meant it could travel faster when pulled by the old mare. Their wagon was great for hauling heavy items, like the new wood stove Caleb had bought a couple of weeks earlier in Sacramento and which was much appreciated by Ruth Anne.

That evening Ruth Anne and Caleb talked about domestic issues: stoves, buggies, the garden, and the next furniture purchase they needed. It marked the first time since she had lost their baby that they had a conversation not colored by the specter of her failure to become a mother. Caleb was relatively happy with his job as a water agent and was starting to think about buying some land when the federal maps were published. But until Ruth Anne was happy in California, Caleb felt unsettled.

As Ruth Anne attempted to master the art of knitting a baby's cap, her head was swimming in the warm feelings of domestic life. Her life's ambition in North Adams had been to be a good wife and mother and to run an orderly and proper household. She had been unaware that California would utterly rearrange and threaten her modest ambitions. For a few quiet moments, with light rain pelting the roof and a fire in the stove warming the house, she felt calm and as though she were close to fulfilling her role in life.

Caleb was a man who liked to learn. He often regretted not having pursued higher education. The flow and energy of the water in the ditch fascinated him. There was so much energy in even the slowest-moving stream of water. He would assist the surveyor as the rod man when a new ditch had to be added or replaced. The surveyor needed to find a line along the hillside or a flat plane that allowed the water ditches' slow declination of 3 feet per mile. Such a small incline allowed the water to flow for over 20 miles from the dam's head gates.

Caleb's interest in science and mechanical arts was not confined to the flow of water, dams, and canals. He was always reading books and newspapers and focused on the stories of scientific advancements. Before Ruth Anne lost the baby, he would frequently read articles to Ruth Anne out loud, in the evening by the oil lamp. For months, Caleb had been quiet with his readings, not wanting to intrude on Ruth Anne's grief, pretending as if everything was normal.

As Ruth Anne murmured under her breath about her knitting, Caleb began reading for her and the baby to hear. The improbable text came from the California Register of 1857, postulating on the causes of volcanoes and earthquakes in the state.

"A small quantity of vapor, almost instantly generated at some considerable depth below the surface of the earth, will produce a wave like motion. The manner in which this motion will be propagated, may in some measure be represented by the following experiment: Suppose a large cloth or carpet, spread upon the floor, to be raised at one edge, and then suddenly brought down again to floor, the air under it being by this means propelled, will pass along till it escapes at the opposite side, raising the cloth in a wave as it goes."

Caleb, a child at heart, jumped out of his chair onto the floor. The baby, sitting on an old cow hide used as a rug, was startled. Caleb lifted one side of the hide, flapping it up and down, calling out, "Earthquake, earthquake, earthquake." The baby began laughing at all the motion and rolled backward, his head landing on Ruth Anne's foot. "Caleb," Ruth Anne sternly addressed him with a smile on her face, "You made him pee. Now I have to change him." Soon, all three of the little home's residents drifted off to sleep with the rain tapping on the windowpanes that evening.

The morning light, filtered by a high overcast of clouds, seeped into the house. The baby, now growing strong and recovered from his head wound, rolled out of the wooden box on the floor where he slept next to Ruth Anne and Caleb. He looked around the room, at windows framed with the morning light, then at the figures soundly asleep in their bed. He crawled on all fours over to the metal framed bed and pulled himself up next to Caleb.

The vocalization of "Papa" came in unison with the child's patting Caleb's face with his hand. Caleb woke up and stared into the eyes of this little creature he had rescued so many weeks earlier. Caleb smiled at the boy and then said, "Ruth Anne, someone is hungry." "What?" came her sleepy reply. She turned to see the baby boy gently tapping Caleb's face and muttering something that sounded like "Papa." With an air of sarcasm that Ruth Anne had not known lived within her, she said, "Oh, I see, I saved your life, but your first words are 'papa'?"

6 Temporary Family

The day came when Caleb and Ruth Anne had to visit the county courthouse to establish some sort of guardianship for the Chinese boy. As they were getting ready, Ruth Anne asked Caleb, "If they want to know his name, what do we say?" Caleb thought for a moment and replied, "Boyton." A little surprised at Caleb's inventiveness, Ruth Anne responded, "Boyton? What sort of name is that?" "Well," said Caleb, "he is a boy, and he already weighs a ton – Boyton."

Ruth Anne was quiet. She really did not want to pursue the conversation. Naming him assumed that they might be keeping the young boy for a considerable amount of time. But she knew there was a possibility that they would have to give the child over to some court officer.

The high, thin clouds had given way to large, white fluffy clouds that quickly moved across a brilliant blue sky pushed by a cold wind. When Ruth Anne stepped outside the house into the sunshine, she was immediately warmed by the bright sun. When one of the big cumulous clouds would pass overhead, she felt the chill of the air cutting through her coat. The road was wet from the night rain. Most people would agree that a few springtime mud puddles were better than the dust of a dry summer road.

Caleb hitched the old mare to the buggy and brought it around to the front of the house. He helped Ruth Anne up to the seat and then handed Boyton up to her. Caleb climbed on to the buggy, grabbed the reins, and asked, "Are you ready?" "Yes," she replied.

The old mare began slowly and then picked up the pace as she got used to pulling the buggy. The canopy was pulled forward as a precaution against any stray thunderstorm that might develop as they rode up to Flagston.

The ride of the buggy was so effortless compared to the old wagon that Caleb was able to drive and talk at the same time. Suddenly the Caleb of North Adams was sitting next to Ruth Anne. From the instant they started their journey, Caleb kept up a running commentary of everything they saw, past, present, and future. The main focus of his thoughts was the Valley Springs water ditch, how it was constructed, what he had built, what he helped maintain, his customers, and the future that all the water would help develop in California.

The buggy traveled down the road, mirroring the twists and turns of the river through the canyon. Several miles south of Carrolton the low hills pulled back from the river. A gap between the oak-studded ridges looked like a horse saddle, hence the name Saddle Gap. Millenia before, the river would swell and spill over at Saddle Gap, out into the valley on the other side of the river canyon. Enterprising miners found that sediment on the valley side of Saddle Gap harbored gold dust. Dry diggings commenced, washed by a small spring of water nearby.

As soon as the Valley Springs water ditch was constructed, a branch line was cut at Saddle Gap to supply the miners. At this point, the water ditch was a couple hundred feet above the river, but a mile distant as the water canal followed the hillsides. Caleb had worked on excavating the landscape for the ditch to service Saddle Gap. To keep the elevation correct and feed the water over the saddle properly, a deep cut was dug.

The area became known as Deep Cut at Saddle Gap. The sides of the deep cut were close to 20 feet high above the crest of the saddle. While much of the cut was through granite, the deep cut was always a constant problem for Caleb and his ditch tender. Small frequent landslides filled the ditch and blocked the water flow. Caleb meticulously conveyed all this history to Ruth Anne as the buggy bounced over the road.

As they crested the saddle and started down the mild descent into the valley, they heard a cry of "Waddy man! Waddy man!" A smiling Chinese man with a wide brim hat was waving his hand over his head. "Ah Fong," shouted Caleb, slowing the buggy to talk with the Chinese man. Caleb leaned over to Ruth Ann and explained that the Chinese miners he sold water to jokingly called him the water man, but it always came out sounding like "waddy man."

Caleb jumped from the buggy and walked over to Ah Fong. Ruth Anne could hear the two men discuss something related to the water and their mining operation, which looked like a jagged gash in the earth meandering around the young oak trees. The Chinese had built an extensive operation of interconnecting sluice boxes. One miner shoveled dry dirt into buckets, then another miner carried each bucket over to the wooden structure filled with running water from the ditch and dumped it into the sluice. Another miner tossed out large rocks from the deposited earth and kept the water flowing toward the end where the water slid out of the sluice, creating a small 4-foot waterfall to the earth below.

Ruth Anne watched all the activity from her position in the buggy. There must have been six or eight Chinese men digging, dumping, and cleaning the sluice box. She did not really understand where the gold was found. Caleb told her later that the bottom of the sluice box had little riffles filled with a thin layer of quicksilver. As the water flowed the length of the sluice, the fine gold dust was trapped in the little riffles and absorbed by the quick silver. After running the sluice box for several days or a week, the miners would perform a clean-up in which they heated the quicksilver amalgam. Heated, the shiny quicksilver metal would evaporate into the air, leaving the gold dust behind.

As Ruth Anne patiently waited with Boyton in the buggy, she heard a shout next to her, "Hi baby, hi baby." Ruth Anne snapped her head in the direction of the voice with an expression like she had just seen a rattlesnake. The voice came from one of the Chinese miners, who was friendly, smiling, waiving at Boyton, greeting the mother and child with "Hi baby, hi baby." Ruth Anne watched the young Chinese man as he made his way around the front of the old mare and down to the mining operation where he started shoveling dirt into a bucket.

This encounter unsettled Ruth Anne, and she was anxious to leave. She did not know if the Chinese men knew that her baby was Chinese or how she came by him, this orphan in her arms. She was relieved when Caleb climbed back into the buggy and started back on the road to Flagston. Caleb told her Ah Fong wanted to know if they could get more water, as they were going to open more ground to mining on the saddle slope. The dirt was paying upwards of $5 dollars per day. It was not an operation that white miners would undertake, because the gold yield for the work was too small.

The ride up the Quartz Hill to Flagston road was pleasant. The slope was gentle, and the road wound around large, imposing granite outcroppings and past green meadows. Parts of the road were lined with large oak and pine trees on both sides. The trees created a canopy above, making the travelers feel like they were passing through a covered bridge. Caleb, less familiar with this part of the country, did note that there was talk of running a railroad from Quartz Hill to Flagston.

Ruth Anne pursed her lips and thought a train would not be a good idea because it would be too noisy and a disruption to the beautiful countryside. This road reminded her of the road between North Adams and Williams Town. Parts of the road were idyllic as it ran next to the Hoosic River, but then a train would come by and break the silence and foul the air with coal smoke. No, a railroad would not be good in this part of the country, she thought.

After a brief series of sharp curves up a short, steep slope, the buggy crested the top of the ridge line. Caleb pulled over and helped Ruth Anne and Boyton from the buggy. They walked over to the edge of the river canyon and looked down at the river over 800 feet below them. From this vantage point, Ruth Anne could trace the river as it roared over rocks in the river and wound its way through the cut it had eroded over thousands of years.

Ruth Anne could see the river motion, the white water, and the spray of the water as it dropped over waterfalls. She could see the river writhing in the canyon, but she could not hear it, as it was too far away. Directly in front of them, she could see little yellow-bellied warblers flitting between the shrubs clinging to the rocky ledge. Floating over the river, swaying back and forth on the air currents, were red-tailed hawks, vultures, and a few bald eagles.

Caleb pointed out a line in the river that was the Valley Springs Water Company dam. She could barely discern the thin line of the water ditch beginning at the head of dam and clinging to the rocky hillside as it traveled to Bretton Falls, Carrolton, and points beyond. Also visible was how the height of the mountains and hills became less as they approached the valley. It was a distinct horizon that transitioned from the green hills to bright blue sky, overseen by the large white cumulous clouds silently moving from east to west overhead.

There was so much motion accompanied by so much silence, high on the brow of the mountain top. "Where is Devil's Den?" Ruth Anne suddenly asked Caleb. "Devil's Den? Well, let's see, down there you can barely make out the town of Bretton Falls. You cross over the flimsy foot bridge that I found you at, and up to that craggy mountain top on the other side of the river," explained Caleb. "How do you know about Devil's Den?" he asked her. She mumbled that she had overheard Caleb and some of the other men talking about it.

Caleb had never probed Ruth Anne about her experience on the other side of river with Boyton. He wanted to let it lapse into forgotten history, and Ruth Anne was comfortable with that prospect. Caleb added, "You can't easily get to Devil's Den from the river below. It's too steep and riddled with splintered ravines. They say a band of Indians still holds out below the den, but no one has seen them for years. The only to access to the area was through Coleville." "Oh," said Ruth Anne, as she counted herself among the few pioneers who had reached the Devil's Den.

The three of them continued their journey into Flagston, which was built in a bowl on top of the hill. Fire had swept through the town a few years earlier and virtually wiped it off the map. Caleb thought that fire should be added to the farmer's almanac, because the eruption of fire that regularly obliterated the little gold rush towns built of wood was as predictable as the phases of the moon or the tides in San Francisco Bay. As they rode up the main street of Flagston, it was evident that many of the town's structures were new. While many of the stores and houses had been rebuilt with wood, there were many new brick buildings and structures of granite and slate blocks.

Ruth Anne was impressed with the state of the town. Many men and women walked up and down the main street, protected from the elements by the wooden awnings above the storefronts. She could see herself living in such a town, except for the risk of fire that terrified her. Flagston was quite different from Carrolton. Dry goods and hardware stores outnumbered saloons along the main street. There was even a store that sold fabric and women's dresses. Civilized people must have founded the town.

Caleb turned down one street and up a slight incline to the new county courthouse. The fine brick structure was still being finished and adorned with woodwork on the outside. Carrying Boyton, Caleb and Ruth Anne entered the courthouse, made their way to one of the courtrooms, and took a seat at the back of the sparse space.

At the front of the courtroom on a raised platform sat a man with a full head of gray hair and a long gray beard. The sight of such an old man was shocking to Ruth Anne. She had not seen an old person since leaving North Adams. California did not have old people. Everyone was young in California. She had seen a few men and women with a little gray in their hair, but not many. The average age of most East Coast, European, and Chinese immigrants to California seemed to be about 35, with the newest arrivals, like Ruth Anne, much younger.

Judge Prewitt, his face illuminated by his gray hair and beard, was presiding over some sort of dispute between two groups of roughly clothed miners. On one side of the room was a group of white miners wearing flannel shirts and suspenders, with hats in hand. On the other side of the room was a group of Chinese miners, their long black hair pulled back into ponytails trailing down their backs. Even though the Chinese miners had an interpreter to communicate their position to Judge Prewitt, many of them were prone to outbursts in Chinese, pointing their fingers at the white miners.

Caleb and Ruth Anne watched the surreal play as the white miners objected and shouted, the Chinese miners protested in Cantonese, and Judge Prewitt periodically banged his gavel to quiet the opposing groups of men. What Caleb and Ruth Anne were able to discern was that the white miners had sold a mining claim to the Chinese miners for $100. The Chinese miners subsequently found there a great pocket of gold at the river's edge. The sellers were now contesting the sale of the claim to the Chinese mining company, saying the sale price had really been $1,000 and they were owed another $900.

To no one's satisfaction, Judge Prewitt held over the mining claim dispute until the next day, when both parties were to present better documents showing the bill of sale and boundaries of the claim on the river.

"Ok, what's next?" Judge Prewitt addressed his clerk. "Your Honor, the request for guardianship by Caleb and Ruth Anne Gibbons of an orphaned China boy," the clerk replied without looking up at either the judge or the petitioners.

Caleb and Ruth Anne approached the table where the Judge was seated. Judge Prewitt observed, "That's not a boy; that's a baby," with a slight smile on his face. Ruth Anne began to relax when she saw the old judge express a little humanity after the stern procedural lecture he had given the quarrelling miners earlier. "You are petitioning for guardianship of this baby of Chinese origin, correct?" the judge asked. "Correct," answered Caleb.

"What is the baby's name, if you know it?" asked the Judge. "We call him Boyton," answered Caleb. "Hmm," pondered the Judge. "Do you know the child's parents or where they might be?" Caleb answered, "We believe the father may have been killed in a rock fall accident at a mining camp on the river. We don't know if the mother is alive or dead." "Okay," replied the Judge, "and you want to assume guardianship of this baby?"

It appeared that the Judge was going to continue his thought, but before he could start the next sentence, Ruth Anne proclaimed, "Yes," her answer ringing loud and clear through the courtroom. Both Caleb and the judge looked at her in surprise when she spoke. Up to now, the Judge had addressed only Caleb, ignoring the woman holding the baby.

The judge then directed his comments to Ruth Anne. "You do know that this baby is of Chinese origin? You are not Chinese. You don't speak Chinese," the judge stated to Ruth Anne in a paternal tone. Ruth Anne flushed at the judge's lecture on the obvious. "The child needs to be with his own people. I don't think it is necessarily a good proposition that Americans should raise Chinese children, and vice versa," observed the judge.

He then sat back in his chair, pondering the situation. "Given that the county has no orphanage for Chinese children, and there is a probability that the mother or father may still be alive, I will grant temporary guardianship of the child to you. Further, I will instruct the Sheriff and Constables to be alert for any Chinese man or woman inquiring about a missing child. When the rightful parents are found, we will be able to reunite the child with his parents. Clerk, please write up the order for me to sign." Then, addressing Caleb and Ruth Anne, he said, "The clerk will have the paperwork for you shortly, and you can pay him $4.50 for the service."

The judge abruptly rose from his chair and, without saying another word, left the courtroom, leaving Caleb and Ruth Anne to wonder what to do next. The clerk told them to return in a couple hours, after the judge had had his lunch, and the temporary guardianship document would be ready. Caleb and Ruth Anne nodded, turned around, and left the courthouse in silence.

It was a rare treat for Ruth Anne and Caleb to eat at a restaurant. They walked into one of Flagston's several restaurants, featuring wooden floors and an open beam ceiling, and sat down at a table. Ruth Anne was careful to keep the blanket pulled over Boyton's head so no one could see he was Chinese. The meal almost seemed like a celebration, but the two were uncomfortably aware it also could be the beginning of the end of Ruth Anne's brief encounter with motherhood, should Boyton's parents be expeditiously found and Boyton reunited with them. After their meal, they returned to the courthouse and picked up the temporary guardianship documents from the clerk.

The horse and buggy trotted up to the top of the hill and turned onto the road back to Carrolton. Before them Caleb and Ruth Anne could see a towering cumulonimbus cloud developing over the Sierras, 40 miles away. As it grew in height and width, the towering white cloud reflected the afternoon sun back to them. Even from their distance, they could perceive its growth, quietly and slowly exploding like a volcano in slow motion. A veil of mist formed on top of the cloud and gently cascaded down its sides, as if the cloud was piercing some invisible ceiling.

As they watched the towering cloud miraculously grow, no doubt raining underneath it, Caleb and Ruth Anne could see the sky becoming dark over the valley. They decided to keep moving down the hill. The large, white fluffy clouds that had resembled floating sheep earlier in the day began to merge. There was less blue sky between them and more dark brooding clouds overhead. Soon there was no blue sky, only ominously dark cloud cover.

As the buggy traveled along the road next to towering oak and pine trees, a flash of bright light snapped in front of them. In that instant flash, Ruth Anne could see the vivid and distinct shadows of the tree trunks, limbs, and leaves on the road in front of them. No sooner had the light faded than there was a thunderous crack and boom. Boyton immediately began to cry. The old mare startled and picked up the pace into a quick trot, the best she could manage, while bucking her head up nervously.

Caleb tried to calm the old mare. Ruth Anne attempted to console Boyton. Just when horse and baby were beginning to calm, the rain began to pour. The buggy canopy, ostensibly meant to shield the passengers from the rain, became a giant funnel, focusing all the rain on the occupants of the buggy. It did not help that the rain was blowing in from the south, the same direction in which the buggy was traveling.

For 10 miles they endured cold rain pouring from the sky and onto the buggy. Small depressions in the road became raging creeks. It was raining so hard and fast that Caleb could barely see the road. The hooves of the old mare along with the front wheels were kicking up mud that found its way into the buggy and onto its passengers. Of all the weather-related experiences Ruth

Anne had suffered through since coming to California, this raging thunderstorm was the worst.

When the buggy finally reached Saddle Gap, they turned onto the road that ran up the river to Carrolton. Now, the wind was at their backs. It was a little comfort that they were no longer being pelted by torrents of rain. They had been soaked by the thunderstorm. Short of jumping in the river, they could not have been more wet or cold. Caleb and Ruth Anne were never so glad to see their two-room shack of a house come into view.

In the morning, the sky was blue and not a cloud could be seen. Ruth Anne looked out the back door and saw the heavy rain had washed out part of her garden. She was mildly irritated because the carrot seeds she planted had just germinated. There was a loud banging on the front door of the cabin. Ruth Anne opened the door to be greeted by Jonah, who spit out, "Is Caleb up? We got to go, a tree came down at mile marker 5 and took out part of the flume." Caleb hastily pulled on his clothes, grabbed a biscuit, and left with Jonah to repair the ditch.

Ruth Anne was sad Caleb was called away: she had been hoping they could talk about the future now that they had temporary guardianship of Boyton. She hated the word "temporary." She felt the term cast a shadow on her ability to care for Boyton. She was not the one who left the child to die. She was the one who walked for miles, crossed a flimsy bridge, and convinced a band of starving Indians to help save the baby from certain death. She was not temporary in her mind. She secretly hoped that she was permanent.

The thunderstorm and wet buggy ride home from the courthouse had stolen any opportunity for conversation Ruth Anne and Caleb might have had about the future. The guardianship and their roles in Boyton's life were fresh, and now was the perfect time to talk. Ruth Anne feared that when Caleb returned home – repairing the flume could take days – they would simply resume their normal lives, and the reality of this temporary parenthood would fade away. They would go on with their lives like nothing happened, caring for Boyton, and not thinking about the future.

With Caleb gone and the baby asleep, Ruth Anne sat down to write her sister a letter with the last piece of writing paper she had.

Dear Martha,

I hope this letter finds you and your family healthy. We have avoided any major illnesses or accidents here in California. Caleb bought a buggy, and we were thoroughly drenched from a thunderstorm while on a ride into the countryside. I was reminded of when during a thunderstorm mother would keep us inside the house because she feared we would be struck by lightning.

The big downpour of rain washed out part of my garden, the carrots had just germinated. The soil is not very good here, very sandy. If you do not water the garden every day in the summer, the vegetables just wilt and die. Some of the neighbors are experimenting with planting fruit trees. One man is planting a whole hillside in grape vines for wine. There seems to be enough alcohol in this town already.

I'm very saddened over this war between the states. We try to contribute to the Sanitary Fund for wounded Union soldiers often. Our little town of Carrolton raised close to $100 for the fund last month. Some of the men have left the area to fight for the Union or the rebels, but not many. Most of the families are from Europe and a considerable number from China.

God has blessed many families with babies up and down the river. We are now part of the Rockrose School District. Caleb helped build the one room schoolhouse on the ridge above the town. The men also improved the trail up to the schoolhouse to make it easier for the children to walk to school. It is nice to see the community work together and build a nice town like North Adams.

There has been talk of opening a hard rock mine across the river. Caleb was talking about having to run a water pipe from the Valley Springs water ditch over the river to the new mine. I guess that work and his other responsibilities will keep us in Carrolton a little bit longer. I was hoping Caleb would take a job closer to Flagston or Quartz Hill. Caleb has been saving money to buy some land when the government maps are released in a couple of years.

Give all my love to Papa and may the grace of our Lord bless him and you, forever. I say a prayer for all of you every night before I sleep. I will write a longer letter when I have more paper.

Love, Your Sister, Ruth Anne Gibbons.

Rereading the letter, Ruth Anne immediately felt shame for not including one line about Boyton. She would never try to write about her trek to the Indian camp or how they had acquired the baby. All of that was too complicated to recite. Without the preface of the arrival of Boyton, it seemed awkward to recount the trip to Flagston for the guardianship hearing. Secrets, so many secrets. It was easier to let her family assume her life in California was no different than it had been in North Adams.

Of course, Ruth Anne's life was very different from that in North Adams. Sometimes she would step out of the little house and forget why she had gone outside. She was having problems with focusing on tasks. Her mind was a swirling tornado of thoughts that did not seem to be connected. She had never experienced such dysphoria.

Her feelings were hard to define, but Ruth Anne did not know what her identity or role was most of the time. In one instant she was a wife cooking breakfast for her husband, then taking care of a baby she had not given birth to, finally writing a letter to her sister full of lies about her life. In addition to her mutating identity, she felt a blanket of paranoia growing heavier every day.

Her and Caleb's guardianship of Boyton was temporary. That meant that any day someone could knock on the door and take her child away. When this stream of consciousness ran through her mind, she would stop, stamp her foot, and remind herself that Boyton was not her child. She did not have a child. The child she had given birth to was buried in the backyard. She attempted to be cavalier with her thoughts and tell herself that she was just Boyton's babysitter until his mother returned for him. The boy was nothing to her. That's when she would clutch her chest, repress a scream, and cry.

After Ruth Anne finished her letter to Martha, she folded the paper into the delivery envelope, addressed it, and prepared Boyton for the walk to the post office. When she stepped out of the front door with Boyton in her arms, Ruth Anne mentally draped herself in a cloak of suspicion. She purposefully pulled the blanket over most of Boyton's face so no one would see he was Chinese.

As she walked down the road to the post office, she studied everyone she saw; was this person the one who would take her baby away from her? If Ruth Anne heard someone speaking Chinese, she stiffened and carefully scanned in the direction of the voice. Was someone pointing her out? That's the woman carrying the Chinese boy. People would greet her on the street, and Ruth Anne, consumed with paranoia, would barely acknowledge their presence.

The one person Ruth Anne could not ignore or avoid was the wild French woman. "*Bonjour, bebe,*" Alma Gosseau greeted Ruth Anne and the baby. Alma's blond curly hair could not be contained or tamed by the headscarf she wore, as though her hair defied all attempts at control. The blond curls burst forth all around the scarf. The curls framed a perpetually wide and inviting smile.

Clothed as usual in a brightly colored patterned dress, Alma was hard to miss. Ruth Anne had dubbed Alma the "wild French woman" because she was like no other individual Ruth Anne had ever met. Ruth Anne was jealous of Alma's gregarious nature, even with strangers, while at the same time cautious of this wild woman. She had to be wild or crazy, Ruth Anne thought, because she was the mother of five children and still exuded more happiness and energy than any woman she had ever met.

"*Bonjour,*" Ruth Anne replied to Alma. "*Tres bien,*" laughed Alma. "Your French is improving," she said, as she stroked Boyton's face with her finger. Alma gazed lovingly at Boyton and sighed, "*Bébé magnifique.*" Ruth Anne relaxed at Alma's kind words and her warm French greeting. She was immediately taken back to her youth in North Adams.

Family trips from North Adams to Williamstown were always exciting occasions. Williamstown was a small college town, and the dress of the people there was different from those in the manufacturing environment of North Adams. The shops down Spring Street in Williamstown were also of a different class than those in her hometown. Even though Williamstown was only 5 miles from North Adams, it had always seemed like a different country to Ruth Anne.

On one occasion, Ruth Anne's father loaded the family into the wagon to collect the tall case clock he had commissioned from Eli Porter in Williamstown. While her father spoke with Eli at his shop and moved the 7-

foot-tall, ornately inlaid clock case into the wagon, Ruth Anne, her sister Martha, and mother strolled down Spring Street.

One of the stores, down an alley, was a bookstore, catering to the college students at Williams College. Ruth Anne and Martha came across a severely weather-worn book for beginning French language students. The leather cover was peeling apart. The pages were stiff and warped as if it had been dropped in water and then left to dry in the corner of the room.

Ruth Anne and Martha were captivated by the book. They giggled as they tried to pronounce the French words. They quizzed one another, "How do you say, 'I would like red wine?'" "How?" Martha asked. "Gee voodrase du vin rooch," replied Ruth Anne. Both girls knew Ruth Anne did not pronounce the sentence correctly, and they both laughed hard. They begged their mother to buy them the book of French dreams. The shopkeeper was happy to let the old decrepit book go for a severely discounted price.

All the way back home, a slow journey as their father did not want to injure the tall case clock in the back of the wagon, the girls read the French translations of English words, idioms, and adages to one another. The French book would provide hours of entertainment for the young sisters and sparked dreams of marrying a French aristocrat and moving to France.

The dreams had ended abruptly two years later when Ruth Anne's mother died. The weather-worn book, a window to a fantasy future, was shut. With the death of their mother, Ruth Anne and Martha had to focus on life in North Adams, finding a local man to marry and caring for their father. All those old daydreams of a French future came fluttering back to Ruth Anne whenever she would meet the wild French woman on the road.

Ruth Anne would occasionally attempt a French word or phrase with the wild French woman, who would gently correct her pronunciation, always with a smile. Through extended conversation in which Ruth Anne was frequently confused at what the wild French woman was trying to convey, Ruth Anne did learn that Alma and her husband, Auturo, were from Fayau. South of France's Bordeaux area, Fayau was a wine growing region similar in climate to California's Bay Area counties.

A group of men from the Fayau region in France had decided to come to California in 1855 together to mine for gold as a company. On arrival in California, they were disappointed to learn that gold was to be found, not in the cooler climates close to San Francisco, but in the hot interior foothill landscape. The men and their families settled along the river in and around Carrolton and took over the mining claim from some Portuguese miners who had given up.

The Fayau mining men were not making the golden earnings they had dreamed of back in France. Alma had taken to being a washer woman, washing the clothes of the miners in Carrolton. The laundress income added to the little bit of gold Auturo pulled out of the riverbank. Some of the Fayau men had moved over to Napa and Sonoma to work in the emerging vineyards and winemaking. Auturo was in conversations with a new vineyard down by Saddle Gap to help make wine and sparkling wine. As the wild French woman explained:

"Not Champagne, sparking wine. Champagne can only be made in Champagne, France. Everything else is inferior, but Auturo will make the best sparkling wine California will ever produce. I wanted to make real French cheese, but there are only cows here, no goats, I need goats for goat milk, it makes the best cheese. I wanted to open a bakery. The flour in California is awful. I need good French wheat, finely ground, to make superior baguettes. So now I wash clothes, and the clothes of my five children, wonderful children, like your baby, what is his name? He is so cute. I heard you were at Mr. Hoxie's getting milked. Oh, that's funny, you got milked, all over you and baby. I must go to see Mr. White the Blacksmith. Isn't that funny, the Blacksmith is named Mr. White? *Au revoir.*"

Ruth Anne muttered "*Au revoir*," as the wild French woman was already out of earshot. Most of Ruth Anne's conversations with the wild French woman were one-sided. Alma Gosseau spoke rapidly, in a mix of French and English, about variety of topics or town gossip.

Part of the reason Alma Gosseau was called the wild French woman was her interminable energy. How was she always so good-natured and full of life with five children, including her husband, who often acted like a child? Ruth Anne wondered. Auturo Gosseau, like his wife, always had a smile on his face. A short man with a round face on a round head of thinning hair, Auturo was always waving hello, telling jokes, and laughing. His laugh could be heard across the river.

The afternoon was bright, clear, and warm for early springtime. Ruth Anne decided to repair the garden that had been partially washed out by the thunderstorm. She spread out the cow hide rug in the back of the house for Boyton to sit on. Over the past weeks, Ruth Anne had acquired a few wooden blocks and trinkets for Boyton to play with.

Boyton ignored the toys and looked around at all the trees and birds. Every red-tailed hawk that floated by grabbed his attention, and he focused on it until the bird moved behind a tree or building. A small lizard had settled on a rock in the sun warming its body. Boyton reached to grab the lizard, but it was too quick for his fumbling grasp.

The sun's warmth was just perfect for the mother and child. Ruth Anne sat there with Boyton, watching him watching the world, soaking up the warmth of child and sun. The family who lived next door had planted some citrus trees to see how they liked the Carrolton climate. Bees buzzed around the fragrant blossoms, and Boyton struggled to focus on the many bees. His head jerked side to side as he tried to follow the bees zipping back and forth.

Near the back of the house, a little Indian paintbrush plant was growing. The hummingbirds would fly in and hover in front of the flowers. One of the hummingbirds decided to investigate Boyton. As the bird approached Boyton,

Ruth Anne noticed him going cross-eyed to see the bird. Boyton startled at the bird, falling backwards in fear. Ruth Anne laughed out loud. "Boyton, no need to be frightened by a little bird!" she told him.

After a period of leisure, Ruth Anne got up to work on the garden. The garden shovel was old and rusty. The wooden handle, while slightly cracked, was smoothed by the hands of miners over years shoveling dirt into their sluices. Ruth Anne worked to move dirt eroded from the downpour back into the garden bed and reposition the rocks that had created the border. It was hard work, and she enjoyed it. She felt productive.

Behind the little cabin house that Ruth Anne and Caleb rented from the Valley Springs Water Company was a nice open space. The water ditch outlined the back of the open space 50 feet from the house. The water ditch ran along the base of the hill that it followed. On the hillside grew the standard collection of oak trees, gray pines, and buckeyes, sometimes referred to as horse chestnut. The underbrush could be thick in some parts and included the dreaded poison oak bush, the oil of which transmitted an itchy, painful rash.

Ruth Anne was calculating how best to arrange the rocks that formed a small retaining wall around the garden when she heard the horrific scream of a child. She looked over at the cow hide where Boyton had been sitting. Frantically searching the terrain, her eyes finally picked up on the sight of the baby being dragged over to the few wooden planks spanning the water ditch that acted as a bridge. The mangy culprit stealing her child was a coyote.

Ruth Anne ran to the crime scene, raising the shovel over her head. She had to stop the coyote before it crossed the water ditch and escaped up the hill into the thick bushes. She screamed and cursed at the coyote as she charged. The coyote abduction was slowed, as Boyton was bigger than the coyote had surmised. Boyton, under Ruth Anne's strict feeding regimen, had been gaining almost a pound a week. As Ruth Anne got close to the coyote, she swung the shovel down like the blade of a guillotine.

The shovel hit the coyote in the neck but did not kill it. The coyote released Boyton from its jaws and ran off yelping, blood dripping from the back of its neck. Boyton's arm ran with blood where the coyote's teeth had gripped him. Ruth Anne scooped up Boyton and ran into the house. She plopped the baby down on the rough kitchen table and reached for a cloth to clean his puncture wounds with soap and water.

After mother and child had calmed down, Ruth Anne realized she had acted in that crisis with the energy of the wild French woman and the instincts of the chicken-killing woman. She also realized that, had her shovel aim been less true, it might have been Boyton who received the blow to the neck and not the coyote. "Dear Lord," she said to herself, "I'm a bad mother. Give me the strength to be better."

In addition to humans, Ruth Anne now had to add animals to her list of potential baby thieves. The only people, so far, who did not want to take the

Chinese boy from her were the generous Indian men and women. Over the next several weeks, Ruth Anne would gradually come to realize that most people she encountered were indifferent to her caretaking of the Chinese child. To the contrary, many of the Carrolton citizens held Ruth Anne in high esteem for her sacrifice and empathy to care for an orphaned child.

Carrolton was an isolated mining community on the river. The major roads crisscrossing the foothills of California as the state grew had bypassed the town, which was situated at the base of steep and rugged hills. The easiest way into town was the long road down by the confluence of the north and south forks of the river system or from the west, over a spot known as Saddle Gap. Carrolton was similar to other Gold Rush river towns that would eventually evaporate into history.

When the Gold Rush blossomed, so did Carrolton. Its river bars were rich in placer gold. Carrolton, along with other small mining villages, developed overnight like weeds. In a brief span of time, most of the other small mining towns had withered away as the easy placer gold was vacuumed out of the bed of the river. Carrolton hung on to its little perch on a bluff above the river.

At the height of its prosperity, Carrolton boasted several butchers, bakers, and wagon makers. There were two express companies and an assay office. Saloons were numerous along the main dirt road through town. The townspeople organized a small schoolhouse as young families who had settled there began to have children.

It was the post office that helped keep Carrolton on the map. At one time, there were five daily stagecoaches stopping at Carrolton. By the time Ruth Anne had settled in the area, the town was down to one daily stagecoach, and it was primarily for the purpose of delivering the mail. If Carrolton lost its post office, the town would lose its daily connection to the outside world.

The beauty of the area was beyond debate. If one could ignore the landscape ravaged by mining along the river, the dramatic granite walls above the town and rugged slate hills across the river were visually stunning. Pines and oaks dotted the hillsides. When the naked rock was wet after a rainstorm, it displayed a subtle rainbow of color, streaks of red, blue, and green as if someone had climbed up the hill and painted the cold granite and slate.

The pallet of color was enhanced by the vibrant green lichen growing on the sides of the oak trees, the ferns growing out of rock crevices, and the hazy blue reflected by the blue oak leaves. In the winter and spring, a small stream of water would cascade over the face of the granite near the summit and disappear into the trees below. The locals named the spot Granite Bluff waterfalls.

Many of the European immigrants who came to the area seeking better lives said they liked Carrolton and its landscape because it reminded them of their native countries. Ruth Anne could not disagree that the little town was a beautiful, if isolated, place. The cabin that Caleb and Ruth Anne moved into when they arrived in Carrolton was owned by the Valley Springs Water

Company. It was a two-room structure that also included a small stable and tack room. The rustic structure was never meant to be a long-term family residence. It was more for a solitary water agent.

Normally, Caleb would conduct his duties through the district on horseback, riding his horse alongside the water ditch. The company gave him a small stipend to feed his horse. Unfortunately, he was frequently without a good horse, as they would either go lame or be stolen. The horse theft was usually blamed on the Indian men, who were sparse in the area and who seemed to be rapidly dying off from a variety of introduced illnesses contracted from the white immigrants.

Shortly after Ruth Anne and Caleb arrived in Carrolton, he took her down to the river, to a massive flat granite boulder protruding from the riverbank out into the water. The huge formation was large enough to be a dance platform for several couples to waltz around its surface. The only problem that Ruth Anne saw with the dance floor were the numerous holes in the granite. The holes were 3 to 4 inches across and 6 or 7 inches deep and perfectly smooth inside.

Ruth Anne asked Caleb what had made the holes. He recounted the story of when he had first arrived in the gold fields and would see naked Indian women smashing acorns in the holes. The women were practicing their people's ancient way of grinding the acorns into a meal used to make a nutritious acorn mush. Ruth Anne had trouble visualizing naked women pounding acorns in the place where she was standing. She decided to banish the image from her mind and instead focus on the sight of the flowing river.

The river seemed to gush from the narrow canyon upstream. Each year, when the snow melted in the spring, the wild river flow was pinched between two opposing granite monoliths, creating a roaring sound accompanied by plumes of white water. The low hills across the river would become a carpet of colorful wildflowers after the rainy season. Even during the hottest summer days, a cool dry breeze floated up the canyon, making life bearable for the inhabitants of Carrolton.

7 Gold Bug

It did not go unnoticed by Ruth Anne that Caleb was trying to acknowledge and support his accidental family. There was the new cast iron stove he had come home with one afternoon, a buggy for easier family travel, and - surprise – a new room addition onto the little house. Caleb received the permission of the Valley Springs Water Company to add a room to their little abode. They agreed to pay for the lumber if Caleb built the addition.

Although construction would take several months to complete, once it was finished, Boyton had his own little room. Ruth Anne suspected that Caleb had wanted the extra bedroom so that Boyton would not crawl up onto his chest in the mornings and wake him up. Boyton had become a little alarm clock, keeping much better time than the old clock they had inherited with the house. Caleb promised Ruth Anne that as soon as he finished the additional room, he would turn his attention to the errant clock. Unfortunately, like any real '49er, Caleb still felt the pull of gold mining.

Once a man has been bitten by the Gold Bug, there is no vaccine that will eradicate the virus from his body. The only treatment for the disease directly relates to the success or failure of the man's mining activity. If a man spends days, weeks, or months digging dry hole after dry hole, he will eventually become disgusted with the pursuit, developing immunity to the "bug."

Alternatively, if a man had the good fortune to find some deep pockets of placer gold, he might be able to leave the mining business comfortably with his profits and pursue other opportunities. California offered many other lucrative endeavors, such as hard rock mining or hydraulic mining, to which many men transitioned after the riverbed placer gold yields declined. All mining pursuits, whether using a pan, sluice, water, pick or drill, were equally hard on a man's body.

Regardless of the final outcome of a man's pursuit for gold or his subsequent occupations, the symptoms of the gold bug virus remained in the body. The virus is never eradicated; it only lies dormant. Even men who had long retired from gold mining still looked upon men pursuing the arduous work with respect, if not with a wee bit of envy. For has there never been a man who did not want to relive his youth, when the body was strong, and he could spend sunrise to sunset mining for gold?

Caleb was no different than thousands of other men who had been bitten by the gold bug. From atop his horse, he would gaze down on the mining companies of Irish, French, German, and Chinese men shoveling dirt into the sluice boxes, hoping for a big payday. If his body and time had permitted, he would happily have joined them. Indeed, Caleb occasionally furnished his labor at some of the mining operations in exchange for a cut of the day's washings.

The man infected by the gold bug was constantly scanning the landscape for a favorable location to mine for gold. It might be a creek bed revealed by a recent fire that had not been thoroughly prospected. Any glimpse of the brilliant white of a quartz vein running through a hillside of granite would freeze the gold-hunting man in his tracks. It was quartz rock that held the gold. All the men had to do was find a way to extract the white rock, crush it, and separate the gold from the white sand and powder.

When Caleb had stopped the buggy at Saddle Gap on the way up to Flagston for the guardianship hearing, part of his conversation with Ah Fong had been in regard to new dry diggings. Both men had noticed the vegetation on the ridges that made up either side of Saddle Gap. When willows and cottonwoods were present in the landscape, there was a good bet for a continual or seasonal water source. Willows often could be found around some of the artesian wells or springs that bubbled up at the base of the hills.

Conversely, stands of blue oaks, notoriously drought tolerant, indicated a lack of soil moisture. It was such a stand of blue oaks, on either side of Saddle

Gap, that was distinctly different from the other trees and shrubs upslope from the tail of the ridges. The tails were just blue oaks and grasses. Ah Fong had walked on top of the ridges and found that just beneath the thin topsoil, the subsurface was composed of round smooth cobble rock. The blue oaks were growing in a landscape with little soil water-holding capacity. There was virtually no soil, just rocks.

Ah Fong and his company of Chinese miners cut a trench down one side of the ridge tail and found a 20-foot-thick layer of cobble stones sitting on a layer of granite bedrock. Caleb agreed with Ah Fong that the area was the site of an ancient river or overflow from the river. The smooth, round cobble stones had been deposited thousands of years ago on top of the granite. Since there was gold in the sediment on the slope below Saddle Gap leading out to the valley, therefore surely, it was assumed, there must be gold on top of the granite under and all around those cobble stones. This conclusion was reasonable, because all the gold mined from the river was found on top of bedrock covered by similar cobble stones.

Caleb struck a deal with Ah Fong. If Ah Fong's mining company would clean out the water ditch, which had become choked with weeds and cattails, Caleb could sell them more water. Caleb was authorized to pay the Chinese laborers $0.75 per day. The prevailing wage for white labor was $1.50 per day. The Chinese laborers did a superior job cleaning out the water ditch, and Caleb was able to sell them a few more miner's inches of water.

Ah Fong started the new mining operation by digging a hole from the top of the ridge down to the granite bedrock. The large hole, large enough to accommodate two men, 15 feet deep. Most of the miners called this a coyote hole. The Chinese miners simultaneously dug a tunnel at the base of the ridge where the cobble layer met the granite. The tunnel intersected with the coyote hole that was approximately 6 foot in diameter. It required a tremendous amount of labor moving all those cobble rocks, ranging in weight from 5 to 20 pounds each.

From the initial hole, tunnel, and interstitial soil around the cobble stones, the Chinese men pulled about $10 in gold. That was not quite a bonanza considering it had taken several weeks of hard labor to dig the coyote hole and tunnel. As the miners were sweeping sand, potentially containing gold dust, out of the mining operation, the unsupported tunnel collapsed, trapping one of Ah Fong's men inside.

The whole mining company frantically worked to free the trapped man. Some men worked at clearing the tunnel, which was hazardous duty. Another group started digging from the top down, to where the man was thought to be trapped. After a full day of nonstop work, the miners finally reached their comrade, who had been killed by the weight of the cobble stones.

After a period of grieving with a ceremony for the man's spirit, Ah Fong returned to look at the mining disaster. What he saw was a rough open trench, 2 feet wide, 15 feet deep and nearly 20 feet in length, that the miners had dug in their desperation to reach the trapped miner. The sight of the excavation gave Ah Fong an idea: Instead of tunnels, which were obviously unstable and dangerous, how about a series of trenches? The mining company set out to create a maze of deep trenches, some no more than 18 inches in width, crisscrossing the ridge.

As their digging expanded, people travelling on the road between Quartz Hill and Flagston would stop and marvel at the trench work of these Chinese miners. Groups would travel out from town to stand on the ridge and watch as the Chinese miners swept up the sand and dirt on top of the granite into sacks deep in the trenches. The full sacks were then handed to another man, who would take them to the sluice to be washed and the gold extracted. The operation was industrious and enterprising. Many of the white miners looked at the operation, shook their heads, and muttered, “I’ll be damned, that’s hard mining.”

8 Broken Time Parenthood

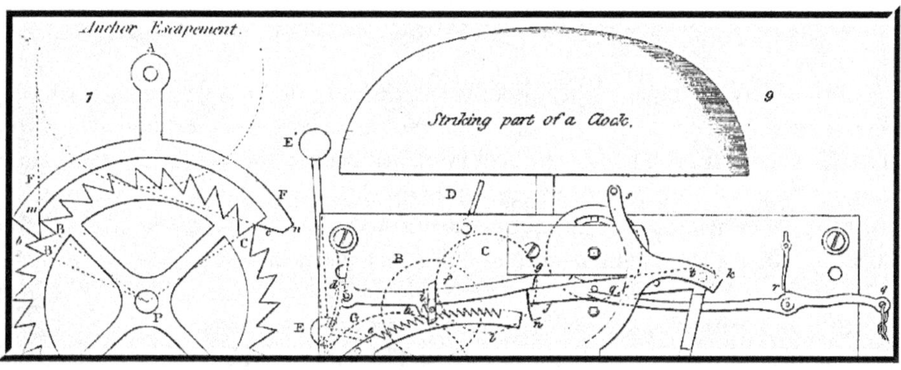

Caleb took Ruth Anne and Boyton out to watch the Chinese trench mining operation as it used Valley Springs water to wash the dirt for its fragments of gold. Caleb was not gold mining, but rather earned his living selling water to the Chinese miners. Ruth Anne expressed the sentiment that she hoped Boyton would not ever have to perform such dangerous work as the Chinese miners did day after day. "Speaking of dangerous work, Caleb," Ruth Anne tossed out, "when are you going to fix the clock, or do we take it up to Flagston to be repaired?" "Boyton and I will work on it later," Caleb replied. Ruth Anne did not know how a 6-year-old child could help fix such a complicated mechanism.

Now six years into their temporary guardianship, the three seemed like a normal family. Ruth Anne would make requests for simple maintenance chores, and Caleb would find excuses not to perform or delay the task. Ruth

Anne knew that Caleb would purposely invoke the Boyton clause of procrastination. Caleb knew that Ruth Anne would grant his excuse of delay if it involved Boyton. Ruth Anne would smile inside when she heard Caleb speak of Boyton in a fatherly manner. Her little family unit brought her more joy than having an old clock keep proper time.

The clock was a rectangular box, 33 inches tall, 18 inches wide, with a depth of 4 inches. It was commonly known as an Ogee design because of the profile of the wood that framed the door. The clock, according to the interior label, had been built in 1835 in Bristol, Connecticut. Ruth Anne felt a common bond with the clock, as they were both about the same age and from New England, now residing in California.

The top half of the clock's door was clear glass to allow the viewer to see the clock's face and time. The bottom half of the door was glass adorned with a hand-painted scene of a colonial New England church on a hill. When the little door was open, you could see the heavy weights on either side that powered the clock mechanism and the little hammer that struck a brass bell to mark the hours. The clock mechanism itself was a series of round gears sandwiched between two pieces of wood. In the small space between the wooden plates, the wheel gears rotated incrementally with each sway of the pendulum.

The arbors or axels of the wheel gears were nestled in little brass bushings or washers on each wooden plate. Caleb could trace the waxed cord from the top of the heavy weight up to a roller at the top of the clock case and then down where it disappeared between the wooden plates. Even though most of the clock mechanism was obscured by the wooden plates, some of the time keeping wheels, clock hands, and wire linkages were clearly visible.

The most fascinating part of the clock for Boyton was the escape wheel with its long, thin, sharp teeth. Preventing the escape wheel from spinning uncontrollably was a thin anchor over it. The ends of the anchor intruded in between the escape wheel teeth. The anchor was connected to the pendulum. As the pendulum swung back and forth, it moved the anchor, like a seesaw. When the pendulum swung to the right, it allowed the escape wheel to tick forward one tooth. On the return swing of the pendulum to the left, the escape wheel locked onto the next tooth, tick-tock, tick-tock, tick-tock.

The clock would run for an hour and then stop. After 20 minutes of fiddling with the clock, Caleb got it to run for an hour, and then it stopped. It was plain to Ruth Anne that Caleb was not enthusiastic about fixing the clock. After staring at the clock mechanism for several hours by the light of an oil lamp, Caleb rose and said, "It is broke. I'll have to buy another one. It's 30 years old. Next time I travel to Sacramento, I'll look for a new clock."

While Caleb may have dismissed the overly complicated contraption of a clock, Boyton continued to study its exposed weights, rollers, wheels, gears, and levers day after day. Ruth Anne had been trying to help Boyton learn to read and write. On the table was a page full of Boyton's exercises writing the alphabet. Ruth Anne turned over the piece of paper for Boyton to begin a new series only to find that he had drawn an illustration of the clock mechanism showing how all the wheels and gears were connected.

Ruth Anne muted her irritation over the waste of the valuable piece of paper with her amusement that Boyton was taking an interest in mechanical objects. He was thinking, and that was good. Boyton was also modestly testing the clock to see how it worked. He found that when he applied a little upward pressure with his hand on the weight that drove the time side of the clock, the pendulum began to swing. When he removed his hand from underneath the cast iron weight, the clock stopped. If he lifted the weight altogether, the clock stopped.

"Papa, Papa, look at this," exclaimed Boyton as Caleb walked into the house. "What you got, son?" Caleb asked. Boyton performed the weight test on the clock and showed Caleb how he could get the clock to start and stop. As Boyton repeated the weight test, Caleb noticed that the front wooden plate would slightly move or flex. He concluded the plate movement might cause the teeth on the wheels to bind with smaller pinion wheels, preventing the clock from rotating.

Caleb was able to adjust the pins that held the front plate so the friction fit was tighter. After he made the front plate more secure, the clock worked without stopping. "Fixed!" proclaimed Caleb, slapping Boyton on the back. Boyton looked up at the tall man, his blond hair thinning, but still with a full beard of red whiskers. He was happy to have Papa's approval. "Does this mean I don't get a new clock?" offered Ruth Anne. "No, ma'am, we'll get you that clock, won't we, Boyton?" said Caleb as he looked at Boyton.

"Son?" Ruth Anne thought to herself. She had heard Caleb call Boyton son. Was that a term of endearment routinely spoken to younger men by the elder, or did Caleb consider Boyton his son? Ruth Anne fought back the welling up of a tear and shouted, "Supper, beef stew and cornbread! Who is hungry?"

Boyton had reached the age where he could help with small chores around the house and in the yard. He helped Caleb with brushing the horses and cleaning the tack. He was always eager to work in the garden with Ruth Anne, although he soon lost interest in pulling weeds and played with the worms and other bugs instead. Boyton was growing into a typical little boy.

After a weekend hunt, Caleb returned with a deer he had shot outside of Coleville. Boyton hesitantly helped Caleb skin the deer and watched as Caleb cut the different pieces of meat to be preserved, given to other families, or prepared that night for supper. When the bloody work was done, Caleb grabbed Boyton, and they both took a bath in the water ditch behind the house. It was over 100 degrees on that September afternoon, and the cool water in the ditch was refreshing.

Caleb did not verbalize his feelings for Boyton. Ruth Anne never asked Caleb how he viewed Boyton. There were certain conversations that were never broached between them. If Caleb were to confess, he occasionally thought about teaching Boyton how to shoot a long rifle or about taking the boy hunting. He tempered these daydreams with the fact that theirs was a temporary guardianship. Any day could bring the mother or father of Boyton to the front door of their house.

The townspeople of Carrolton were in a buoyant mood when they learned of the new bridge over the river to be built at the foot of their community. In addition to some hard rock gold mining operations, a significant deposit of lime had been found south of Coleville. The wagon, stagecoach, and foot traffic over the bridge would surely help their struggling little community. The construction of the wire rope suspension bridge harkened back to the days of '49 when the town had been bustling with people.

The river was the dividing line between counties and geology. It was very plain to anyone who paused to look at the landscape that the banks on the Carrolton side of the river were mainly granite, and on the eastern side of the river the mountains were composed of metamorphic rock like slate. The diverse geology created a juxtaposition between the terrains on the two sides of the river.

The granite around Carrolton was relatively smooth, round, or flat. The large boulders or plutons looked like big balloons rising through a thick sea of mud. When they reached the surface, they just floated in the landscape. In contrast, the slate rock on the other side of the river had sharp angles and poked out of the ground angrily.

The original native inhabitants, Indians, knew the difference. The grinding holes used by the Indians to pulverize acorns and other seeds were found almost exclusively in the fine-grained granite outcroppings and had sides as smooth as porcelain cups. The jagged slate rock on the opposite side was too hard to fashion a smooth hole, difficult to use to create mortars and pestles for grinding.

It was the jagged metamorphic rock that held the deposits of minerals that the immigrants were after. Deep within the slate mountains were lodes of gold and silver. Occasionally, a prospector would come across a white mineral called limestone, or calcium carbonate. A nice deposit of limestone had been found up in the hills close to Coleville. By itself, limestone was not of great value, but it could be transformed into quicklime used in cement. Cement was used to make concrete. The immigrants wanted to build more permanent structures in California, and cement was cheaper than hauling big rocks for building foundations.

A big steam engine had been hauled in to work on the bridge construction. Chiefly, the steam engine was used to drill into the granite and slate rock for the anchoring posts of the wire cable. The steam engine was of great fascination to Boyton, and each day Ruth Anne would take him down to the river to watch the steam engine operate. All the children and many adults would gather on the bluff above the bridge site to watch the construction.

Many of the local Carrolton men also worked on the bridge construction.

On this day Ruth Anne had found a nice spot to sit and read while Boyton watched the steam engine and scrambled over the river landscape with the other children. In her hands was the book *Walden; or, Life In The Woods*, by Henry D. Thoreau. It was not a book she would have chosen to read. In lieu of a library, locals would circulate books among themselves. Katherine Lewis, wife of the wagon maker, had given Ruth Anne the Thoreau book. Katherine was also from Massachusetts and thought the volume might be of interest to Ruth Anne.

For Ruth Anne, it was a struggle to read a book about a man who sequesters himself on a pond away from civilization. This Thoreau fellow lived next to Walden Pond, isolated, by choice. Ruth Anne lived with her small family in the wilderness, not by choice. Her concentration was broken when Boyton yelled, "Mama, Mama, I found ice." To literal-minded Ruth Anne, ice on an 80-degree day seemed as impossible as a man voluntarily living alone next to a pond.

"Show me," said Ruth Anne. Boyton brought her a flat rock, the size of his little hands, studded with pointy, clear crystals. Yes, they did look like ice crystals, but they were not. Ruth Anne was able to grab Mr. Thompson's attention to ask his opinion of the crystals. Thompson was the engineer who oversaw the steam engine operation and lived in Flagston. "Oh, that is a nice specimen of quartz crystals," said Thompson.

Mr. Thompson went on to explain, much to the Boyton's delight, how hot molten quartz was pushed up from the earth's depths between the balloons of granite. As the liquid quartz cooled, the six-sided crystal would grow with a sharp point at the tip. The quartz crystals were not valuable, but they were pleasant to look at as they reflected the light and sometimes created little rainbows.

After delighting Boyton with this short lesson in geology, Mr. Thomspon went back to working on the bridge. The construction of the bridge was as complex as the crystals were simple. The structure was designed to be 8 feet wide, with the ability to handle heavy wagons full of ore or supplies. The bridge would be supported by four towers, built of logs milled to 12 x 12 inches square, sited two on each side of the river.

The wooden towers were held erect, pointing to the sky, by massive, quarried, square blocks of granite placed to surround and support the wood. Anchored on either side of the river, the 2-inch diameter wire rope was draped over the towers, forming two distinct visual lines. Boyton pointed his finger at the wire rope and traced it as it extended from up to the top of the tower, then sagged in the middle, and then rose to the top of the other tower, then back down.

The suspension cables dropped from the 2-inch wire rope down to the deck of the bridge. All the lines and waves created a beautifully graceful structure. It was much larger replica of the little foot bridge Ruth Anne had to cross when she was searching for the Indian village several years earlier. The solid nature of the structure did not give Ruth Anne any cause for concern, as the previous footbridge had.

Of course, one just could not walk across the bridge without paying a toll. While the structure was referred to as the Carrolton bridge, it was officially constructed and owned by two men, Phineas Jackson and Michael Treat. Luckily, there was no charge for looking at the bridge. Once the bridge was completed and open to traffic, Ruth Anne and Boyton would spend hours watching all the people, animals, wagons, carriages, and stagecoaches crossing. Ruth Anne used bridge-watching time to incorporate school lessons such as counting and spelling for Boyton.

The day came when Ruth Anne, Boyton, and Caleb crossed the bridge together on a family carriage ride up the hill on the road to Coleville It was a warm spring day and Caleb left the folding top down on the larger carriage he had purchased to replace the smaller buggy. Sandwiched between Caleb and Ruth Anne, Boyton sat in the middle on the bench seat. He was growing so fast his boots now rested on floor of the carriage. Perched on Boyton's head was the round-crown, wide-brim brown felt hat that Caleb had bought him and resembled the hat Caleb wore.

Their objective was to tour the Cathedral Cave, discovered a couple of years earlier by Phineas Jackson, one of the owners of the Carrolton bridge. After paying the 10-cent crossing toll, Caleb drove the carriage onto the new, and dusty, road to approach the summit. They passed several hard rock mining operations, identified by large wooden head frames over a deep hole out of which mounds of rock tailings were spilling. Boyton thought the mines looked like mouths coughing up the rocks from deep inside the mountain.

At a meadow with a little creek running through stood Jackson's lime kiln. It was a large stone structure with three arched openings. This is where Jackson would bring in the limestone, have it crushed, and then heat the crushed rock in the kiln until it was transformed into quicklime. Jackson would then sell the quicklime as a form of cement, which combined with sand, rocks, and water, created the concrete so valued by gold country builders. Limestone was not as lucrative as gold, but Jackson avoided gold mining.

Phineas Jackson had been driven out of town in Mariposa County five years earlier for a gold mining operation he promoted that had gone bust. He had even persuaded the local people to rename the town in his honor. After a year of hard rock mining, with no valuable metal found, the community ran him out of town and renamed the town Pinch'emtight. Jackson, broke and humiliated, wandered the California wilderness for months, until he stumbled across this extraordinary cave complex.

To Jackson, it was obviously a sign from God that he should be the first white man to view this surreal white cave that looked like a cathedral. He called his find the Cathedral Cave and immediately knew it would be a tourist destination. Later he learned that the white rock in the cave was limestone and had commercial value when converted to quicklime.

Caleb knew Jackson from his early years in California. Caleb did not think much of him, someone who was a constant self-promoter, a person to keep at arm's length. There was no denying that Jackson had finally stumbled across a viable money-making operation. Caleb pulled the carriage up to the arched entrance to Cathedral Cave and greeted Jackson. A large open area was filled with horses and carriages that had carried people from as far away as San Francisco to see the cathedral.

"Caleb, how is my favorite water agent?" greeted Jackson. "Well, we came up to see your grand cave," stated Caleb. "Cathedral, Caleb, it is a cathedral, imbued with the spirit of God," replied Jackson. So absorbed was Jackson in his own presence and renown, he barely acknowledged Ruth Anne or Boyton. Jackson explained that after they paid their admission fee, he would give them a personal tour.

The tour party entered the cave through an enlarged opening in the side of the hill. Once inside, standing erect, with the light of numerous oil lamps and candles strategically placed through the cave, the view was truly impressive. Ruth Anne began thinking about how she would describe the cave, cavern, or cathedral to her sister Martha in a letter. It was something between the inside of a house coated with snow and ice and the drippings of candle tallow. Plus, the interior of the cave was not universally white. There were different colors infused into the cool, white walls and long, ceiling-to-floor stalactites.

Jackson guided the group through the different rooms of his cathedral. There was the rainbow room, where the limestone had been shaded with different hues of red, green, and blue that seemed to flow from the ceiling. Jackson called it the rainbow room because it reminded him of the rainbow Noah saw after the flood in the Bible story.

With each room, Jackson embellished his Bible stories to fit his particular Christian perspective of redemption and salvation. Next, they came to the whale room. Phineas thought the equally spaced ribs of limestone resembled the belly of the whale that had swallowed Jonah, who lived for three days before being spit out on shore. Like Jonah, Phineas prayed to God and had received his grace and mercy when He led Phineas to the Cathedral Cave.

The cathedral room was the largest room in the cave and had the highest ceiling. Two thick columns of limestone had formed from the ceiling to the floor. In between the columns was a rock smothered in limestone that appeared to Jackson to look like an altar. With all the candles, lamps, and smoke from the wicks, the ambience did bear a faint similarity to a Eucharist celebration in a church as it seemed to Ruth Anne.

The final room they entered was the lion's den. Jackson imagined it resembled the den into which the King throws Daniel to his doom in the Old Testament story. Daniel was protected by God and not eaten by the lions. Boyton, who had been quiet so far, piped up and said, "I don't see any lions."

Jackson replied, "True, but at the top of the lion's den was a door," he explained, as he pointed to the opening on the cave wall above them. The tourists were able to climb up to the jagged opening and look out.

Ruth Anne took her turn to climb on the stairs carved into the limestone to peer out of the porthole in the side of the hill. The brilliant light of the sun shining through the hole created a shaft of light that made it difficult for Ruth Anne, whose eyes were adjusted to the dark interior of the cave, to focus outside. When she was able to look out, she saw the steep gorge and ravine below the opening, she immediately realized this was the entrance to the creator's cave the Indian men had told her about. She struggled to look down into the ravine to see if she could spot any of the Indian men or women. She thought she saw a wisp of smoke from the Indians' campfire but could not be sure, as she was ushered along for the next visitor to peer out the portal.

Their tour guide proclaimed that no man had visited the Cathedral Cave until he, Phineas Jackson, had found it. Ruth Anne wanted to challenge Jackson about his assertion of being the first man to view the interior of the cave. Instead, she demurred and let the fiction stand, as it pleased the other participants on the tour, who believed they were treading on virgin, holy ground, white man soil.

When the group left the cave, Ruth Anne could see how everyone's boots, hands, and clothing were dusted with the white lime dust. The Indian men had shown similar white dust on the soles of their feet, knees, and hands after visiting the creator's cave. This was confirmation that the Cathedral Cave had to be the creator's cave. As they left, they could see how Jackson had begun excavating a side of the mountain and was extracting the white lime to be burned and converted to quick lime for cement, and eventually concrete.

Perhaps channeling Thoreau, Ruth Anne thought the Cathedral Cave was a metaphor for California. Immigrants came to this newfound world of California and set about to extract the natural resources, earn lots of money, and leave behind holes in the ground, with no regard for who called it home before their arrival. Before Ruth Anne could explore her philosophical thoughts, she heard Caleb holler.

"Boyton, get out of there now!" As Boyton walked from among the tall growth of some shrubs, Caleb grabbed him, threw him on the ground and began rolling him around. Ruth Anne flew into a panic, wondering why Caleb was assaulting Boyton. After all the Bible talk from Jackson, Ruth Anne's mind flickered onto the Old Testament story of Abraham offering his son Isaac as a sacrifice to God. Boyton was crying, his hat on the ground, with dirt in his hair, as Caleb began to stand him up.

Ruth Anne ran over to the stand of shrubs, which was in full sunlight. They looked like little twigs of oak trees, growing, trying to reach the sun. They appeared to be odd-looking oak saplings with leaves of three to each leaf stem. The leaves were shiny in shades of green and red. There was a strong aroma of oil in the air. The scent was vaguely familiar scent, like that of cloves.

"Caleb," yelled Ruth Anne, "what's going on? Is Boyton hurt?" From behind her, Ruth Anne could hear Phineas Jackson laughing, the other tourists staring at Caleb and the dusty boy, who now was caked in white from the limestone dust of the earth that he had been rolled in.

Caleb pointed at the stand of shrubs and said, "Poison oak." Caleb had been trying to protect Boyton by covering his exposed skin in dirt in the hopes that it would stop the poison oak from spreading. On the ride home, Boyton did not get to ride on the bench seat next to Ruth Anne and Caleb in the carriage. He had to ride in the back so that, if he was coated in poison oak oil, it would not be transferred to either Caleb or Ruth Anne.

When the trio returned to Carrolton, Caleb got some soap, took Boyton down to the river, and gave him the most thorough bath the boy had ever received. They returned home, and Boyton was once again happy. He was always happy to spend time with Caleb, as Ruth Anne could be a little overprotective.

Life returned back to normal for about a week. Then Boyton started to scratch his arms, neck, and face. Within a couple days of the itching, Boyton broke out in a horrible poison oak rash with the excruciating urge to scratch. The poor boy could not sleep or sit still for his school lessons from Ruth Anne. He could not focus on anything except scratching the bumps up and down his arms, neck, and face. He was tired and given to just breaking down in tears.

Ruth Anne knew she had to find help for Boyton. She went down to Dr. Waddle's home office. His first line of treatment was just to wait, and the poison oak would eventually fade away. Waiting for the rash and constant itching to fade away did not sound like an acceptable treatment or remedy to Ruth Anne. At her insistence, Dr. Waddle sold Ruth Anne a thick white substance that smelled like rancid tallow. Whether the white noxious substance had any medicinal effect, Ruth Anne could not determine, because shortly after applying it to Boyton's arms, both he and Ruth Anne vomited at the smell of the ointment.

Ruth Anne knew she had to visit the merchants she had been avoiding for years. There were two Chinese merchants in Carrolton. One of them sold vegetables and the other dry goods and some Chinese herbs favored by the Chinese men to cure certain illnesses. Ruth Anne, as a rule, avoided Chinese people, as she clung to an irrational fear that they would help take Boyton away from her.

As she entered Ah Chee's little wooden shed of a store, she was surprised and shocked when he greeted her, "Good morning, Miss Gibbons." Ruth Anne should not have been surprised that the Chinese men knew her as she was the wife of Caleb Gibbons, the water man. In addition to the position of her husband as the purveyor of the all-important resource of water, everyone knew Ruth Anne was raising the orphaned Chinese boy.

"Hello," replied Ruth Anne, "my son, uh, Boyton…" Ruth Anne stumbled over how to reference Boyton to Ah Chee. She wondered if he would be offended by the name that wasn't Chinese in origin. Somewhat flustered, Ruth Anne pushed forward, "….poison oak rash, he has bad poison oak…" Before she could finish the explanation, Ah Chee chimed in, "Yes, a help for bumps." He then went into another room where Ruth Anne could hear him crushing something in a mortar and pestle.

After a few minutes he returned with a jar that looked like a mixture of olive oil, salt, and dried leaves. Ah Chee told Ruth Anne to smear the poultice of sorts on the bumps one to two times per day. Ruth Anne offered to pay, but Ah Chee shook his head and with a smile said, "No, no, all good." Ruth Anne left the little shed and walked back home wondering how she could repay Ah Chee for his assistance.

Ruth Anne then applied the salty, oily, leafy concoction on Boyton's arm as a test. He said it stung and felt hot, but a stinging sensation was better than an itching sensation. The observation both Ruth Anne and Boyton made was that the treatment smelled far better than Dr. Waddle's rancid tallow ointment. Then Boyton asked, "Did you get this from Ah Chee?" Ruth Anne, again surprised, asked, "You know Ah Chee?" While rubbing the oily salty stuff on his arms, Boyton replied, "Yes, I talk to him all the time. He is a funny old man."

When the poison oak rash had finally subsided, Boyton's badgering began again. "Mama, can I go to school? Mama, when do I get to go to school? Mama, all the other kids go to school," was Boyton's insistent refrain. For the past several years Ruth Anne had avoided interacting with the normal institutions of life that might cause friction or anxiety when it came to Boyton, a Chinese boy circulating in a white world.

Boyton was correct, all his pals in Carrolton had already started attending the one-room Rockrose school house up the hill. His playmates and fellow explorers of old mining sites, pranksters, dog chasers, tree climbers, and other mischievous acts the young lads could find to divert themselves, were all attending school. They wanted to know when he would join them. School was boring, they said. Boyton would make it more fun, as they fought imaginary battles as they hiked up the hill to the schoolhouse.

One summer afternoon, before school was to begin in a couple weeks, Ruth Anne told Boyton they would walk up to the school to inquire about his attendance in the fall. They set out on the foot trail to the ridge top. The trail began next to a creek that was mostly shaded during the year. The air was always cool there, as water from the little creek splashed about keeping the ferns green and the ground moist.

Even in the summer, the ferns were abundant and green. Moss covered the rocks next to the creek. There were big granite boulders one could sit on and gaze down on Carrolton below. As the trail ascended to the ridge, the landscape transitioned to more oak trees and gray pines. Just over the ridge line was an open area next to the road up to Flagston. The Rockrose school house had been built by the community on a small plot of flat land near the trail.

Ruth Anne entered the schoolhouse as Boyton remained outside, playing, and exploring the landscape. Miss Doolittle, the teacher hired a couple years previously, was sitting behind a desk facing the door next to a large cast iron heating stove. "Hello," said Ruth Anne, "I would like to enroll Boyton in school for the next year."

Miss Doolittle was not from Carrolton. She lived in Flagston and was only slightly familiar with the families and community of Carrolton. Miss Doolittle was younger than Ruth Anne and displayed the energy level of a young, unmarried woman. "Wonderful," exclaimed Miss Doolittle, with a big smile on her face. Ruth Anne relaxed, as Miss Doolittle was cheery and seemed willing to help.

"What grade will your son be?" asked Miss Doolittle. "Well," started Ruth Anne, "I have been schooling Boyton at home, and he is very good at reading, writing, and we started on the multiplication tables last year. But I don't have the English and History books for him. I think he might be 3rd or 4th grade level." "I see," said Miss Doolittle. "I often see new children who have been crossing the country to California, and it can be hard to judge what grade level they are."

"Oh, we are not new arrivals. We've been in Carrolton for nearly 10 years," explained Ruth Anne. From outside the schoolhouse, there was wild yelling and laughing. Another boy and girl, who lived close to the schoolhouse, had wandered over, and Boyton and the boy were using tree branches as swords in a mock battle. The young girl saw a lizard scamper out from under a log she was sitting on and screamed. The boys laughed.

Miss Doolittle and Ruth Anne moved over to the window to see what was causing the commotion as the three youngsters played and ran around. Miss Doolittle pointed to the white boy with a stick and asked, "Is that your son?" "No," said Ruth Anne, "Boyton is the boy with the hat." Boyton never left the house without the wide brim felt hat Caleb had bought him for Christmas.

"Okay," started Miss Doolittle in a subdued tone. "We don't accept colored or Chinese children. I'm afraid we won't be able to accept the boy." In an instant, the friendly and cheery Miss Doolittle had turned sour and dour. Ruth Anne realized that Miss Doolittle had stopped referring to Boyton as her son and was calling him "the boy."

"My husband helped build this schoolhouse,"," countered Ruth Anne. "I'm sorry, I don't make the rules. The school trustees made the rules several years ago," explained Miss Doolittle.

Ruth Anne had grown flushed with anger, unsure whether her distress was visible or not. She had nothing more to say to Miss Doolittle. She turned around and left without saying goodbye. She walked outside and called Boyton. They were going home.

"Mama, when do I start school? That boy was fun. The school looks nice. Papa helped build it, he said," Boyton rattled on and on, but Ruth Anne could not hear him, her head was too stuffed with emotions.

Ruth Anne took off toward home, walking at a faster pace than normal. Boyton trailed behind. "Mama, why are you walking so fast?" She was practically running down the windy trail, trying to push the anger out of her head. As she made a turn on the trail, she suddenly heard the buzz, the long buzz of warning and caution. She stopped, turned around, and told Boyton to stop.

"Don't move," she yelled. Already perplexed at Ruth Anne's behavior since leaving the schoolhouse, Boyton looked at her in utter confusion and fright.

Ruth Anne scanned the ground. Finally, she saw the flicker of the tongue. The rattlesnake was perfectly camouflaged between a rock and a log, among the dry oak leaf litter, coiled, ready to strike. Ruth Anne, so immersed in her emotions over Miss Doolittle, had not been paying attention to the trail with its inherent dangers.

The coiled rattlesnake was between her and Boyton. She could not risk either her or Boyton walking past the snake, as the rattler had forewarned her that it was ready to defend itself with its bite and venom. Ruth Anne looked around and found the branch of a gray pine, small enough for her to hold with two hands and long enough to strike the snake at a safe distance. Ruth Anne picked up the branch and, letting out a scream of frustration, brought the tree branch down on the snake.

The rattlesnake quickly slithered off to the side over the log and vanished. But Ruth Anne kept swinging and slamming the tree branch on the log, the rock, tree trunks, shrubs, and wildly in the air. Out of breath, her clothing all out of order, her hair sticking out from under her bonnet, she finally stopped still, Boyton staring at her with his mouth open.

"Come here," she said. Boyton ran over to her and hugged her. "Let's go home," she said in a tired tone.

When Caleb came home later in the evening, Boyton's excited talk was not about school, but about how Ruth Anne had battled a rattlesnake and won. Unfortunately, Ruth Anne felt she had battled a snake and lost. The snake in the schoolhouse.

Few of the residents of Carrolton enjoyed a leisurely life. To sustain oneself and one's family, one had to work in Carrolton. Men worked as gold miners, merchants, and tradesmen, with a growing number of people turning toward farming and ranching. Women had little spare time, as maintaining a cabin, washing, obtaining food stuffs, and cooking monopolized most of their days. If a woman had children, it was if she replicated herself – or at least her energy level – to attend to all the needs of the children as well.

Consequently, the hard-working populace embraced any holiday or festivity as a special event, including attending church services, even if you did not believe in religion. When George Bailey, a new California vineyard owner, invited the town to celebrate his new wines, brandy, and sparkling wines at a gala fete, few in Carrolton could decline the invitation.

Bailey had come to California in 1849 and mined for gold at Carrolton in those early days. He had acquired enough gold to segue into farming, his real passion in life. In the 1850s people all over California were experimenting with different crops. If a farmer had water, his crops could survive the regular summer droughts. Men were planting trees, grain, alfalfa, and vegetables. The Valley Springs water ditch provided the water for farming and ranching operations along the river and out into the valley.

After several years of agricultural experiments, Bailey settled on grape vines. He planted over 100 acres with different varieties of grape vines. Within a couple of years, he was shipping table grapes to market and drying hundreds of pounds of grapes for raisins. Next, Bailey set his sights on making wine, which led to making brandy and sparkling wines. Bailey called his winery Blue Oak Vineyards after the stand of blue oaks on the ridge above his property.

When the day of the celebration arrived, the townspeople of Carrolton, including Ruth Anne, Caleb, and Boyton, piled into wagons and carriages for the trip down to Bailey's Blue Oak Vineyards. There they were greeted by Bailey and his wife, Caroline, a most jovial and welcoming couple. There was a small musical ensemble within the winery playing a variety of contemporary music. Bailey had put his Chinese employees to work serving food and drink.

Ruth Anne, Caleb, and Boyton strolled through the vineyards and around the small pond Bailey had stocked with fish. Boyton was in awe of all the activity; he had never seen so many people, heard such music, or tasted such food. Boyton and Caleb studied the large copper pots and tubes of the brandy still. Caleb explained how the grape wine was heated and the wine vapor condensed in the copper tubing and dripped out as brandy.

Caroline Bailey approached Ruth Anne and thanked her for caring for the orphaned Chinese boy. She told Ruth Anne that the Chinese people were excellent people, loyal, hardworking, and honest. That was why her husband employed so many of them, she said. Ruth Anne asked Caroline if she and her husband had any children, and Caroline replied that they had not been blessed with that part of marriage.

Ruth Anne was enamored of Caroline. While several years older than Ruth Anne, Caroline seemed like a sister, mother, or special girlfriend to Ruth Anne. She could relate to Caroline on so many levels of life. On top of all that, Caroline was a gracious and welcoming woman. Caroline made Ruth Anne feel comfortable, like she belonged, as though she was not an outsider with a Chinese boy for a son.

Someone handed Ruth Anne a glass of red wine. She had never before drunk any alcohol, except small sips of communion wine. Caleb mentioned that it would be rude if she did not at least taste the wine. She took a sip and thought it tasted like tart cherry juice with some alcohol in it. Next, she tried to sip some brandy, but, as she raised her glass, the concentrated alcohol vapor hit her nose, creating a stinging sensation. She opted to put it down.

Finally, in order to be a polite guest, she took a sip of the sparkling wine. The cold liquid felt so refreshing in the hot winery, with the little bubbles exploding in her mouth and tickling her throat. She continued to sip on the sparkling wine, and, when another glass was offered, she did not decline it.

Ruth Anne was feeling a little lightheaded as the ensemble struck up a waltz. Neither she nor Caleb really knew how to dance, but, in the spirit of the evening, they decided to be close and step together in the music. Another glass of sparkling wine had her and Caleb dancing to the galop music, and then to a quadrille. Several of the musical pieces had been commissioned by vintner Bailey to market his just released sparkling wines. In addition to drinking newly created wines, Ruth Anne was listening to new music, never before played outside of California.

On top of one of the immense wooden wine barrels, formerly used as water tanks, Ruth Anne saw the wild French woman dancing with her husband Auturo. They were waltzing, spinning, and swaying to the music. They were the happiest couple in the winery. With each dance step, one of Alma's blond curls sprung out from beneath the beaded head dress attempting to hold it in place. Between reels, Alma shared the news with Ruth Anne that vintner Bailey had agreed to sponsor Auturo to become a naturalized citizen. The night was a *magnifique* celebration.

As Ruth Anne and Caleb danced, Ruth Anne felt it; she felt California. She was enjoying the fruits of California transformed into wonderfully tasting refreshments. The dreams of hard-working young couples were coming true. She was dancing to music that had been composed by a local man and that reflected the California climate and energy. She felt as never before the freedom, opportunity, and happiness that California offered to her residents.

Outside, standing among the young grape vines, Ruth Anne looked up at vintner Bailey's imposing three-story house on the ridge. The Victorian-inspired design of a white house reflected the setting sun's orange glow. The house looked as if it was on fire in the light and jumped out at the viewer among the oak and pine trees surrounding it.

Vintner Bailey strolled over to Ruth Anne as he noticed her gazing up at his house. "That house cost me more than this vineyard and winery," said the short, round man with a long beard. While holding a glass of his sparkling wine, vintner Bailey gazed up at the house and added, "It's really just for Caroline."

"Just the two of you must get lost in that big house," said Ruth Anne. With a chuckle, vintner Bailey said, "Several of our Chinese workers live with us; they are kind of like family." Ruth Anne had never heard the term family and Chinese coupled together in the same sentence. What a foreign and novel idea, that white people and Chinese people could be a family.

While Ruth Anne and Caleb were dancing, drinking, and conversing with the other guests, Boyton gravitated to the corner of the winery where the Chinese men were preparing the food and pouring the libations. The little Chinese boy was dressed like the son of a white couple, which seemed odd to them, but they also realized that a white couple was caring for the orphaned Chinese boy. The Chinese men smiled at Boyton and tried to talk to him in their native Cantonese language.

Boyton did not always understand what the men were saying to him. He smiled just the same. Boyton was learning that Chinese men did not drink or dance. Chinese men did the work. Understanding that he, too, was Chinese, Boyton decided he should help the Chinese men. They let him sweep the stone floor, move some crates of glassware, and cut some bread.

As the evening came to a close, Ruth Anne and Caleb decided not to ride back to Carrolton in the wagons. They would walk the long road back to town on this warm evening, as the full moon began to crest over the mountains. As they walked, not saying much, Caleb held Ruth Anne's hand, in part to steady her, but also as a small token of affection. Ruth Anne held Boyton's hand. As they walked, with the moon in front of them, their shadows formed the silhouette of a family.

9 Future Railroad

A true sign of progress was approaching in the Golden State, the railroad. A railroad line from Sacramento to Quartz Hill had been completed. Theodore Grainger, superintendent of the Valley Springs Water Company, was also on the Board of Directors of the fledging 22-mile railroad company that built and operated the line from Sacramento to Quartz Hill. In Grainger's possession were complimentary train ride tickets for the inaugural opening day of the line. Caleb was invited to come to Quartz Hill with his family and ride on the train.

Boyton was a bundle of exuberance when he learned he would not only see the huge railroad engine but get to ride the train. In the days before the big adventure, his questions were nonstop about how big the train was, how fast it traveled, how many cars it had, and on and on. All Caleb could say was, "We'll see when we see it." Ruth Anne was secretly happy at Boyton's excitement and anticipation, especially after the debacle of the school admission attempt.

It was a long carriage ride from Carrolton down to Quartz Hill, made longer by Boyton's incessant questioning about the train trip. As they crested the last rolling hill and looked down at Quartz Hill, it was apparent this was a special day. Hundreds of people milled about the town waiting for the train to arrive. The town was festooned with red, white, and blue bunting and American flags. A podium had been erected where local and state dignitaries could make long, boring speeches about progress in California.

On the horizon, to the west, they heard the familiar steam engine roar pushing the train wheels with a rhythmic pulse. Black smoke billowed in the still air in the distance. Then, finally, the piercing sound of the train's trumpet whistle, along with the clapping of the bell. The train pulled into the station at the foot of the town and was immediately thronged with people inspecting the steam locomotive and cars.

Boyton and Caleb circled the train so many times looking at all the pipes, wheels, boiler, and passenger cars that Ruth Anne lost count. Ruth Anne was a little apprehensive over whether there would be a problem with a Chinese boy riding the train. As it turned out, there was no problem; this was a commercial venture. If one had a ticket or could pay the fare, one got to ride the train. Ruth Anne sat in one of the passenger cars as Caleb and Boyton stood in the open-air car at the end of the train.

Once the train got up to speed on the trip into Sacramento, Ruth Anne saw Boyton spread his arms out like wings, pretending he was flying through the air. The surrounding countryside as they passed was flat and dry. The grass of the valley was yellow and reflected the brightness of the sun. As the train travelled on the new rails, people tending their gardens or cattle along the railroad stopped to wave. The combination of the heat of the day and smoke from the train's engine made Ruth Anne nauseous. She was happy when they finally arrived in Sacramento.

Because the train was making numerous round trips during the day to promote the line's grand opening, Ruth Anne, Caleb, and Boyton had time to walk around Sacramento. Ruth Anne was not impressed with Sacramento. They fought constant dust being thrown up from the horses on the dirt streets. The air smelled foul, a combination of sewage, animal waste, cigar smoke, whiskey, and stagnant water.

Many fine homes and buildings had been erected since Ruth Anne's last visit. Caleb visited Sacramento once or twice a year for the water company, but Ruth Anne had not ventured into the city for many years. The trio strolled along the waterfront looking at the large paddle wheeled steamers, which were almost as interesting to Boyton as the train was. They walked down J Street and then over to I Street, where Ruth Anne found the origin of the stagnant water.

To the north of I Street lay a stagnant pond of water initially christened Sutter's Lake. Lately, it had become known as China Slough. The slough was a stagnant branch of water from the Sacramento River. Between the slough and I street stood the homes and businesses of the Chinese community in

Sacramento. The Chinese washerwomen would use the slough water to wash clothes for Sacramento families.

The buildings in the Chinese community were ramshackle and interconnected, making it difficult for the viewer to know where one building stopped and another began. The area looked like a labyrinth of clustered buildings whose internal path was only known to its dwellers, populated by lots of saloons on one side of the street and obvious opium dens on the slough side. Many Chinese men and women were visible, walking between the buildings, across the street, hauling vegetables, dry goods, and the like.

Ruth Anne had harbored an uneasy feeling ever since they had arrived in Sacramento. She was feeling a touch claustrophobic. She felt surrounded by big buildings, people, horses, steam engine noise, men cursing and fighting, with few places to run. She had never imagined that she would long for the isolation of Carrolton. She also felt as though the three of them were being watched, maybe even followed. All were crazy thoughts that would only subside once she was back on the train.

As their train home pulled into the depot on the Sacramento waterfront, Boyton and Caleb had time to inspect the steam locomotive again. At the front of the engine was the tall conical shaped smokestack with a screen on top to keep the embers from escaping. There were four pilot wheels at the front of the engine. Above and between the pilot wheels on either side were large cylinders that contained pistons. Steam from the boiler entered the cylinder and pushed the pistons back and forth.

Each piston was attached to a large articulating driving arm linked to the drive wheels. The massive drive wheels, directly under and in front of the cab, were close to 6 feet in diameter, almost twice the height of Boyton. In front of the cab and over the wheels sat the long boiler and fire box. The next car behind the cab was the tender car, full of split wood to feed into the fire box to boil the water into steam.

The steam locomotive engineer, Mr. Leonard Robinson, saw Caleb and Boyton seriously studying all the parts of the engine. He came over and offered additional information on how the locomotive functioned. Boyton had a look of awe on his face, not only at learning the steam engine details, but at the fact that a real train engineer was standing in front of him.

Boyton asked questions that impressed Mr. Robinson. How many times did the pilot wheels rotate to the large drive wheels? How did the alternative valve work in the cylinder? How much wood was burned between a run from Sacramento to Quartz Hill? How much water was used? Mr. Robinson took a liking to Boyton and tried to answer all his questions before it was time to return to Quartz Hill.

On the return trip, Boyton and Caleb sat with Ruth Anne in the passenger car. There were few people in the car on the return trip and that gave Boyton the opportunity to snoop around. He opened boxes, looked under the seats, worked the windows, and opened the door to a little utility closet. As they got off the train, Boyton ran up to Mr. Robinson and asked if he could work for the train company when he grew up. "Of course you can," bellowed Mr. Robinson, with a big grin and a laugh.

On the carriage ride back to Carrolton, Ruth Anne thought to herself about how Boyton was treated like any other child by the engineer and by all the other people they had encountered on their expedition. Sacramento was not as bad as she wanted to believe it was. When the buggy crested Saddle Gap and moved into the river canyon, Ruth Anne felt good to be home. Home was a rushing river, tall mountains, oak and pine trees, coyotes, and rattlesnakes. It was beautiful, and it was dangerous, but somehow Sacramento seemed more dangerous.

After a year of being in service, the new railroad, like so many other projects in California, was running out of money. The grand revenue projections from freight and passenger service did not meet expectations. The optimistic promoters felt that if the line could just make it up the hill to Flagston, they could overcome their financial deficits.

One reason for the line's lack of profitability was that the rail line from Sacramento to Quartz Hill was relatively flat, and wagons could easily haul goods and people for less money, even if the travel time was slower. In contrast, the road up to Flagston was steep at points, and teamsters had to break up wagon loads to get the mules or oxen to pull the loads up the grade. A railroad to Flagston would solve that problem for many shippers of goods and people from Quartz Hill and Sacramento.

The owners of the railroad turned to Chinese men for labor to work on the line up to Flagston. The Chinese men worked just as hard as white men for less than half the cost. There had always been an underlying tension between working white men and the Chinese immigrants since shortly after the Gold Rush began. In addition to hiring Chinese labor to build the railroad, Chinese mining companies had acquired more mining claims along the Valley Springs water ditch and were having modest success at gold mining.

Some of the white East Coast immigrants to the region began to grumble that the manifest destiny of California was accorded exclusively to "Americans." The bar for entitlement to the state's natural resources was lowered to include white immigrants from Europe but not immigrants from other countries.

One such favored immigrant, Augustus Brannan, originally from Ireland, had been in San Francisco during the period of the Committee of Vigilance in the 1850s, where he had learned the rhetoric of how to demonize your opponents, especially if they were foreign-born. Brannan conveniently ignored his own foreign Irish roots.

When times were good, Brannan had little enmity towards the Chinese men. When everyone was working and earning a living, no one cogitated over how a man talked or dressed, or who they worshipped. When there was no work – or when you did not want to work as hard – then the tribal nature of men grew within white workers' minds like thorns on a blackberry cane. Brannan, like many of the white men who came to California, had done some gold mining, worked at a lumber mill, worked as a teamster, and worked in building construction.

Everyone could feel it: the California economy had slowed down. Since the conclusion of the Civil War, the East Coast had been enjoying a building boom and economic rebirth. California, on the other hand, was running out of steam. Gold mining had moved up into the mountains with hard rock mines and hydraulic mining, not enterprises that a group of poor immigrants, like Brannan, could undertake. That had been the beauty of the Gold Rush. A man got him a pick and pan, went down to the river, and began to work. There was no "big man" dictating to him when to work and how much he would be paid per day. His fortune depended solely on his own labor and his own luck.

There was a tinge of envy and jealousy on the part of the white population toward the Chinese men who were still working under the old rules. The Chinese men formed little companies and went to work, mining, farming, clearing weeds from the water ditches, and now, laying the grade for the new rail line up to Flagston. The Chinese men also shared a different perspective on life in California than that of the white residents: The Golden State was not their forever home. They were here to work and then return to China. In contrast, many of the white men saw California as a permanent home, if not their eternal resting place.

Brannan was typical of many men who were not happy about the control of resources in California either. The Valley Springs Water Company controlled the water to the miners in the valley. Years earlier, Brannan had sold his little mining claim at Saddle Gap because he was only washing out $2 a day in gold, when the water had cost him $1. He sold his claim to a company of naïve Chinese men led by Ah Fong. Within a year of sluicing the ground, Ah Fong's company was pulling out $5 a day in gold. Even after paying the foreign miner's tax, the Chinese miners were able save some money, construct some nice cabins, and buy warm clothing for the winter.

Now, the focus of the growing anti-Chinese rhetoric around the region was how the Chinese men were taking jobs and opportunities away from white men. Brannan found it easy to demonize a population group that was not white and Christian, although many white men did not adhere to the latter characteristic either. Brannan was good at organizing the landless, underemployed white men into a mob with his oration skills. The original focus of action was to boycott businesses that employed Chinese men for labor. Organized violence against employers or the Chinese immigrants was an implicit threat.

Brannan's anti-Chinese rhetoric and organization was no secret. He was routinely holding meetings of his newly formed Quartz Hill Anti-Chinese Society. Brannan and his cohorts were able to raise some money to place advertisements in the local newspapers to alert the residents of their meetings, usually held at saloons sympathetic to their cause. The Valley Springs Water Company was monitoring the anti-Chinese society because they were a target of the rhetoric, as well as their Chinese mining company customers.

Within a few decades since bursting onto the national scene, California had morphed from a tradition of rugged individualism to monopolistic corporate control of resources. At least that was the feeling of many men who had chosen to settle in the Golden State. Water canal companies controlled the water. Private landowners controlled the timber that could be cut down. The railroad companies were controlling how much a man could earn by paying low wages to Chinese men.

The tipping point for anti-Chinese society members was the railroad hiring Chinese men to work on the new line. From a saloon in Quartz Hill, with the whiskey flowing, it did not take much encouragement from Brannan to mobilize the mob to march on a mission of driving the Chinese immigrants from the area. The route of the mob march was along the new railroad line from Quartz Hill up to Flagston.

Caleb was riding back from Bretton Falls when he noticed the Chinese merchants in Carrolton hurriedly packing up their stores and hiking into the hills above town. Caleb asked Ah Chee what was happening, and he said the mob was coming for them. Caleb quickly rode to the house and told Ruth Anne to stay inside with Boyton and block the door. From there he rode down to Quartz Hill where he encountered the mob approaching Saddle Gap.

"Brannan!" shouted Caleb from atop his horse, "What are you doing?"
"Gibbons, we are taking back our land," Brannan replied with a scowl and alcohol induced slurring of words. "It is time the water monopoly is broken and people like you protecting and raising the Chinese are driven off our land."

Caleb tightly held the reins of his horse. He was afraid that if he let his grip go, he would withdraw the pistol from his holster and shoot Brannan.

There was nothing to say to Brannan. Caleb was outnumbered as he surveyed Brannan's mob of 50 men knocking over the sluice runs of the Chinese miners, setting their cabins on fire, and battering Chinese men who tried to protect their property. He spun his horse around and kicked the horse to gallop up to the top of the ridge. The sun was setting, and the hills across the river were brilliant in the evening light. Smoke from the burning Chinese mining operations drifted up over the ridge and down toward the river.

Caleb maneuvered his horse around the Blue Oak vineyards, which were dense with foliage and heavy with fruit. As the horse walked toward the river, Caleb heard the shout of "waddy man." Suddenly, several Chinese men and women stood up from under the cover of the grape vines. When the Chinese, refugees from the mob violence at this point, saw it was the friendly water man, Caleb, they could continue their exodus down to the river for, hopefully, safety from the Brannan mob.

This was not California, Caleb thought. This was not the California that had lassoed his heart and imagination and pulled him back to the West Coast. The fires, destruction, and irrational hatred of people was akin to European wars and crusades he had read about. What had gone wrong in the Golden State of California? Caleb rode down to the river trail and went back to Carrolton. He spent the rest of the night outside the house, pistol in hand.

The mob never reached Carrolton, as they ran out of steam before they could walk or ride that far. They also ran out of whiskey, and some simply fell asleep after an exhausting day of marauding and terrorizing the countryside. However, in the aftermath of the violence, many of the Chinese men who operated shops and businesses in Carrolton left town with as much of their goods as possible. The next day, the smell of the smoldering fires of the Chinese cabins drifted into Carrolton like the stench of a skunk on a hot day.

Ruth Anne was frantic and agitated. She did not know what to do. Should they leave Carrolton? Where would they go? Was Boyton in danger? Were Ruth Anne and Caleb in danger? What was clear was that she had underestimated the hatred of some men toward the Chinese population. All her fearful actions to avoid white people when she was with Boyton had been validated.

The information that filtered into Carrolton was fractured and tainted by unsubstantiated reports and biases. In the days following the attack, Ruth Anne, who had never given newspapers a second glance, scrambled to acquire every newspaper that had printed a report on the anti-Chinese mob violence. Boyton noticed Ruth Anne's new fascination with newspapers and asked what she was reading. She told him she was trying to learn why men were so mean to their neighbors.

The newspapers she obtained fell into two categories: those who favored driving the Chinese out of California, and those papers that abhorred the violence and breakdown in civil society. Superintendent of the Valley Springs Water Company, Theodore Grainger, submitted a long letter to the Valley Record newspaper explaining how the water company did not favor Chinese miners over white men. Everyone was charged the same rate for water, he wrote. Vintner Bailey was quoted as saying his Chinese laborers were gentle, hardworking, and loyal men. It was vintner Bailey's hope that the perpetrators of the violence be brought to justice.

After reading all the newspaper accounts, none of it made sense to Ruth Anne. She understood, as the Mountain Herald out of Flagston wrote, that there was a criminal element within the Chinese community. There were gangs, prostitution, and opium use. Ruth Anne was certain she knew the section of Sacramento that the newspaper was referring to when it exaggerated the threat of the Chinese to white Christian families. Her retort, had she been able to voice it, was, who was it that had gotten drunk and proceeded to attack Chinese men and burn down their homes? Not Chinese criminals!

Boyton knew there were troubles. He could see it on the faces of Ruth Anne and Caleb. None of them talked about it. Boyton realized Ruth Anne was being more protective of him than usual. Before he ran out of the house to explore with his friends each day, she quizzed him on where he was going and who he would be with. Boyton lost a certain amount of innocence after the anti-Chinese mob violence down at Saddle Gap.

When the Chinese merchants who had fled Carrolton finally returned, Ruth Anne made a point to visit each of their stores and apologize. All she could say was that she was sorry for the incident. The Chinese men simply nodded and went about their business.

Several months after the anti-Chinese mob violence, Carrolton was jolted again when a large plume of smoke rose into the sky down by Saddle Gap. Only a large conflagration could cause so much billowing, black smoke. The dark smoke cloud continued to ascend into the evening sky, the underside glowing orange. "Not again," thought Ruth Anne. "Not another mob marauding, setting buildings on fire."

As Carrolton's townspeople gathered to view the spectacle of the large smoke cloud, they all wondered if the mob would make it to Carrolton this time. Some of the men and women armed themselves in anticipation. They did not want that violence in their community.

One of the young teenagers hopped on a horse and rode down to Saddle Gap to see what was happening. The young man returned after dark and reported that vintner Bailey's home and winery were fully engulfed in flames. The heat was intense, and he could only get so close to the flames. Men were running around, throwing water on the flames. Vintner Bailey's house on the hill had completely collapsed in a heap of rubble, a total loss.

While the winery fire sounded like an unfortunate event, at least there was no concerted march on Carrolton to drive out the Chinese. Later in the day Ruth Anne heard a woman's piercing screams. Her immediate reaction was that someone was being killed in the street. She ran down the dirt road and found Alma Gosseau screaming and crying. Alma had completely lost control, yelling and hitting anything she encountered: houses, buildings, and horses.

Eventually Alma collapsed in the street, and Ruth Anne was able to run up to her and wrap her arms around her. "He's dead!" Alma cried. "Who?" Ruth Anne asked. "Auturo, he's dead," Alma muttered, as her five children looked on at the pitiful scene of their mother in a state of inconsolable shock. Auturo, Ruth Anne would learn, had died at the winery the night before. He had been working there for vintner Bailey. When the fire started, he was trapped in the winery.

Ruth Anne would spend the next few weeks shuttling between her house and that of Alma Gosseau. Alma was virtually catatonic, unable to speak or eat. Ruth Anne, with the help of Alma's daughters, cooked meals, cleaned the house, and got the younger children ready for school. Ruth Anne also learned how to wash clothes, as that was now Alma's sole source of income. Alma was a better washerwoman than Ruth Anne, but the local men who brought their clothes to be washed gave Ruth Anne some leeway, as they knew she tried her best.

The gossip that floated up from Quartz Hill was that the fire had been retribution for vintner Bailey hiring Chinese men at his Blue Oak winery. Vintner Bailey took out an advertisement in the newspapers offering a $500 reward for information leading to the arrest of the arsonist. No one was ever arrested for the crime. If the mission was to drive vintner Bailey out of business, it succeeded. Bailey could not recover from the losses he had sustained, even with his fire insurance.

It took several months, but Ruth Anne got Alma and her family back into a stable environment. Ruth Anne no longer needed to spend all day at the Gosseau house, and she could once again focus on Caleb, Boyton, and her own home. She was exhausted from attending to Alma and organizing Auturo's funeral.

Alma was crushed at the loss of Auturo. The wild French woman would not reappear in Carrolton. No more big grins or sing-song greetings in French. Alma was not sure she would stay in Carrolton. Ruth Anne understood Alma's desire to leave behind all the heartache.

10 Separation

It would happen without warning. First, the snap, then the crack, and finally the whoosh and boom of a large branch plunging to the ground.

The crash was inexplicable, and no one knew why the oak trees would shed massive branches without warning. "Widowmakers" were a known hazard to living around the oak trees that provided protective shade during the brutally hot summer months. The separation of branch from trunk typically occurred when the air was calm. If a person was lounging or sleeping under the several-hundred-pound branch when it fell, death or serious injury was the inevitable result. It was part of life in California.

Ruth Anne heard a carriage pull up to the house. She knew it could not be Caleb, as he rode the old mare on his water collection route in the morning. Responding to a stout knock on the door, Ruth Anne opened it and stared at Sheriff Jebediah Royster. Ordinarily, the only time the sheriff came to

Carrolton was to collect the foreign miner's tax, selectively, from the Chinese miners, never from the European miners. Since many of the Chinese miners had left their river claims after the Brannan mob raided Saddle Gap, she did not understand why the sheriff was at the door.

The first words out of Ruth Anne's mouth were, "Has something happened to Caleb?" "No, ma'am, I'm here to collect the Chinese orphan boy," stated Sheriff Royster.

Ruth Anne tilted her head and strained to comprehend what the lawman was saying. Boyton was not an orphan; he had a mother and father, Ruth Anne and Caleb. Sheriff Royster could see that Ruth Anne was confused about the purpose of his visit.

The sheriff pulled out some papers and started to explain the situation. "Judge Prewitt of the county district court granted Caleb and Ruth Anne Gibbons temporary guardianship of an orphaned Chinese boy until his mother or father presented themselves to regain their custody. With me today is Jun Ho, who has sworn a statement that she is the boy's mother." Sheriff Royster opened the front door further so Ruth Anne could see the Chinese woman sitting in the carriage.

Unknown to Ruth Anne, Boyton had joined her at the front door. When the Chinese woman saw Boyton, she started shouting, "My boy, my boy, Sheriff, my boy."

The sheriff started talking to Boyton. "Son, that is your Chinese mother, and I'm going to give you and her a ride back to her home in Sacramento to live." Boyton shook his head violently and began screaming, "No." Sheriff Royster grabbed his arm and started to drag him out of the house.

Ruth Anne screamed, "You are hurting him." The sheriff picked up Boyton and handed him to a waiting deputy, who put Boyton in a bear hug to control him. Sheriff Royster explained, "I know this is not easy for you, but it is best to make a quick and clean break, so you can move on with taking care of your husband."

Holding the struggling child, the deputy managed to climb into the back of the carriage. Sheriff Royster climbed onto the driver's seat, tipped his hat to Ruth Anne, and urged the horse forward. Boyton screamed, "Mama, help, help, help." Ruth Anne saw the Chinese woman put her hand on Boyton's head to try to console him. Jun Ho had now become an evil Chinese woman to Ruth Anne.

As the carriage rode off down the road, Ruth Anne collapsed. She could not breathe. She could not stand. She now knew how Alma felt; anything less than death was torture. Caleb returned and found Ruth Anne still on the ground, unable to communicate. She tried to tell Caleb what had happened, but she wasn't sure if she told him everything.

Once Ruth Anne saw the evil Chinese woman in the carriage, the event started to become a blur. All she knew was that she had failed to protect Boyton. Ruth Anne could battle rattlesnakes and coyotes, but the evil Chinese woman was too powerful for her. The Chinese woman must be evil, because no woman would inflict this sort of pain on another woman.

Ruth Anne lay awake all night, running the loop of endless questions through her mind. How did the evil Chinese woman find Boyton? How did she know where they lived? How does she know she is the mother? Why would the sheriff believe her? Why did she want Boyton back now, after more than ten years of separation?

Sacramento, it must have been when they were in Sacramento. Ruth Anne knew someone was watching her, following her. If they had not gone to Sacramento on the train, none of this would have happened. Caleb listened to all of Ruth Anne's recitations of the events, theories on how the Chinese woman had found them, and incoherent ramblings signifying a deep depression was descending upon Ruth Anne.

"I never got to say goodbye. I never told him I loved him," she moaned through her tears and trembling hands. Love? Caleb wondered if he had ever heard Ruth Anne utter the word love. Love was unspoken at best, he thought. For a minute, Caleb entertained the thought of whether he had loved Boyton. He decided he didn't really know what love was when it came to children.

Caleb reassured Ruth Anne he would work to get Boyton back. He tried to remember the name of the lawyer in Quartz Hill he was acquainted with. Was the name Muncie, Manson, Mumford? He couldn't remember. He told her he would ride to Quartz Hill or Flagston the next day to hire a lawyer and get Boyton back.

When Caleb returned from his efforts the next day, he had met with the lawyer. Their situation did not sound promising. The lawyer told him that the evil Chinese woman had signed a sworn statement attesting that she was the boy's mother. The legal guardianship granted to Caleb and Ruth Anne was only temporary. California courts did not really want to get involved in disputes of a family nature within the Chinese community. The lawyer said they could file a petition to have the court review the suitability of the boy's new home, but they would only succeed if the mother was found to be negligent or unfit. In other words, if the boy was in danger of being harmed.

After Boyton was taken from them – snatched – Ruth Anne became quiet and melancholy. She rarely spoke. She was not impolite to Caleb; she just had nothing to say. He kept his distance and let her grieve the loss of her son.

Caleb kept telling her he would find a way to get Boyton back. But she knew he was just placating her. The justice system was against them. She had no recourse. Ruth Anne thought of going to Sacramento to find the boy, but Caleb always discouraged it. He had heard Boyton was still with the woman in Sacramento. She was a laundress. Caleb tried to rationalize the situation, to tell himself that it might be best for Boyton to live in his own culture, with his own people.

His "own culture"? His "own people"? Ruth Anne found Caleb's stream of logic ridiculous. The two of them were Boyton's own people. Life in

Carrolton was the only culture he had ever known. He spoke English, not Chinese. The situation was senseless to Ruth Anne. Her head began to spin. Her thoughts became an endless stream of recurring events, replaying the scene of when Boyton was taken from them. She thought of all the things she should have done and said in that moment. She fantasized how, if she had possessed a gun and knew how to use it, she would have shot the Sheriff and the woman right there on the spot.

Caleb had to travel to Willow Bluff for a meeting with the Valley Springs Water Company. He saddled up the horse and asked Ruth Anne if she was going to be alright. She looked up at Caleb, so tall sitting on the horse, those pretty blue eyes conveying a sense of pity on her, and tried to smile, but all she could muster was a blank stare. She bowed her head, wiped her hand on her apron, and walked back to the cabin as Caleb rode off.

Ruth Anne's ears were ringing or buzzing, she could not tell which. The sound was so loud she stopped noticing the tick-tock of the clock. She was alone. Caleb was gone. She was alone in this miserable little town populated by miserable little people. She had no one to talk to. The other women in town, consumed with their chores and their very present children, could not begin to understand what she was going through.

The New Testament of the Bible is all about hope. Hope that even while your life may be hell and drudgery today, in death you will be with your Father in heaven. It struck Ruth Anne, for the first time, that the Bible was about obtaining happiness after you die. The implication was that you were destined to be miserable and unhappy while you were alive.

If it was written in the Bible, it must be truth, she thought. After all, the teachings of Jesus were commonly referred to as the "Good News." Through a maze of disconnected thoughts and illogical arguments, Ruth Anne concluded that only death would bring her some peace.

She went and found Caleb's rifle he kept for shooting coyotes. Because of its length and weight, she discovered there was no way she could point the gun at her head or chest and pull the trigger. "Damn these men with their long guns," she thought. How was a woman to reach eternal happiness if she could not reach the trigger? Caleb's pistol was not an option, as he had strapped it on to his hip before he left for Willow Bluff.

Ruth Anne remembered that Jim Wheeler's wife had committed suicide a couple years earlier. She had gotten herself a rope, thrown it over a big tree limb, wrapped the other end around her own neck, and jumped off a tree stump. What could have caused Mrs. Wheeler to commit suicide? she wondered. Obviously, she too had lost a child, or maybe…maybe…. Ruth Anne could not think of another reason to commit suicide. Even if Caleb died, she would not kill herself. Only the loss of a child could drive a woman to such an extreme measure to find peace without her child.

Ruth Anne did find a rope. She wrapped it around her waist and went walking, looking for a suitable Valley Oak tree from which to hang herself.

Valley Oaks were tall, with big thick branches. She was afraid if she used a blue oak or live oak tree, their thinner branches may not hold her weight. She kept walking. She walked along the water ditch. She traversed over the tall wooden flume, not looking down to make sure each next step landed on one of the boards over the water.

She walked into Bretton Falls. She found the house where the chicken-killing woman had lived. Ruth Anne stood by the side yard where the woman had unceremoniously killed that chicken. She just stood there. A young woman walked out of the house. Ruth Anne asked if the older woman still lived there. The young woman said no, her mother had died a few years back, of fever.

The daughter of the chicken-killing woman asked Ruth Anne if she could help her with anything. Ruth Anne, looking disheveled and disoriented, her hair escaping her bun and flying around her face, said nothing. She gave the woman a blank stare, turned, and walked toward the river.

The old wire rope suspension bridge was still standing. The cables were rusty, and the boards seemed more rotten than ever. Ruth Anne was glad the boards were rotting. She figured she would walk across the bridge, a board would break, and she would go falling into the rushing river below. Unlike her first crossings, this time Ruth Anne had no fear of walking on the bridge as it swayed back and forth in the wind.

Once over the river, and finding herself still alive, she made her way to the path to the Indian village. The trail was overgrown with intruding bushes and small trees. Why weren't the Indians keeping the trail clear? she thought to herself. Ruth Anne fought through the overgrown trail and finally reached the clearing where the Indian village had been situated.

There were no Indians. The village was a ghost town of sorts. The huts had fallen in on themselves. Acorn-crushing pestles were scattered about in the dirt, along with arrow heads, strips of fabric and leather, shards of glass, and tin cans. The Indian village had been abandoned. Where did the Indian men, women, and babies go? Were they alive or dead? They were gone and could be of no use in bringing back her son. The only sound that could be heard was the cry of a young red-tailed hawk, screeching at his mother for food high in a gray pine. Ruth Anne stared at the hawks. "Feed the boy," she said to the hawk mother. "Feed the boy. Too soon he'll be taken away from you."

Ruth Anne made her way back to the main road. She walked along the road past a small garden being tended by some Chinese men. They rose up and looked at her. Ruth Anne looked at their faces and began to cry. She saw her son in their faces. She saw his black hair, high forehead, beautiful eyes, and crooked teeth. She saw her son as a grown man, the man she would never know because some crazy Chinese lady had taken her child away.

The Chinese men watched as this woman cried and her hair, no longer contained in a neat bun, flew around her face. They watched as she muttered to herself about a chicken-killing woman, Indians, and a little boy. They thought maybe the chicken-killing woman or Indians had killed her son. The truth was the exact opposite; the woman and the hidden Indian village had saved her son.

Ruth Anne turned, slightly disoriented, and continued walking. She left the road and walked through tall, dry grass and around the oak trees scattered across the savannah. She walked up the bluff overlooking Bretton Falls. There were no salmon jumping over the waterfalls. Ruth Anne looked around and could see none of the beauty of the countryside that had once been so prominent to her. Several Chinese men, concerned and somewhat fascinated by this wild-looking woman, followed behind her.

Without a word, Ruth Anne stepped off the bluff and dropped into the pool of slow-moving water that lay below the rocks of the waterfalls. Her descent was almost like a pen dropped straight down into the water. She entered the cold water and felt her feet hit the rock below. She pushed herself up and came out of the water gasping for air. She flailed about, not knowing how to swim. Her object, she briefly remembered, was not to swim, but to drown.

The rope around her waist had come loose and was floating downstream. She heard loud voices shouting incomprehensible words at the river's edge. The Chinese men who had followed the wild woman had grabbed the rope as it floated by and were shouting to Ruth Anne, albeit in Chinese, to grab hold of the rope. Ruth Anne's instinct to obey the command of a man's voice resulted her in grabbing the rope, unthinking. The Chinese men pulled her out of the river. Ruth Anne, no longer so wild, sat on the stony bank and cried.

Ruth Anne's saviors walked her back to their little cabin, where they stoked the stove to help get her dry and warm. As she sat warming in the tiny cabin, she proceeded to tell them the story of how Boyton had come into her life. The two Chinese men remembered that a fellow Chinese man had died when a boulder crashed into his cabin. The men began squabbling over whether the man had been crushed by the boulder, drowned, died of fright, or was killed by that woman.

"What woman?" inquired Ruth Anne. "Oh, the crazy woman, she had an evil spirit in her," replied one of the men. "Did she have baby?" asked Ruth Anne. The men looked between themselves, shook their heads, and said no. "Baby would be crazy like her, I think.," added one of the men.

Ruth Anne did not believe in evil spirits. She was convinced that Boyton was not possessed by any demon or devil. However, the woman who claimed to be Boyton's mother was most certainly crazy, possessed or both. If she could kill the man in the cabin and leave her child to starve to death, she was capable of harming Boyton. Ruth Anne was now fueled with a new energy. A reason for life, with maybe a little spark of hope mixed in. "Thank you," Ruth Anne said to the men, "But I must leave now and save my son."

The long hike back to Carrolton gave Ruth Anne ample time to ruminate on all the recent events. The dominant theme coursing through her thoughts was that she was mad. She was mad at everyone. She was mad at Sheriff Royster, mad at the evil Chinese woman, mad at Caleb, mad at everyone. All these men talked about manifest destiny. What about her destiny? Why was it taken from her? Her destiny had been to care for Boyton. Snap, crack, boom, no warning, separation.

Ruth Anne wandered into Carrolton looking more like a stray dog than a woman, with cockleburs and weed stickers stuck to her dress. Her hair was disheveled. She was tired and felt old. As she neared home, she saw Caleb's horse in the corral. She figured she would go in the house, and Caleb would have another excuse for the delay in finding Boyton. Caleb, what was he good for? she thought. Men, they make lots of promises. She decided she would travel to Sacramento to see this mysterious lawyer Caleb had talked to about Boyton.

Before she opened the door, Ruth Anne had made up her mind to be stern with Caleb and let him know she wanted action, and she was travelling to Sacramento to get Boyton. Anticipating a confrontation, she opened the door, only to be greeted by Boyton running up to her and hugging her waist.

"Oh, my sweet boy, how did you get home?" exclaimed Ruth Anne. Caleb asked Ruth Anne, "What trail did you take to get home?" Ruth Anne looked up at Caleb with a smile on her face and tears in her eyes, "The wrong trail."

Ruth Anne's irritation at Caleb had dissipated. A short time later she was shocked to hear the sounds of Caleb and Boyton at the wood stove, frying up some meat for supper. Caleb never cooked. He never so much as boiled coffee. After Ruth Anne got cleaned up, the trio sat down at the table to eat and to hear how Boyton had found his way back home. The question in Ruth Anne's mind was, was his stay temporary or permanent?

Boyton devoured his meat and potatoes. "All she fed me was rice and vegetables, it was awful," Boyton offered.

Boyton then shared his version of events of his daring escape, sprinkled undoubtedly with a little embellishment and hyperbole, reminiscent of Phineas Jackson. He described how after the Sheriff Royster delivered him and the Chinese woman to Sacramento, he was taken to a room in one of the shacks along China Slough in Sacramento. The shack also housed a couple of Chinese girls a little older than he was. They all spoke Chinese, and he did not understand what they were saying unless they spoke to him in sparse English.

After a couple of days, the girls instructed him on his work. He was tasked with some laundry washing, cleaning the rooms, and taking food to the evil Chinese woman. The girls were bossy, he remembered. He was told his new name was Wen Ho, and from then on, that is what everyone called him. Sometimes he had to work with one of the Chinese men moving sacks of rice or other dry goods from wagons to one of the stores on I Street. The only time he was allowed to go outside by himself was when he was told to sweep the wooden planks that constituted the walkway in front of the stores and shacks.

Boyton relayed that nighttime was the most terrifying part of his captivity. The shack and surrounding alleyways were thick with all sorts of strange smells and sounds. He did not even have so much as a candle for light in the little room, which felt at night as cold as a cave. The only light that entered the shack was from the gaps in the wood siding between rooms and the outside. He had hated the place and did not want to go back.

One curious incident Boyton recounted was that the sheriff had come and visited the evil Chinese woman almost every evening. She was nice to the sheriff. Sometimes late at night it sounded like they were wrestling around in the room next to his. At this part of Boyton's captivity story, Ruth Anne and Caleb looked up at one another, each with a blank stare that conveyed their comprehension of the situation.

The hypocrisy of some people in the anti-Chinese movement was plain for most people to see, had they cared to think about it. Law enforcement officials had the power to shut down the opium dens and prostitution within the Chinese communities if they had wanted to. It was the case that some law enforcement men were in cahoots with the Chinese purveyors of the vices, either taking bribes or partaking themselves in sins of the flesh at Chinese establishments as payment for their protection. The result was that law enforcement looked away from many of the crimes committed in the Chinese community, unless a white person was involved. Boyton was not white.

Clearly, Sheriff Royster fell into this category of anti-Chinese agitators. He was a vocal proponent of any legislation that sought to expel the Chinese from California. He attended anti-Chinese Society meetings. Sheriff Royster's ardent support of the anti-Chinese movement made him popular with many voters in Sacramento and those who would give money to his election campaign for county sheriff.

Sheriff Royster was also smart enough to know that nothing would ever change in California despite local lawmakers' anti-Chinese efforts, because foreign immigration was controlled at the federal level. Chinese immigration to the U.S. was governed by the Burlingame Treaty between the United States and China, and it was not changing anytime soon.

Although Boyton spent only limited time outside during his Sacramento captivity, he told Ruth Anne and Caleb that he was able to observe that when a train arrived at the same time as a paddle wheeled steamer, there were lots of people, horses, carriages, buggies, and wagons on the street. There was so much traffic and noise, a person could easily move into the crowd and disappear. He reckoned the building where he was being held was about three blocks from the waterfront where the train and steamer depots were located.

One afternoon, as he was sweeping the uneven planks by himself, he noticed the crowds of people on the street swell with passengers departing from the train and the steamer. He just meandered to the other side of street and started walking toward the waterfront and Sacramento River. He was short enough to hide among the adults in the crowd, so that none of the Chinese men who might be watching could see he had left and was walking away.

At the train depot, Boyton recognized Mr. Robinson, the train engineer, and said hi to him. Robinson was surprised to see the little Chinese boy who asked so many questions about how the steam locomotive operated. Robinson asked Boyton if his parents were around, and Boyton told him he had gotten lost. "Hmmm, okay, hop on the back passenger car, and I'll collect the fare from your Pa when we get to Quartz Hill," said Robinson.

Before the train left the station, Boyton told Caleb and Ruth Anne, he crouched down so none of the Chinese people could see him through the window. He could hear the evil Chinese woman calling out his name, "Wen Ho, Wen Ho, where you at Wen Ho?" Once the train got out of Sacramento, he sat up in his seat and enjoyed the rest of the trip back to Quartz Hill. When he got off the train at Quartz Hill, he saw Mr. Hoxie and got a ride with him back to Carrolton.

"Oh, my goodness, Boyton, you are so brave and smart! You are such a little man," praised Ruth Anne. Boyton, with a grin, basked in the glow of his parents' approval of his daring escape from the clutches of the evil Chinese woman. In the succeeding days, Ruth Anne was torn between keeping Boyton safe in the house or letting him run outside with his pals. The first few days passed easily, as all Boyton did was sleep and eat. He had obviously been deprived of both while in captivity at Chinatown in Sacramento.

Eventually, the energy level of a 12-year-old boy blossomed again. Ruth Anne took Boyton on a short trip into town to pick up some flour, milk, and eggs. From every house, store, and barn came shouts of, "Hey, Boyton, glad to see you are back!" As Boyton waved and said hi, Ruth Anne had a hard time keeping the tears from running down her face. "Oh, my goodness," she thought to herself, "this town really cared about him."

"Ma, can I go with John down to the river? He says salmon are jumping all over the place. Maybe I can catch one for dinner," Boyton asked. "Sure, run along and play, be careful," replied Ruth Anne. She doubted Boyton would catch one of those large salmon on their spring run up the river to spawn. If nothing else, watching those giant fish leap out of the water was a spectacular sight. That was the difference between Carrolton and Sacramento, she thought. In Sacramento, all you had to watch were the drunks falling over themselves. In Carrolton, you had all sorts of deer, mountain lions, coyotes, eagles, hawks, and salmon to watch. Ruth Anne would take the dangers of lions and snakes over the corrupt humans inhabiting Sacramento.

Ruth Anne had seen Ah Chee, the Chinese dry goods merchant and herbalist, return from Sacramento the day before with a wagonload of goods. She walked to Ah Chee's little shack of a store to buy some of the black tea he was stocking. The black tea tasted better to Ruth Anne than coffee. After a conversation with Ah Chee, she learned that she could apply the wet tea leaves to a flaky little rash on her arms she had developed over the years. The tea leaves soothed the rash, a bonus after a nice cup of tea.

Ah Chee was bagging the black tea for Ruth Anne when he quietly said, "They are coming." "Pardon?" replied Ruth Anne. "They are coming, Miss Gibbons," said Ah Chee intently staring at her as if to telepathically convey the message of danger to Boyton. She blinked her eyes a couple of times and understood what Ah Chee was communicating. Ruth Anne paid for the tea and rushed back to the house.

"Boyton! Boyton! Where are you?" Ruth Anne shouted as she approached the house. The Chinese boy was at the back of house working on his school reader. "Get inside, quick!" Ruth Anne commanded.

Boyton thought he was in trouble. He wondered if she had found out about the lizard he put in Maria Gosseau's dress pocket. It had been funny to see her scream when the lizard started crawling up her dress. She had then chased Boyton down to the river as he laughed uncontrollably.

Now, out of breath and shaking, Ruth Anne grabbed Boyton by the shoulders, bent down and looked him straight in the eyes. "Listen, the evil Chinese woman is coming back," Ruth Anne said. "Okay," he said," let's run away! We can go up to Flagston or some other town; they'll never find us up in the mountains."

Ah Chee's surreptitious message had revealed to Ruth Anne the web of Chinese informants and communication that perfused the region. Suddenly, no place seemed safe. She also was afraid of committing a crime, by absconding with the boy, in defiance of a court order to return him to a woman who was posing as his mother. At this point, Ruth Anne felt she could easy kill the woman without any hesitation. Of course, she knew at heart, that solution would only make matters worse for everyone.

Ruth Anne's panic was interrupted by Caleb's return from his rounds upriver at the Valley Springs Water Company dam. Caleb could see the fear on Boyton's face and the look of consternation in Ruth Anne' eyes.

"What's going on?" Caleb greeted them. "She's coming back for me," shouted Boyton in alarm. "What are we going to do, Caleb?" asked Ruth Anne. Boyton looked at Caleb and thought, "Pa can fix anything."

Ruth Anne looked out the open front door, its weathered boards framing a beautiful landscape. White wispy clouds passed slowly over head, and she could see the gleam of the river as it came around a big curve in the canyon wall. The fruit trees were dropping their white blossoms and pushing out bright green leaves. A few eagles soared above the river looking for the last of the salmon. Ruth Anne simply stared out the door. She could not hear Caleb or Boyton discussing possible plans.

Suddenly, Ruth Anne turned around and said, "We have to let them take Boyton." "Ma," protested Boyton. "Then what?" asked Caleb. "I'm not sure, we need more time to make this right," replied Ruth Anne. But there was no time left.

As they looked at one another helplessly, a carriage came into view bearing Sheriff Royster and the evil Chinese woman, with a deputy at the reins. Following the carriage was a buggy driven by two Chinese men.

Boyton recognized the two Chinese men from his brief captivity in Sacramento. They were part of Jun Ho's operation. Both were both dressed in the traditional Chinese garb of collarless quilted jackets buttoned up to their necks. Their pants were billowy and would be considered beautiful by Ruth Anne in any other circumstance. The bulges visible at their waists were either knives or guns, thought Ruth Anne. The two men had expressly been brought by Jun Ho to intimidate her, she thought.

Sheriff Royster stepped down from the carriage and walked over to Ruth Anne and Caleb. "Mr. and Mrs. Gibbons, we don't want problems. However, you can't abduct Wen Ho from his home," he stated sternly to Ruth Anne.

Boyton started to explain that he had run away, only to be interrupted by Ruth Anne, "Hush, child!" Then Caleb started to speak about a misunderstanding, until Ruth Anne jabbed him in the gut with her elbow.

"You are correct, Sheriff," began Ruth Anne. "It was wrong of me to collect Wen Ho and bring him back to Carrolton. I apologize. It will never happen again."

Caleb and Boyton were bewildered at Ruth Anne's admission of guilt over an event that had not happened. "Sheriff, if you will give me a minute with Wen Ho, to collect some of his clothes, he will leave peaceably with you," requested Ruth Anne.

Jun Ho started shouting with an angry look on her face, "Wen Ho don't need your clothes." Sheriff Royster abruptly turned and shot Jun Ho a look telling her to be quiet.

"Certainly, Mrs. Gibbons, take all the time you need," replied Sheriff Royster. The sheriff explained to Caleb that he would not file any charges against Ruth Anne, but if she repeated the abduction, he would have to arrest her.

Inside the house, as Ruth Anne stuffed clothing into a burlap sack, she informed Boyton of her incomplete plan to help him escape from Jun Ho. "Boyton, just go with them, be very nice and polite," she said. "Give them no reason to suspect you might run away. Keep a watch for me because I'll be down there in a day or two. It's going to be alright. Mama will make this right. We just have to play their little game right now."

Boyton reluctantly climbed into the back seat of the carriage with the sheriff and the Chinese woman. "Thank you for your cooperation, Mrs. Gibbons. Caleb, good day," said Sheriff Royster, as the carriage pulled away, followed by the two Chinese men in their buggy. Ruth Anne looked on, stoic and stone-faced; she refused to reveal any fear or anger in front of the evil Chinese woman.

When the carriage and buggy had rolled out of sight, Ruth Anne began throwing anything that would break and make noise. Clay pots, bottles, dishes became instruments of anger release. Caleb stood by and let her release her emotions in and out of the house. When she became exhausted, she collapsed into his arms. "What am I going to do? I just gave my son away to that evil Chinese woman," cried Ruth Anne.

The best words Caleb ever spoke at that moment were no words. Silence, that is all Ruth Anne wanted. She did not want words of comfort. She wanted silence. She just wanted to be alone with the gaping wound in her heart until she could begin to breathe again. Before the oil lamp was extinguished for the evening, Caleb said, "I'll head to Flagston in the morning and hire a lawyer I found. Then we'll head down to Sacramento."

In the morning, Ruth Anne hated the silence in the house. It was never quiet when Boyton was awake. She wanted her little boy who would not stop chatting and asking questions back under her roof. There were times when she was fixing breakfast that she would shiver and seethe with anger at the evil Chinese woman. She wanted to hurt that woman as she had been hurt. She took a deep breath and prayed for calmness and guidance. She prayed for forgiveness for her sins of the past and for those she might commit in the future.

As soon as Caleb had saddled up his horse and started toward Flagston, Ruth Anne threw a few coins in her waist pocket and a biscuit, without much thought of any other provisions she might need, started off to Sacramento. She was able to get a ride to Quartz Hill with Mr. White, the blacksmith. At Quartz Hill she went to the train depot and purchased a ticket to Sacramento. She looked around the passenger car and wondered where Boyton had sat when he escaped from captivity in Sacramento.

After four hours of travel from Carrolton, Ruth Anne arrived in Sacramento, still without any plans for helping Boyton escape from the evil Chinese woman. First, Ruth Anne had to find Boyton. She remembered that Boyton had said he was held captive about three blocks from the waterfront. Ruth Anne assumed that was along I street in Chinatown Town, in one of the shacks fronting China Slough.

As Ruth Anne walked up J street, she caught a glimpse of herself in a window. She was wearing a calico striped dress that Alma Gosseau had given her in appreciation for Ruth Anne's caring for her family after Auturo died. The dress had always looked so pleasant on Alma, a compliment to her bright personality. On the small-framed Ruth Anne, however, it looked baggy and not at all flattering. Caleb had once mentioned it looked like Ruth Anne was wearing a potato sack.

Ruth Anne had not yet started altering the pretty dress to fit properly. She also realized that she was wearing a dark-colored bonnet that did not match the dress. Instead of her proper lace ups, Ruth Anne had pulled on her work boots. The window reflection revealed how tan Ruth Anne's face had become from working outside in the garden. Her hands were calloused, and there was dirt under her fingernails. Suddenly she was embarrassed at her appearance.

Alternately, she rationalized that her rough exterior might bring her less attention as she wandered around Sacramento searching for Boyton.

There was a light wind blowing as she walked, and the cottonwood trees were shedding their fluffy cotton-like seed pods. Ruth Anne followed the trail of cotton until she was standing under a large cottonwood on the eastern edge of China Slough. The cotton fluff coated the surface of the slough and descended all around like summer snow. She waited next to the giant cottonwood until she caught a glimpse of a young boy she thought might be Boyton.

She could see a lot of activity on the slough and along I street in Chinatown Town. Wagons and horses were moving up and down the dirt roads. Ruth Anne was not conspicuous to anyone. But, she worried, if she looked just like another pedestrian going about a woman's business, how would Boyton recognize her? She walked slowly down I street, hoping to catch a glimpse of him.

After several hours, Ruth Anne spotted him. He was wearing more traditional Chinese attire of a young boy. He did not have his wide brim felt hat that he loved so much. She walked up and down the street, as Boyton moved some sacks and boxes out of a wagon. When he finally saw her, he stopped still. Ruth Anne violently shook her head to indicate to him not to say anything. "Just keep working, Boyton," she thought to herself. A small smile crossed his mouth, as his mother made visual contact. Ruth Anne kept walking.

The first part of her plan was accomplished: to let Boyton know she was in Sacramento. She heard one of the men who had come to Carrolton with the evil Chinese woman shout something at Boyton in Chinese. Boyton kept working and averted his eyes from Ruth Anne. A woman walked toward them down the street, and Ruth Anne recognized her as Jun Ho, the evil Chinese woman. Ruth Anne quickly turned down an alley and out onto J street.

All of sudden, Ruth Anne realized Jun Ho was following her. "Did she recognize me?" wondered Ruth Anne. The familiar feeling of paranoia returned. Quickly, she opened the door to the nearest business and darted inside. She peered through the window to assess if Jun Ho was truly following her. "Good afternoon, madam," a familiar voice spoke from behind her. "Can I interest you in one of Bailey's famous patent-pending butter coolers?"

The small round man, with a long dark beard, dressed in a handsome suit, continued his sales pitch in a booming baritone voice, much to Ruth Anne's dismay and annoyance. "This butter cooler is made of the finest terracotta, manufactured right here on the premises," the man continued. "All that is needed is for you to fill the hollow bottom and top with water. Then from the extraordinary evaporative properties of this pottery, it keeps your butter rounds cool, even on the hottest day."

Without waiting for Ruth Anne to ask any questions, the man whose voice was as rich as the smoothest butter continued, "This is a wonderful opportunity for a woman of your intelligence, grace, and poise to earn a little extra money. I'm willing to supply you with ten of these fine butter coolers to sell to your fellow housekeepers. You will keep 20 percent of the sales price." The man stopped, looked at Ruth Anne and said, "You look familiar. Have we met before?"

"Hello, Mr. Bailey. I am Ruth Anne Gibbons. We met at your winery several years ago," replied Ruth Anne. "Ah yes, Mrs. Gibbons, I'm so glad you stopped and are interested in my butter cooler," Bailey said. "My apologies, Mr. Bailey, I'm not interested in a butter cooler. I'm in Sacramento to get my son back," explained Ruth Anne. Now it was Bailey who had the perplexed look on his face.

To break the awkward silence, Ruth Anne asked, "How is Mrs. Bailey, Caroline, your wife?" "Oh, my dear, Caroline died in the house fire out at the vineyard several years ago," said Bailey. "The same fire that killed Auturo Gosseau," added Ruth Anne. "Yes, and several of my Chinese employees, brave men trying to save Caroline, the house, and the winery. Sadly, all gone now," said Bailey in a somber tone.

Bailey's sales veneer dropped away. He walked over to a chair and sat down and looked at the floor. Without looking up at Ruth Anne, Bailey remarked, "And you came to Sacramento to… to get your son back. Back from what? He is a mere lad." "Jun Ho," was all Ruth Anne said. "Jun Ho, ah, I see," said Bailey. He rose from his chair, walked to the door, and turned the sign hanging in the window from open to closed.

"She is an evil Chinese woman who claims to be Boyton's mother and renamed him Wen Ho," Ruth Anne said summarizing the situation she found herself in. "So, Boyton is now housed at Chinatown with Jun Ho?" asked Bailey. "Yes, and I have to try and get him back home, or something," replied Ruth Anne, looking out the window onto J street at the passing buggies and carriages.

"Well," began Bailey, "I would not say Jun Ho is evil. I've known her for many years." Dread struck Ruth Anne's heart. She had been sure Bailey would sympathize with her situation. Now, she was learning that Bailey was on the side of Jun Ho.

"I see," said Ruth Anne, a chill in her voice. "I must leave now." "Wait," implored Bailey, "I might be able to help." "How?" Ruth Anne shot back at Bailey. "Let me explain," Bailey replied.

"After I had finished my mining operations up on the river, Caroline came out to Sacramento, and we settled into this town," he continued "An old mining partner, James Hardesty, had improved some property out by Saddle Gap. He was tinkering around with planting grapes and some fruit trees. But Jim really did not like farming. He decided he wanted to return to Australia. He offered to sell me his spread between the Valley Springs Water Company ditch and the river, about 300 acres."

Ruth Anne grew even more annoyed. She did not want to hear a recitation of the early pioneer days. She only wanted to move forward with getting Boyton back. How was any of Bailey's history with gold mining, land, and vineyards connected in any way to the immediate concern for her son?

"I wanted to get back to the wild country, the Gold Country," Bailey went on. "I did not want to mine anymore – too old – but I also like farming, from the days when I lived in Stamford, Connecticut. Anyhow, I built a nice house for Caroline and started planting the vineyard, starting with raisins, and moving into wines, brandy, etcetera.

"Before we left Sacramento, Caroline had become acquainted with Jun Ho, who was then just a young girl. She worked at a vegetable stand and sold some tea my Carolina enjoyed. Chinatown in Sacramento at that time was not as rough, a little safer than it is today. Caroline could see that Jun Ho, like many of the young girls brought from China, was virtually held captive by the man who owned her. I say 'owned' because they paid for the girls in China and then brought them over to California like some bag of rice – chattel – that they could sell.

"Caroline developed a tentative friendship with Jun Ho and learned that she really wanted to leave the men who held her. Her life was not her own. If Jun Ho walked anywhere in Sacramento, maybe to deliver some laundry, she had to be accompanied by one of her captors. She was closely watched and, I assumed, abused at night.

"Once Caroline and I were settled in the new house at Blue Oak Vineyards, we felt we could offer a safe place to Jun Ho, a sweet innocent young girl. We developed a plan to distract the men at her Chinatown shanty, then got her into a hackney coach so she could not be seen. The coachman drove her to the edge of town, out by Sutter's Fort, where we picked her up in our carriage and took her to Blue Oak Vineyards to live with us.

"What amazes me is the communication web within the Chinese community. Something can happen in Redding, and the next day, before the newspapers have reported on it, all the Chinese people know what happened," Bailey said with a chuckle. "Anyhow, there was no train out to Quartz Hill in those days. The roads were not as good. It was difficult to reach Blue Oak Vineyards and even to attempt to abduct someone. We felt Jun Ho was relatively safe.

"Unfortunately, Jun Ho learned that her sister Mai Ho had been bought and brought to Sacramento. Her desire to protect her sister was too great, and Jun Ho went back to Sacramento. I cannot blame her.

"No, Jun Ho is not evil. She is a victim, a captive, just like Boyton. She is doing their work to survive." No matter how Bailey painted Jun Ho as an exploited young woman, Ruth Anne was never going to relent and grant her an ounce of sympathy.

"Well, Jun Ho was not the only Chinese person to become a slave of these foul men," Bailey continued. "Other Chinese people approached us to see if we could accommodate other Chinese men and women who wanted to escape

Chinatown and the abuses they were subjected to there. We helped several Chinese people escape. They then helped us at Blue Oak Vineyards or moved on to safer places. For the record, I did pay a fare wage to any Chinese man or woman who worked for me.

"I guess our little underground railroad became a burr under the saddle of men like Wong Bang, Chu Lung, Chung Kit, and Lee Fook, who are the principals of criminal activity in Chinatown. I suspect it was one of them who set Blue Oak Vineyards on fire."

Ruth Anne sat in amazement at Bailey's story. She had never had any notion that those sort activities were occurring in California. She had been insulated in her small town of Carrolton until the outside world intruded on her family. Ruth Anne tried to put all the pieces of California's complicated social structure in place. She kept coming back to one question, "How was any of that story of any help to Boyton in escaping his captivity?"

"What about Sheriff Royster?" asked Ruth Anne. "Royster? He is a Copperhead of the first order," replied Bailey. "What do you mean?" asked Ruth Anne. "Well, Royster, was a Copperhead during the war. One of those people who professed loyalty to the Union, but secretly, sometimes openly, was a Confederate sympathizer. He hails from Texas, dyed-in-the-wool Democrat, who never had any compunction about slavery. Royster puts himself first, everyone else is second," explained Bailey.

"Now," began Bailey, "getting back to the Boyton situation. The combination of Sheriff Royster with the Chinese gang at Chinatown means Boyton will never be safe in the Sacramento area. Your best proposition is to get him to San Francisco and to the Presbyterian House. There is a large enough population of good Chinese men there to protect safe places like the Presbyterian House," Bailey offered.

"What is the Presbyterian House?" asked Ruth Anne. "It's a religious mission that takes in young Chinese women escaping exploitation. They should be able to protect Boyton, if not there, then at another location, and he will be safe," explained Bailey.

"But I can't move to San Francisco. There is no work for Caleb there. How could I live, survive?" asked Ruth Anne.

"Perhaps this is more about the survival of Boyton," Baily said. "If you are connected to Boyton, they will track him down. They don't give up easily. Look what they did to me, to Caroline, to the winery," Bailey said with a somber expression on his face.

A Chinese man entered the doorway from the pottery room, startling Ruth Anne. Bailey introduced Ruth Anne to Sam Fong. Sam was tall, skinny, and young, with a hint of an adolescent moustache. Bailey told Ruth Anne that Sam had learned pottery-making skills in China before immigrating to California. More importantly, Sam Fong was Bailey's accomplice when it came to moving Chinese women out of Chinatown captivity. Sam had been a valued employee at Blue Oak Vineyards before the fire.

Bailey then sketched out a plan to extricate Boyton from Chinatown. There was always some risk, especially when it came to the police officers and the judge at the police court, but Bailey felt they had a high probability of success. "Okay," agreed Ruth Anne.

"Do you have a place to stay this evening?" asked Bailey. "Uh, yes," stammered Ruth Anne. She did not have a place to spend the night, but she was determined to figure it out. She did not want Bailey to think she was completely incompetent.

Bailey and Ruth Anne agreed to meet at 9 o'clock in the morning. Ruth Anne then walked toward the waterfront, not knowing exactly where she was going to spend the night. She remembered Caleb said he stayed at the Eagle Hotel on the embarcadero, so she decided to try that option. It was a pleasant evening for walking. As she got closer to the waterfront, she could hear the trains running up the tracks and steam paddle wheelers splashing through the river.

The air was heavy with smoke from not only the transportation engines, but from all the different establishments burning wood to heat water or cook food. The smoke and stench fouled what otherwise would have been a nice evening stroll. When Ruth Anne reached the Eagle Hotel, she was pleased to discover a nicer establishment than she had expected.

Ruth Anne walked through the double doors of the hotel and was struck by the fine dark wood of the wainscoting and banister. Beautiful tapestry rugs covered the highly polished wood floor. Big, red velvet chairs surrounded a mahogany table, with bright brass spittoons next to each chair. In the corner was a clock taller than her father's. When the clock struck the hour, it played a Westminster tune on tubular chimes, filling the foyer with wonderful sound.

"If this is where Caleb stayed on business while in Sacramento, why would he ever come home to our little cabin in Carrolton?" Ruth Anne wondered. She approached the front desk and asked for a room for the night. The clerk told her the room would cost $2 a night, meals extra. Gripped with fear, Ruth Anne realized she had about a dollar in change in her waist band. "May I charge the room to the Valley Springs Water Company?" she calmly inquired. "Oh, yes," came the reply from the short balding man at the front desk, who was wearing a crisp white shirt, tie, and dark vest.

"To whom should I charge the room?" asked the clerk. "Caleb Gibbons," replied Ruth Anne. "Mr. Gibbons, wonderful, we have not seen him for a while. Would a river view room work for you?" the clerk asked. Ruth Anne did not want a pleasant view. She was not on holiday. She wanted a room where she might be able to see where Boyton was sleeping. "No, a room in the back along J street will be fine," replied Ruth Anne. "Those rooms can be a bit noisy from the establishments below," cautioned the clerk. "It will be fine," she assured the clerk.

Ruth Anne collected her room key, and, before she could leave, the clerk asked, "Do you have any bags that we can bring up to your room." "No," said

Ruth Anne. "My husband will be along later, but thank you for your concern." As Ruth Anne began to ascend the stairs to the third floor, she realized what a compulsive and adroit liar she had become. Every time she was questioned by someone, she seemed to utter a lie. This is what California had made of her: a liar, a bad mother, and, probably, a criminal.

At the top of the staircase was mounted a full-length mirror. Ruth Anne studied her appearance, disheveled hair, baggy dress, dusty work boots, a tinge of gray in her hair, and lines in her face. This is what California had bestowed upon her, she thought. As much as she felt depressed over her appearance, she was surprised at Caleb's reputation. Everyone she encountered knew Caleb Gibbons, or so it seemed.

Ruth Anne walked into her room, which she had lied to get and fell on the bed. She was tired. She felt old. She had to prepare for a fight against a community of Chinese men so well versed in subterfuge. Where was God? Where was Caleb? Caleb, the man who many people thought resembled William Tecumseh Sherman, albeit with a fuller face and gentler smile.

Caleb had always wanted to be an explorer like Kit Carson or John Fremont. He felt living in Carrolton, almost wilderness, was as close as he was going to get to being a professional wanderer, explorer of new lands and frontiers. Ruth Anne cried, thinking she had failed Caleb. She was not a real frontier or pioneer wife. She could not have children, and the one she did have had now been lost. It would have been better had she succeeded in her dive from the bluff into the river to terminate her life.

The sun set, and the gas lights were lit along the streets beneath Ruth Anne's room. She looked out the window to see if she could see Chinatown. She could barely make out some of the roofs of the shanties and the stagnant and fetid slough behind them. Her child was in that miserable living space. "I'm coming for you, Boyton, Mama's coming for you. Be strong, I'll be there soon," she said to the window.

The clerk was correct; the room was noisy. The carousing of drunken men went on into the early morning. There were shouts from the gambling halls. There was a fight or two that spilled out into the street. The tinny, out-of-tune music of pianos and brass instruments was a constant background annoyance of noise. "Dear Lord, how do people live in Sacramento?" whispered Ruth Anne. She pulled out a pulverized biscuit she had put into her dress pocket before she left Carrolton, ate it, and then drifted off into a fitful sleep.

11 Ticket to Freedom

Ruth Anne was standing next to Bailey's butter cooler pottery shop when he and Sam arrived to open up. "Have you had breakfast, coffee?" asked Bailey. "No," replied Ruth Anne. "Sam, please make us some tea, and I think we have some bread and jam. I know we have some butter kept in the Bailey butter cooler that will be nice and sweet," Bailey said, with a little twinkle in his voice. Ruth Anne was having problems finding any humor in Bailey's comments, but she appreciated his attempt to lighten the mood of the morning.

"Your role in this charade, Mrs. Gibbons, is to be seen but not heard," began Bailey. "We want Boyton to see you and know that everything is good. We don't want your presence alerting the Chinese men that something is amiss," continued Bailey.

"But how are we going to communicate with Boyton?" interjected Ruth Anne. "Have no fear, it will be through a series of overt and covert acts and communication. We must attempt to try to time this so that we can get Boyton on the 3 o'clock train to San Francisco," explained Bailey.

"I still don't understand what is going to happen," Ruth Anne protested. "Mrs. Gibbons, you will have to trust me," Bailey said. "What if things go wrong, what then?" Ruth Anne asked. "Well in the worst case, either you, myself, or both of us will be spending the night in the county jail, but I do not foresee that happening," Bailey said. "I think this little gamble will work and give us enough time to secrete Boyton away from Sacramento."

Ruth Anne was terribly apprehensive about the whole affair. She had faith in Bailey, but the lack of details he was willing to share with her was concerning. "What is the first step?" Ruth Anne asked.

"The first step is to wait until Boyton comes outside. With luck, he won't be watched too carefully, and I'll be able to apprise him of the events that will be taking place," explained Bailey. "Don't the Chinese men know you?" asked Ruth Anne. "Yes, some do know me, but to others I'm just a bumbling old pottery salesman," Bailey quipped.

"What happens if the Chinese gang learn you were involved? Won't they attack you or burn down your pottery shop?" asked Ruth Anne.

Bailey gave a cynical chuckle and shook his head. "Ma'am, I've already lost everything. My beloved wife, Caroline, taken from me. What else is there to lose?" he replied. Then Bailey sat back and began to muse philosophically.

"Do you know who the most dangerous men are in this world?" Bailey asked. Ruth Anne shook her head. "I'll tell you; the most dangerous men are those who have nothing to lose, nothing to live for. And you are looking at one of those men," he said.

Ruth Anne did not know what to think. Was Bailey dangerous, or was he just trying to explain why he had little fear of the Chinese gangs? "With that, let's commence with our little plan to rescue your son," Bailey said with his charming and reassuring smile.

Sam Fong was upstairs working on pottery pieces, his body positioned so he could look out the window to see if Boyton had come outside. For a short period, Boyton helped some men unload bags of tea and rice. There were too many Chinese men milling about for Bailey to approach. Late in the morning, Boyton came outside with a shovel and bucket. His job was to clean up the horse droppings next to the plank sidewalk. The horse poop always attracted lots of flies, which wasn't good for the vegetable vendors.

Sam and Ruth Anne were stationed across the street at the opening to the alley. Sam stood on one side of the alley, flipping through a Chinese newspaper. Ruth Anne stood across from him, hands folded, looking up and down the street as if she was waiting for someone to arrive. Boyton was engaged in shoveling the horse poop, which was covered in cottonwood fluff, into a wooden bucket.

Bailey came walking down the plank sidewalk with purposeful steps, as if he was late for an appointment. When he reached the point where Boyton was working, Bailey tripped, his short round body flopping on the wooden planks as the contents of his valise scattered across the sidewalk and into the street.

"Boy, help me," commanded Bailey. As Bailey pulled himself onto his knees, he began to whisper to Boyton. "Listen carefully, Boyton, across the street is your mother. Next to her is Sam, the Chinese man," said Bailey.

Boyton looked across the street and thought he saw Alma Gosseau. Then he realized the woman did not have Alma's wild, blonde curls. It was Ruth Anne, wearing Alma's dress. Boyton looked at Bailey and thought he looked familiar.

"The next time you see Sam, go with him; he'll take you to safety," instructed Bailey.

Together Boyton and Bailey gathered the pottery trinkets that had spilled all over the street and sidewalk. Before Bailey stood up, he clasped Boyton's hands and placed something round and smooth into the right one. "Hide this in your pocket, it is your ticket to freedom, and if asked by the police, you indeed did take it from me," said Bailey as he rose to his feet.

As Bailey started walking, he shouted at the Chinese vendors to fix the rotten wooden planks on which he had tripped, or he would report them to the city.

Boyton finished cleaning up the horse poop. He looked across the street, where neither Sam nor his mother were anywhere to be seen. He ran to his little cave of a room to inspect the ticket to freedom.

In the dim light, Boyton could see that the round smooth object Bailey had given him was a gold pocket watch. Engraved on one side of the case was a wreath of grape vines and leaves with a plump brunch of grapes in the middle. On the other side was engraved a swift-looking racehorse. He pushed on the crown used to wind the watch, and the front cover popped open to reveal a glossy, smooth, enameled dial face. At the 6 o'clock position was a recessed circle where the second hand moved in time with the clicks of the escapement.

Boyton could feel the pulsing and quick clicking of the watch's escapement making the little second hand rotate. The back cover had a small lip, and with his fingernail Boyton was able to flip the back cover open. He figured he had broken the watch, and all these springs and wheels would explode out of the pocket watch. Instead, he found himself gazing at the intricate inner workings of the pocket watch. He could see the tiny hair spring as it compressed and then expanded several times per second. The small wheels were slowly turning with each click of the escapement.

The myriad arms and plates that held the gears in position formed a complicated swirl pattern. The stem of each gear passed through a red ruby placed in the plates and arms of the pocket watch. Boyton held the pocket and watched in amazement as it ran. He was holding a little engine in his hands. His fascination was interrupted by angry shouts in Chinese and the sound of his name, "Wen Ho," that meant he was wanted and probably in trouble.

He stuffed the watch in his pocket and ran to the front of the building. As

Boyton stuck his head out the entrance to see who was commanding him, he saw Bailey pointing at him, yelling, "That's him, that's the scoundrel that stole my pocket watch."

Next to Bailey stood a police officer. The officer told Boyton to step forward and empty his pockets. On top of a small bench, Boyton placed the gold pocket watch.

"Arrest that boy! He stole my pocket watch," demanded Bailey. With great reluctance, the police officer told Boyton he would have to take him down to the Police Court. The officer could not put such a young child in the county jail. Because of the perceived value of the gold watch and the seriousness of the crime, the officer wanted direction from the Police Court Judge Thaddeus Farnsworth.

As the officer, Boyton, and Bailey marched over to the Police Court a few blocks away, Ruth Anne and Sam watched from the second story window of the pottery shop, then quickly moved downstairs to follow the trio. They could hear shouts in Chinese alerting the bosses and Jun Ho that Wen Ho had been arrested.

Boyton and the police officer were seated on chairs near the judge's bench. Bailey and Ruth Anne took seats a couple of rows back on a flat wooden bench. All had to wait as Municipal Court Judge Thaddeus Farnsworth adjudicated a few cases related to public drunkenness, an unlicensed vendor, and vandalism, all misdemeanors. By that time, Jun Ho, Wong Bang, and Lee Fook, along with a cadre of other Chinese men, had crowded into the courtroom.

The chatter of the Chinese attendees was beginning to irritate Judge Farnsworth. He banged his gavel, "Quiet back there. I don't know why all of you are here, but I will not have this court disrupted by a lot of foreign talking and squawking. Is that understood?"

The Chinese men quieted down. The angst of the Chinese crowd was that yet another Chinese resident would be found guilty of a crime he did not commit. Whenever there was theft, fire, or murder, the crime was always blamed on the Chinese community, or so it seemed. California's rough justice system was tilted against the Chinese population, from their experience.

"Next," ordered Judge Farnsworth. The police officer next to Boyton stood up and recounted how Mr. Bailey had accused the young boy of stealing his pocket watch. The police officer confirmed he had found the watch Boyton's possession. "Son, did you take the watch?" asked the judge. "Yes, sir," answered Boyton.

Judge Farnsworth frowned and said, "Deputy, please hand me the pocket watch." Bailey, following the proceedings, grew tense. "What's wrong?" whispered Ruth Anne. Bailey answered, "We need this to be petty larceny, not grand larceny. That could delay everything by requiring that the District Court Judge hear the case."

Judge Farnsworth examined the engravings of the gold pocket watch. He popped open the front cover to reveal the pure, white enameled dial.

Judge Farnsworth looked up. "Mr. Bailey, is the case of this Waltham railroad watch gold filled?" "Er, uh, no, it is solid, 14 carat I believe," Bailey replied. "The watch was a gift from my wife before she died." Judge Farnsworth continued to examine the watch and commented, "I would say this is quite an expensive watch, falling into the grand larceny category."

Bailey groaned, leaned over and whispered to Ruth Anne, "He is going to kick the case up and release Boyton back to Jun Ho, I can feel it. We need to delay this somehow." The judge continued, "However, the boy has admitted to taking the watch and…."

Before the judge could finish his sentence, Jun Ho stood and shouted, "Wen Ho no thief. I'm his mother, he don't steal Bailey's watch." The Chinese crowd roared in agreement with Jun Ho's statement.

In an involuntary response, like raising a hand to stop a blow from an opponent, Ruth Anne stood up. All of her pent-up fear and anger was expressed in the only way she knew how to fight back, like a person who had nothing to lose, with her words.

"You are not Boyton's mother," Ruth Anne shouted at Jun Ho, pointing her finger at the Chinese woman. "I am his mother. You abandoned him shortly after he was born. I nursed him back to life when he was dying. I raised him. I protected him from wild animals and snakes. I took care of him when he was sick or injured. I taught him how to read and write. You are not his mother. I am his mother."

The court room erupted into a harangue of Chinese shouts rebuking Ruth Anne and in defense of Jun Ho. Judge Farnsworth banged his gavel. "Order, order in this courtroom, or I'll have it cleared out," he commanded.

When the room became quiet, the judge rubbed his forehead and continued, "Deputy, can you take the boy to the back holding room, he doesn't need to hear all of this. We will take a 10-minute recess while I consult some statutes, and none of you, Mr. Bailey, the two mothers, are to leave, or I'll have you arrested. Understood?"

"Deputy," shouted Judge Farnsworth. The deputy stuck his head out of the room where Boyton had been taken. "Yes, Judge," replied the deputy. "Stay out here and watch these people, make sure none of them leave," instructed the judge. "But the boy….," answered the deputy. "The boy isn't going anywhere; he's probably eating my lunch as we speak," chuckled Judge Farnsworth.

The judge banged his gavel and retired to his chambers. Ruth Anne could see Jun Ho looking down at her hands as Lee Fook spoke to her. "What happens next?" asked Ruth Anne of Bailey. "We wait until the time is right," he responded. Ruth Anne sat trembling. She had never shouted at anyone with such vehemence and vitriol in her life. People were shuffling in and out of the courtroom, but Ruth Anne, like Jun Ho, was focused on her hands.

Judge Farnsworth returned to the courtroom, banged the gavel, and announced court was back in session. The judge turned to Ruth Anne and said, "Ma'am, please stand. You claim to be the mother of...," the judge consulted his notes, "...of Wen Ho, or Boyton, uh, the accused. Do you have any legal representation?"

Before Ruth Anne could answer, a strong voice from the back of the room boomed, "Yes, she does, your honor." "Who are you?" asked Judge Farnsworth, with a perplexed look on his face. "I'm Caleb Gibbons, husband of Ruth Anne Gibbons, father of Boyton Gibbons, and this is our lawyer Addison Crane."

"Oh, this is turning into quite a little complicated mess....," started the judge. In the middle of his sentence a series of booms, bangs, and cracks rang out. "Damn it!" exclaimed Judge Farnsworth. "Why are those Chinamen setting off firecrackers? It is not the Chinese New Year. Now, where was I?"

Bailey squeezed Ruth Anne's hand and smiled at her as she sat down. "What's wrong?" asked Ruth Anne.

"Good news, Sam has Boyton, and they are on their way to the railroad depot," Bailey explained. "The firecrackers were the sign. Boyton must have climbed through the back window, where Sam was waiting."

Judge Farnsworth continued where he had left off. "This boy is obviously of Chinese origin. I'm not sure how Mrs. Gibbons can claim to be the child's mother. If you have such a claim, you can file an action with the District Court. On the charges, the theft of the gold pocket watch is serious and needs to be reviewed by the District Court. In the meantime, I will release the boy to the Chinese mother on the condition that she must, with the boy, attend a subsequent hearing on a date set by the District Court. Deputy, please bring the boy out," directed the judge.

The deputy opened the door, went into the room, quickly came back out, and leaned to whisper into Judge Farnsworth's ear. With a quick look of anger, Judge Farnsworth addressed the Chinese crowd. "What have you done? Did you take the child? If I find out that any of you participated in his escape, there will be serious charges," he exclaimed. "Deputy, alert the police officers to watch for the child and return him to his home. What a day!" The judge banged his gavel and said, "Court adjourned."

As the crowd streamed out of the courthouse, the group of Chinese men ran back to Chinatown, while Ruth Anne and Caleb rushed down to the train depot. When they arrived, they could see Boyton was already on the train, sitting next to Sam in a passenger car. Ruth Anne yelled, "Boyton, Boyton, I love you. Mama loves you." Boyton saw Ruth Anne and started waving his arm widely out the window.

The Chinese men from the courtroom had figured out what was happening and arrived shortly at the depot. The air was thick with steam, wood smoke, and the cacophony of Chinese men talking and shouting. Lee Fook, the Chinese man who appeared to be their leader, approached the steps to board the passenger car where Boyton and Sam were seated.

Before Lee Fook could take another step, Caleb stepped in between him and the train. Caleb towered over small Chinese man. Lee Fook looked like a coyote stalking a lamb. His eyes were big and locked on to Boyton at the train window. It was apparent Lee Fook was ready to pounce. Caleb was a guard dog between the coyote and lamb.

Lee Fook, with a shaved head and perpetual scowl on his face, pulled a short dirk from underneath his quilted coat. Caleb pushed back the right side of his oil cloth jacket and drew his pistol from the holster. The crowd of people at the depot had gone quiet and surrounded the two men like school children awaiting a fight in a school yard. Would Lee Fook lunge at Caleb? Would Caleb pull the trigger?

Lee Fook's eyes darted between Boyton on the train and Caleb's gun. He was sizing up the situation. Ruth Anne saw that Bailey's assessment that the Chinese gang men never let anything be taken from them was correct. Everyone could see that Lee Fook was calculating the odds that Caleb was bluffing.

If Lee Fook were white, chances were that Caleb would not pull the trigger. Because Lee Fook was Chinese, Caleb would most likely be allowed to kill the Chinese man, with few consequences, and be feted by some white people. Lee Fook backed down; the dog had won. Fook stealthily returned the dirk to his waistband. Waving his hand and speaking in Chinese, he motioned the other Chinese men away from the train.

Ruth Anne could see Jun Ho in the back of the crowd, standing with arms folded. The Chinese woman who had been so vocal in court that she was Boyton's mother was quiet now. If she were the real mother, Ruth Anne surmised, she would have pushed Caleb out of the way to board the train. That is what Ruth Anne figured she herself would have done. No, Jun Ho could not have been Boyton's mother.

From a distance, Ruth Anne could see Lee Fook approach Jun Ho and start berating her in Cantonese waving his arms around. Jun Ho bowed her head and followed Lee Fook back toward Chinatown. The train trumpet whistle blew, indicating an imminent departure.

With loud puffs and releases of steam, creaks, groans and the clang of the bell, the engine began to pull the train forward. Ruth Anne, Caleb, and Boyton were wildly waving at one another. Ruth Anne began to cry. The train rolled along the tracks around a sweeping curve. The engine pulled the cars through the curve as it began its approach to the long wooden bridge over the Sacramento River toward Davisville and eventually San Francisco.

The wooden trusses of the bridge quickly obscured Boyton and his arm waving out the window. The depot crowd had returned to milling around as if nothing had happened. Something of monumental importance had happened. Ruth Anne had simultaneously saved her son and lost him at the same time.

12 Imaginary Lines

Upon returning to Carrolton, Ruth Anne stared at the Bailey butter cooler on her kitchen table, thinking how it did not work very well. It was not a refrigerator. It only retarded the rate at which butter melted into oil and milk solids. Ruth Anne was like the butter cooler, she thought. "Everything I touch melts away from me." She had several butter coolers stacked in the corner of Boyton's room, unlikely to be brought out anytime soon.

Ruth Anne wanted to write to Boyton but did not know where he was. She wanted to travel to San Francisco but was paranoid that the Chinese men would follow her, and she would inadvertently expose Boyton's location. She settled on silent prayer for his - someday - safe return.

With the face of a woman who was mourning the loss of a loved one,

Ruth Anne pushed herself to be normal, to return to taking care of home and garden, going into town for supplies. As she walked down the road, she longed for the time when she assumed people were staring at her because of the Chinese boy next to her. Now, they were only staring at a lonely, aging woman walking to the market.

She went to Ah Chee's store to buy some rice, which she had started eating because she thought Boyton probably was being fed rice, vegetables, and tea. As Ah Chee bagged up her goods, he quietly said, "The child is safe." Safe, Ruth Anne heard the word "safe." The one immutable truth Ruth Anne had experienced was that the covert Chinese communication system was never wrong. "Thank you, Ah Chee," was the only reply Ruth Anne could utter, as she held back tears of joy.

She passed Mr. Hoxie as he was loading some milk cans for delivery. "Hello, Mrs. Gibbons. The kids miss Boyton." "So do I," replied Ruth Anne. "I remember when he was a baby, and you brought him over here for the cow's milk. Oh gosh, I think you two left with more milk on your clothes than in his belly," reminisced Mr. Hoxie. Ruth Anne smiled at him. "I know you loved that boy," said Mr. Hoxie. "I still do," replied Ruth Anne.

Back at her silent home, the knowledge that Boyton was safe, somewhere in San Francisco, was comforting to Ruth Anne. But she still had a huge ache in her heart. She did not know if the pain would ever go away.

There was a light knock on the door. When she opened the door, Alma Gosseau was standing there wearing a big smile and holding a plate. Her blond curly hair was battling the scarf trying to contain it.

"*Bon jour*, I bring you cheese," greeted Alma. "Please come in, and let's sample it," replied Ruth Anne.

Alma explained that she had gotten the milk from a hotel owner in Quartz Hill, who kept a small herd of goats to keep down the weeds on his property. As Ruth Anne attempted to spread the crumbling cheese onto some bread, Alma chatted nonstop. The cheese was a little tart for Ruth Anne's palate. She told Alma it was *magnifique*. Alma giggled knowing the cheese was a poor imitation of real goat cheese.

"Have you heard any word of Boyton?" Alma asked. "He is safe, and I miss him terribly. Someday, I know we'll see him again," Ruth Anne replied. "That is good news. You will see him again. I must wait until death to see my beloved Auturo in heaven," Alma said. The two women sat in silence pondering the cruel world of California that they had been brought to.

"Your clock has stopped," Alma noticed. "Yes, Caleb is not interested in it, and Boyton is not around to fix it. So, there it sits, a reminder that time has stopped in Carrolton," Ruth Anne explained.

"I'm thinking of moving to Quartz Hill," Alma sprung on Ruth Anne. "Really? When? How?" Ruth Anne asked. "The hotel owner Mr. Fitzpatrick, he needs someone to cook and clean for the boarders. It would be steady money. The clothes washing here in Carrolton keeps dropping every month as more and more miners give up on their claims. And the Chinese men don't bring me their laundry," Alma said.

"Did you know that Miss Doolittle, the schoolteacher, won't let my children speak French at school? She demands they speak only English. My children will lose their language, their culture, their heritage, if they can't speak French, like I taught them, and they forget their native tongue," Alma complained.

Ruth Anne did not point out that all but one of Alma's children were born in America. She wondered if Boyton was being forced to learn Cantonese. Would he forget English? Would he forget her? Was he Chinese or American?

Caleb returned from his north end water ditch rounds as Alma was leaving. "Hello, Alma," greeted Caleb. "Caleb, you look fine this morning. We'll talk later, Ruth Anne, *au revoir*," said Alma as she walked out to the main road. Ruth Anne snickered that Alma found Caleb was looking fine. After the night before, she was surprised he had even risen in the morning.

Caleb, like most men, was good at bottling up his emotions. That was, until he found his feelings in a bottle. Quite out of character, Caleb had drifted down to Carrolton's last operating saloon. There, he drank whiskey, by himself, for several hours. Caleb then regurgitated the contents of the evening's therapy session onto the dust of the road outside. His frugal nature bothered him that half the whiskey he had bought that night was now flowing across the dirt road.

The night's full moon meant that Caleb could stumble home and not into a dark ditch along the way. Once home, he collapsed into bed. Ruth Anne could smell the whiskey, cigar smoke, and vomit on him. Before she also lost the contents of her stomach, she got up and moved to Boyton's room. She had a good sleep, dreaming that she was hugging her little son, who was asleep in the foreign land of San Francisco.

San Francisco was continuing to grow and flourish, even as the mining districts and communities that brought the peninsula into existence were fading away. Most of the water sales from the Valley Springs Water Company had shifted to farmers, ranchers, and little towns outside of the river canyon. Theodore Grainger had been encouraging Caleb to consider taking over his job as superintendent of the water ditch operations. Of course, to do so Caleb would have to move out of Carrolton and closer to Quartz Hill.

The mental diversion of contemplating a different job at the water company and moving was welcomed by Caleb. He could only allow his mind to be consumed with thoughts of Boyton's safety and memories of the past for so long before he needed to wash them away with whiskey. Still, Caleb felt guilty that he might be forging forward in life when Boyton was no longer part of his decision-making process. He concluded that he had to close that barn door and move on, whether or not Ruth Anne understood or liked his decision.

It was late summer, after a rare rainstorm had passed through Carrolton, when Caleb walked into the house one afternoon and announced to Ruth Anne that he had bought Samuel Tarbot's ranch above Quartz Hill.

Caleb was wet and smiling. Ruth Anne had not seen Caleb smile for months. The rainstorm appeared to have reinvigorated him, washing away the haunting memories, offering a small prospect of new growth. Suddenly, Ruth Anne was confronted with the prospect of moving out of Carrolton. She did not hate Carrolton. She liked Carrolton, or at least its landscape.

Caleb explained that Samuel Tarbot was from Nova Scotia and could no longer endure the heat of California's interior valley. In the summer months, Tarbot would hide in a hollow he dug out on the side of a hill. When the heat subsided, he would come out and do his chores around the ranch at night. Unfortunately, Tarbot's attempt to avoid the summer heat meant he was not really caring for the ranch and cattle. He decided to sell and go over to the coast or back to Nova Scotia.

The next day, Caleb took Ruth Anne on a long carriage ride to the Tarbot Ranch. They went down the river, through Saddle Gap, over to Quartz Hill, and picked up Deer Valley Road, until they came to a little shack next to a grove of giant valley oaks. With a fierce north wind blowing and in an agitated state from the long buggy ride and the irritating wind, Ruth Anne was not impressed. "What do you think?" asked Caleb with a big grin on his face. "It's very flat. I bet it is nice in springtime," was the only response Ruth Anne could muster.

Suddenly, the Caleb of yore, his youthful exuberant self, had resurfaced, along with his giddy talk of the future. Ruth Anne saw the man she had fallen in love with so long ago in North Adams. She had followed his dreams to California, and those dreams had not panned out as she had expected. There was no gold in the pan, the Golden State. Now, Caleb was pitching another journey in life, one wrapped up with less adventure, but, she hoped, with a little more happiness as they grew old together.

"Over there, do you see that mountain sticking up on the horizon?" Caleb asked, pointing to the southwest toward San Francisco. "That's Mount Diablo. It is what they call the base line meridian for the new government maps. Once the final government land office maps are released in a couple of months, I can file a preemption and then buy the land from the federal government," Caleb explained.

"Wait," Ruth Anne started, "I thought you already bought the ranch from Tarbot. Why do you need to buy it again?" "Well…," Caleb started before Ruth Anne rattled off more questions. "I don't understand what this preemption is. Where is the money coming from to buy the ranch twice?" The wind whipped around Ruth Anne and Caleb as they stared out on an open prairie of yellow grass.

Ruth Anne remembered gazing at the snow-covered Sierras from San Francisco when they first arrived in California. The mountains had seemed so far away. On this day she was on the other side of the valley looking back at the Bay Area. She wondered if Boyton could see from San Francisco this patch of dry prairie grass where they stood. It did not matter. She had no part in any of these decisions.

"Well," Caleb attempted to restart his answer, "I still have some of the gold from the early mining days. Plus, I've been saving money from the water agent job." As he spoke, the wind roared and flipped Caleb's hat from his head. He went running after it through the dry grass. Ruth Anne laughed at the big man, who looked like a child chasing after a lizard. To see Caleb stripped of his hat and running like a little boy, the hat seemingly smarter than the man at eluding capture, was worth the long buggy ride to this barren plateau.

It then occurred to Ruth Anne that they had been living frugally, sometimes in a state of poverty, when they did not have to. Caleb had money. Why did they have to rent that drafty, rotten cabin for so many years? She had done everything possible to stretch their food budget. She had counted every penny, never bought any new clothes. She altered other women's hand-me-down dresses to fit herself. The same with Boyton's clothing, always hand-me-downs from some other boy in town who had outgrown them. She was tired of being a pioneering wife in the California frontier.

Caleb had won the race and regained his hat. He returned to Ruth Anne, and they walked over to the shack by the valley oaks for some protection from the wind.

Ruth Anne surveyed the wooden shack and, without opening the door to look inside, she told Caleb, "I'm not living here." It was a declaration of independence that she had never made. Caleb did not object to her statement. "No, I'm going to build you a proper house," Caleb informed her.

Under a majestic valley oak tree, its branches reaching down and sweeping across the ground in the wind, Caleb pulled out the handwritten deed to the property. The property description was written in the metes and bounds format. "Commencing at the oak at the northeast corner next to the Deer Valley Road, blazed with a T, running four hundred forty yards, due south, to Willow Creek, thence west to the white rocks above Quartz Hill…."

Caleb would read from the deed as he and Ruth Anne walked the entire perimeter, noting each of the boundary markers. On the north side of the property were some rolling hills that contained the valley oaks. Most of the property was flat, sloping gently down to the town of Quartz Hill. Tarbot had dug a well at the base of one of the hills next to the shack, and he swore it never went dry. Down at the far end of the property, where Willow Creek drained the hills to the east, a collection of willow and cottonwood trees had taken root.

From appearances, it was a little valley or dale, like God had taken a spoon and scooped it from the rolling hills above Quartz Hill. Caleb floated the name Willowdale for the homestead. He had visions of raising cattle and maybe some fruit trees if they would grow. Ruth Anne asked how many acres were contained within the piece of paper he just spent $1,000 to purchase. The rough calculations would approximately total 160 acres, more or less, he explained.

Ruth Anne then asked, "How much is it going to cost to buy the land from the federal government?" "I reckon it will be in the neighborhood of $2.50 per acre, unless it falls into a school township section, which I don't think it will from the maps I've studied," replied Caleb. Ruth Anne was shocked that Caleb would be spending over $1,300 for what looked like a barren wasteland of a ranch.

Ruth Anne and Caleb had not had a proper conversation since Boyton's escape to freedom. Caleb would usually come home, they would eat dinner, and then Caleb would spend hours reading newspapers, documents, and maps he had obtained. He had maps, lots of maps; he was becoming a map collector. He would study the maps for hours by the light of the oil lamp. Ruth Anne would go to bed with Caleb sitting at the table reviewing any one of the numerous maps he had, comparing them, plotting distances, and scribbling notes.

All of Caleb's intent study was now coming into focus for Ruth Anne. In a sense, Caleb was plotting out a new map for his life, one that left the past behind. Employment at the Valley Springs Water Company was still central to his plans. Ruth Anne was comforted that she was also included and considered a part of Caleb's new map of life. While she did not have much input in his decisions, at least Caleb considered her presence in his calculations.

As the north wind started to subside, Caleb took on the air of a schoolteacher, and tried to explain how all the maps and preemptions figured into the equation. When Mexico ceded California to the United States, virtually all the land was owned by the federal government. Apart from Spanish or Mexican land grants, all of California was wide open. Men from all over the world flocked to California to mine for gold without the worry they were on someone's private property. It was all government land, and the government was not going to stop anyone from mining, erecting dams, or digging water canals. Manifest destiny.

The federal government did have a way to sell land to new residents, but the land had to be surveyed first. The Public Land Survey System created townships that were six miles by six miles square. Each township contained 36 sections, and each section totaled 640 acres. Mount Diablo was the base line, or starting point, for the townships in the region around Quartz Hill.

The congressional Homestead Act allowed men to a file a preemption when the federal government land office maps were published for a particular township. The preemption guaranteed that the government would sell the land to the man who met all the conditions for the preemption. The preemption was based, in part, on a man settling on the land and improving it with a house, fences, and activity such as farming or ranching operations.

Samuel Tarbot had filed a property description with the county and paid taxes, but he technically did not own the land, just the appurtenances and improvements upon it. The land itself was still owned by the federal government. Caleb had bought the property description and its improvements. Caleb could now file for a preemption for a homestead with the federal government at a set price per acre up to 160 acres. That translated into a quarter of section of a township.

Some of the issues Caleb was concerned about were the school sections, county lines, and land grants. There were two sections in each township set aside for the state to sell to raise money for the public school system. If the Tarbot land fell in section 16 or 36, he'd have to deal with the state of California.

The other issue was the Mexican land grant to the south of the property. Willow Creek was noted as the northern edge of the land grant, but until government land maps were official, it was unclear what the final acreage would be for the property.

Ruth Anne's head was swirling in the extended school lesson on the machinations concerning maps, townships, sections, preemptions, and land grants. She asked Caleb about the Indians. "What land is set aside for them?"

"Indians? They've all been rounded up and put on reservations. They are not American citizens anyhow, so they don't qualify for homesteads," Caleb explained.

What Ruth Anne could comprehend was that there were all these imaginary lines being laid down over the landscape. Some people, the chosen people, could buy land within these imaginary lines, and others could not.

Ruth Anne tried to connect all the parts and pieces. A Canadian fellow from Nova Scotia had improved the land with a flimsy shack. Caleb had bought the shack from the Canadian. Caleb filed for the homestead and acquired land not available to the men who had lived on the land for thousands of years. There was no use for Ruth Anne to ponder how the Chinese immigrants fit into the puzzle; she just assumed they were not part of the equation. The new imaginary lines were taming California, making it docile, making it hospitable to East Coast immigration.

Imaginary lines were nothing new. There were imaginary lines setting the boundaries of Sacramento and San Franciso. There was an imaginary line between California and Nevada. What was bothering Ruth Anne was the imaginary difference between people. It was imagined that Indian and Chinese people were different from the white people from the East Coast. But her time with Boyton underscored for her that, outside of skin color, there was not much difference between people. Some Chinese people were good, while others were evil incarnate, as were some white people, like Sheriff Royster.

The horse pulled their carriage back to Carrolton at a good trot. Caleb told Ruth Anne that he would start the superintendent job in the next couple of weeks when Grainger left. They would rent a house in Quartz Hill until their new house was ready at Willowdale. Ruth Anne realized that if they moved, and Boyton came back to Carrolton, she and Caleb would not be there. Would Boyton ever come home?

13 Reconciliation

Ruth Anne and Caleb moved into a small, rented house a short way down from the Episcopal Church in Quartz Hill. Other than the convenience of easy walking to Sunday worship services, Ruth Anne did not like Quartz Hill. The people who lived there were provincial. She had been told, without any supporting evidence, that the townspeople had been secret supporters of the Confederacy during the Civil War, sending money to the southern states. Rumors and gossip were the driving forces in Quartz Hill. She knew for a fact that the main street in town, Davis, was not named for Jefferson Davis, president of the Confederacy. However, some people in town liked to believe the South lived on with Davis Street.

Quartz Hill was home to a larger Chinese community than Carrolton's. There was still some placer gold to be mined at the south end of town and down on the riverbanks.

Ruth Anne avoided the Chinatown of Quartz Hill. She did not know if any of the Chinese there were connected to Lee Fook and his gang in Sacramento. She knew Ah Chee in Carrolton was on her side. She could not tell in Quartz Hill whether the Chinese men and women she met were friend or foe.

The train that ran into Quartz Hill was also annoying to Ruth Anne. The locomotive engine was noisy, belching thick wood smoke that darkened the air. It did not help that the rented house she was living in lay directly in the path of the steam engine's smoke whenever the prevailing southerly winds blew. She concluded the stifling smoke was the reason the former tenants had left the house. In addition to the steam engine smoke, the air was filled with the dust of the horses, buggies, carriages, and stagecoaches constantly driven through town. Consequently, everything in their house was coated with a layer of dust and wood ash.

When Ruth Anne lived in Carrolton, she had not felt as if she belonged. She was in the minority there, as most of the residents were born in other countries. In Quartz Hill, those demographics were reversed. Foreign-born residents were dwindling in the area, as U.S.-born individuals became the majority. Ruth Anne missed the eclectic mix of people in Carrolton. She also missed the river canyon, the eagles flying overhead, and the background noise of the river flowing through the canyon. She did not miss the rattlesnakes.

The move to Quartz Hill meant she no longer encountered the many little landmarks that triggered sadness over Boyton's loss. Ruth Anne no longer had to see the wire rope suspension bridge over the river where she and the boy stood for hours watching its construction. She no longer had to see the Carrolton kids running around the streets without Boyton. The tightness around her heart was starting to loosen as time passed.

It was welcome news when Ruth Anne learned that Alma Gosseau, the wild French woman of Carrolton, also would be moving to Quartz Hill. Alma took a job cooking and cleaning at the American Hotel, owned by Patrick Fitzpatrick, a native of Ireland. Ruth Anne and Alma would often joke that the American Hotel was truly Californian because it was owned by an Irishman and run by a French woman.

Alma and Patrick bonded over his little herd of goats. He wanted sheep, to remind him of his native home, but thought sheep might get too hot in the valley heat. Alma was happy to get some goat's milk with which to experiment in making cheese. Patrick was delighted to have the cheery French woman at the hotel. In fact, he was so taken by her personality and work ethic that he asked Alma to marry him.

Alma had never imagined herself being married again after Auturo died. She was realistic enough to know that she would never be able to save enough money to meet her expenses as she grew old and could no longer work, whenever that might occur. Patrick was a good and honest man; he was also Catholic. Alma agreed to marry him and permanently join the staff of the

American Hotel, officially making it an international affair.

Ruth Anne was happy for Alma. Plans for a future wedding created a nice distraction from the monotony that living in Quartz Hill offered. Caleb had secured his preemption and was moving forward with finalizing his purchase of the Willowdale ranch. He had also started construction on the house sited on the small knoll overlooking the property. Caleb routinely asked Ruth Anne to join him in traveling out to Willowdale, and she always declined.

For Ruth Anne, the time had not yet come to swim in daydreams of the future. She was racked with guilt whenever her attention turned to something pleasant, even briefly, when she did not know if Boyton was safe and healthy. She felt by getting on with life she was abandoning him, forgetting him, leaving her child to fend for himself in the wicked city of San Francisco. She was in her own prison, helpless at not being able to help him.

More than a year after Caleb and Ruth Anne had moved to Quartz Hill, he came into the little rented house and told her to get in the carriage. "Why?" she asked. "It's time to go. The horse is hitched to the carriage, and it's time to go," Caleb said. "Where?" was Ruth Anne's one word reply. "Ruth Anne, if you don't get in the carriage, I'll pick up, take you out there and strap you in if I have to, and don't think I won't do it," Caleb's warned Ruth Anne sternly.

The carriage ride out to Willowdale was quiet, with nary a word spoken between them. Ruth Anne did not want to be pushed out of her comfort zone of depression and boredom. The buggy turned off Deer Valley Road and pulled up to a new house. Ruth Anne did not recognize where she was, having not been out to the ranch for over a year. "Whose house is this?" asked Ruth Anne. "Yours, ours. It's the Willowdale ranch house," Caleb said.

Lying before Ruth Anne was a beautiful two-story house with a wide porch that wrapped around the house. White pillars supported the porch overhang. Stair steps made of granite slabs led up to the wood plank porch. The roof featured multiple gables and ridge lines. The exterior wood shiplap siding was painted a light blue with the trim in crisp white. Several brick chimneys could be seen poking out of the roof. Behind the house was a stable for the horses that matched the design of the house.

The house was not of any identifiable architectural style. As it was being built over the past year, different craftsmen would make suggestions to Caleb. The man from Massachusetts suggested porch columns with a colonial flair. The framer from Maine thought shiplap siding would evoke a New England coastal cottage feel. The men who worked on the foundation, who were from New Hampshire, encouraged Caleb to use exposed granite slabs as stairs up to the porch.

When finished, the attentive observer could see multiple design and style influences in the house. For some architectural purists, who mainly resided in San Francisco, the house was a mishmash of conflicting design elements. To Caleb, and ultimately to Ruth Anne, the house on the knoll at Willowdale represented California. The Golden State was defined by people from all over the United States and the world. The state was a mishmash of different cultures, religions, and languages. It seemed fitting that their California dream home reflected the diversity of the state's residents.

"Can you ever forgive me, Caleb?" asked Ruth Anne. "Forgive you for what?" he asked.

"I've been so terrible to you these past couple of years. In spite of my indifference to you and the ranch, you have built a beautiful house… for us," she explained.

"What's done is done. We can't change the past. We can only move forward," Caleb said. He then took her inside the house, leading her through its parlor, dining room, separate kitchen, and four bedrooms.

Ruth Anne tried not to think how much the house had cost to build. It was obvious that Caleb had saved more gold from his mining days than he had told her. Four bedrooms! What were they going to do with so many rooms in the house? As Ruth Anne walked through the mostly unfinished interior of the house, she began to let herself slip back into the California spirit. Caleb took her up to the attic and showed her how, on a clear day, she could see Mount Diablo.

Overcome with emotions, Ruth Anne just began to cry. How was this good fortune happening to her while her son was living in unknown circumstances? She did not speak of her emotions and thoughts to Caleb. She was determined she would not be the cloud on his sunny day. He was correct, she had to find a way to move forward.

The path forward was asking Alma if she wanted to be married at Willowdale. Alma and Patrick's wedding day was a festive affair, and it seemed as though all the residents of Quartz Hill had come to enjoy the ceremony. Musicians from Sacramento traveled up to play some traditional Irish and French music. Ruth Anne was not even bothered by the voluminous amounts of beer, wine, and sparkling wine being served. She did halt any plans to have hard liquor for the guests - no whiskey allowed.

Willowdale was similar to that of Saddle Gap, in that it was an ancient overflow deposit from the river. At the tail end of Willow Creek, down by Quartz Hill, some men were still mining placer gold from the cobble rocks under the topsoil. In the spring, the flat prairie of the Willowdale ranch hosted numerous little shallow pools of water. In between the pools of water, a carpet of small wildflowers of white, yellow, and blue would bloom. Ruth Anne had never seen such color within such a fragile landscape before.

She was enchanted by the wildflowers and commanded Caleb not to run any cattle over the areas until after they had finished blooming. She could not help but remember the times when she and Boyton would sit in the garden and watch the bees and hummingbirds come to the different flowers and citrus blossoms. Ruth Anne had not thought she would ever live in a place as beautiful as Carrolton. Willowdale was certainly different from the river canyon, but when she looked hard enough at the landscape, there was similar natural beauty, just not on as grand a scale.

Caleb had settled into his new position as superintendent of the Valley Springs Water Company. He was not prepared for the amount of time the job would take. If he was not in the office reviewing property tax assessments or customer accounts, he would frequently be required to travel to Sacramento on company business. These duties were on top of his work out in the field, along the water ditch, assessing maintenance and improvement projects that were needed to keep the old ditch operating.

The net result was that Caleb could not spend as much time as he wanted to establish the cattle herd at Willowdale. He did hire Thomas Laughlin, a young man from up the road, to make sure the cattle were fed and watered. Ruth Anne could see that Caleb's California dream was growing weedy because of his lack of attention. She figured she had extra time in the day and started helping with ranch chores.

Ruth Anne quickly realized that her long dresses were more of a hindrance than a help when working outside. The full skirts were always blowing in the wind and would catch on an exposed nail or splinter of wood on a fence post as she passed. She dealt with the annoyance, until one day her dress caught the edge of fence while she was walking. The fence held tight to the hem of her dress, and she fell, headfirst, into a fresh cow pie.

With that humiliation, the search was on for more appropriate women's work clothing. Ruth Anne had read about the bloomers or pantaloons that some women were wearing, in limited situations, usually outside of public view. It took her several attempts, using various fabrics she could acquire in Sacramento, to fashion a pant that would work.

Ruth Anne's version was a pant of heavy cotton fabric, which narrowed above the boot, with a drawstring around the waist. She would then layer a shorter skirt over her pantaloons that stopped just at her knees. She never wore the work garb off the ranch. Caleb, when he first saw Ruth Anne in her new work clothing, had a difficult time containing his amusement and laughter. "First you are wearing pants; next, you'll want the right to vote," snickered Caleb. He was rewarded with a well thrown turnip that Ruth Anne had just pulled out of the garden.

Since Ruth Anne had moved to Willowdale, she did not mind visiting and shopping in Quartz Hill. Before the move, it had been painful to move about Quartz Hill. She was a stranger to most people except at the local church she and Caleb had begun attending. She had just felt uneasy shopping for necessities in the small town.

Now, visits into town gave her the opportunity to stop by the American Hotel and chat with Alma, still the wild French woman even after her marriage to Patrick. Since the big wedding at Willowdale, whenever Ruth Anne was in Quartz Hill, people greeted her on the street, "Hello, Mrs. Gibbons."

As Ruth Anne passed a newsstand on Davis Street, the main road through town, one headline caught her eye, Royster Convicted of Embezzling Gold. Could this Royster be the same person as the vile Sheriff Royster who had conspired to kidnap her boy? Ruth Anne bought the newspaper and sat down on the plank sidewalk with her feet in the dirt gutter to read the story. So intent was she on her reading that she ignored the horse poop next to her feet, the horses and carriages trotting by, and the loud drunks shouting from the saloon next to the newsstand.

The headline was in fact about the same man Ruth Anne knew as Sheriff Royster. She read the lengthy news story several times so as not to miss a single detail. What she gleaned was that Royster had propelled his success in the county's sheriff-tax collector position to be nominated for the state office of Treasurer. In most counties, the sheriff also served as tax collector, traveling around to the different townships to collect local taxes and the foreign miners' tax.

In exchange for a sheriff's tax-collecting efforts, he was allowed to keep a percentage of the tax receipts. The commission, approximately 10 percent, provided a great incentive for sheriffs to be diligent in collecting taxes from county residents. Sheriff Royster had been a top tax collector in the state. The conventional logic went that a good, albeit greedy, sheriff-tax collector would make for a great state Treasurer.

Royster had won his race and was elected California's state Treasurer. No less than a year into his tenure, problems arose with the shipment of gold bullion being sent back to New York to meet the state's interest payments on bonds the state had issued. Royster claimed there were no problems in his office, and the fault for any missing shipments of bullion lay with the express company that had handled the shipments back to New York.

As a few more short and missing debt payments occurred, the California Attorney General, a good friend of Royster and a fellow Democrat, was forced to investigate. The investigation led to an associate of Royster's, who was operating as an intermediary between the state and the express company. Royster's associate, Thomas Leggett, would provide the Treasurer's office with a bond for the gold bullion, and then transfer the gold to the express company to be sent back to New York.

However, in several instances the full amount of gold was not delivered to the express company, if any gold arrived at all. Leggett stated that he would honor the bond he provided to the state, even though it was his assertion that it was the express company that was at fault. After a couple of weeks of investigation, Leggett disappeared.

Royster was livid, not that Leggett had disappeared, but that he did not get his cut of the gold transfer scheme. Royster never admitted he was conspiring with Leggett. There was plenty of circumstantial evidence regarding the long-time friendship and gold dust dealings from Royster's time mining with Leggett up in Trinity County. Royster was charged with embezzling gold bullion, and a jury convicted him.

The news of Royster's conviction brightened Ruth Anne's day, and she had to show the story to Caleb. The door creaked open as Ruth Anne entered the offices of the Valley Springs Water Company and was greeted by Jonah. "Good morning, Ruth Anne, Caleb's in the back office." Ruth Anne was glad to see that Jonah was settling into his new clerk position at the company and, thankfully, out of her house.

Several months earlier, Jonah, one of the original ditch tenders on the Valley Springs water ditch, had slipped and broken his leg. He had been walking on the ditch along a remote and steep part of the river canyon. The ditch had been recently cleaned out of weeds and muck that was left on the side of the ditch.

Jonah, who swore he had not been consuming alcohol, slipped on the slick weeds and went tumbling down the steep embankment toward the river. He rolled over several boulders, which caused some of them to come rolling down over him as he lay near the river. Dazed and injured, Jonah knew that few people would be traveling through this part of the river canyon, as it was steep and rocky.

Jonah resigned himself to the understanding that he would probably die where he lay. He was able to push himself into a sitting position, but the pain from his broken leg prevented him from moving much further. He sat by the river all day and made it through a chilly night.

The next afternoon Jonah saw a person climbing over the rocks on the other side of the river. He yelled and waved his arm over his head in a desperate attempt to get the man's attention. Eventually, a Chinese man who was out prospecting walked down the river across from Jonah. The river canyon was narrow at this spot, and the river coursed over the rocks with astonishing speed.

Although he could see Jonah lying hurt, there was no way the Chinese man could attempt to ford the river to reach him. The Chinese man waved at Jonah and then continued his prospecting journey. Jonah cursed the wretched Chinese immigrants. He was hungry, cold and he, assumed, near death.

The next day, several men from the Valley Springs Water Company came down the ditch and found Jonah. On reaching his side, they told Jonah that a little Chinese man had told them he saw the ditch tender sleeping below the ditch, or that was how they had translated it. The men were able to get a splint on Jonah's leg and hoist him up the side of the embankment. The men took turns carrying him on their backs, an incredibly humiliating experience for a proud and aging '49er like Jonah.

The group eventually got Jonah to Doctor Ferguson's office in Quartz Hill, who cleaned up the wounds Jonah had suffered from tumbling over the sharp granite boulders and made a stronger splint around his leg. Caleb offered Jonah a room at his place to recuperate. Caleb did not ask Ruth Anne if she was willing to be Jonah's nurse.

Jonah had been deeply appreciative of Ruth Anne's attempt to make him comfortable, at least for the first few days. Her cooking was good, but Ruth Anne would not let him drink or chew tobacco in the house. He was in too much pain to get outside and could not really put any weight on the broken leg. Thus, his recuperation at Caleb and Ruth Anne's also was a de facto detoxification period for Jonah.

The first weeks, as Jonah went through alcohol and tobacco withdrawals, were miserable for both him and Ruth Anne. He was constantly agitated, and nothing Ruth Anne provided would calm him down. After two weeks of what Jonah considered hell on earth, his focus returned. He started to read the newspapers, and Ruth Anne happily gathered more newspapers from Sacramento, San Francisco, and the East Coast for Jonah to read in bed.

Ruth Anne was surprised that Jonah could read. She had always thought he was illiterate. She was even more astonished to learn that he could write and that his penmanship, while shaky, was pretty good. It took a solid six weeks before Jonah was able to put weight on his leg and begin the slow process of learning to walk again.

It was evident from the type of injury, and from the permanent limp that resulted from the improperly healed leg break, that Jonah could never go back to being a ditch tender. Caleb suggested Jonah might consider working in the company office, as the young gentleman Caleb had hired as clerk was leaving for a job at a bank in Sacramento.

Jonah expressed a lack of confidence to Ruth Anne about taking the job and performing the tasks. He could read and write, but he felt his math skills were lacking. Ruth Anne volunteered to tutor him on the basics of addition and subtraction. With patient instruction, Ruth Anne was able to get Jonah to a rudimentary level of basic bookkeeping tasks sufficient for writing receipts for the water customers.

Jonah had a rough start at the water company office. He made lots of mistakes, but the customers loved him. He knew almost all the water consumers, and they enjoyed coming into the office to pay their water bills and chat with Jonah about the early days of California mining.

A bonus of the job was that there was a saloon two doors down from the water company office. Jonah swore to Caleb that he would only drink after closing the office each day.

Ruth Anne talked to Alma about getting Jonah a permanent room at the American Hotel. Alma was able to fix a small room on the ground floor that had been used as storage space. The little room was cramped, but Jonah proclaimed it was perfect and much warmer than his draughty cabin up by Carrolton.

Now Jonah was all set with a new job and place to live. He could hobble the couple blocks from the American Hotel to the Valley Springs Water Company office on Davis Street in Quartz Hill six days a week. He could drink and chew his tobacco. And Ruth Anne was ecstatic that Jonah was out of her house. He was a nice man, but his incessant chatting about anything and everything was annoying to Ruth Anne, who found silence to be sacred.

Now, Ruth Anne moved past the front counter of the water company's office and back to Caleb's office. It was discomforting to see Caleb behind a desk, reading through a report on the possibility of extending the water ditch to Sacramento. While he liked to read, he found dry engineering reports tedious going. Behind a desk in an office was not Caleb's natural environment.

"Caleb, I thought you might like to see this story on Sheriff Royster," she said, as she handed him the newspaper with the details of the crime and conviction. "Hmm, at least he was convicted of something. It was bound to happen when you are a crook at heart," Caleb replied.

Ruth Anne was disappointed that Caleb did not seem to find as much joy in Royster's downfall as she did. While Caleb did not attend church often, he always seemed to be the better Christian than she, in that he resisted the temptation to gloat over others' misfortunes.

"I'm going over the Lawson's Feed Store to order more feed for the cattle. Is there anything else you need?" asked Ruth Anne. "No, I think you have it covered," Caleb replied, as he looked at the engineering drawings for pipeline over the river.

"Oh, and I'll probably order the first batch of chicks," Ruth Anne added. Caleb looked up at her, smiled, and nodded his head in agreement.

She left the office in a conflicted emotional state. On one hand, she had enjoyed seeing Caleb during the day, however brief it might be. On the other hand, she did not like that this superintendent's job absorbed so much of Caleb's attention and made him so tired. Ruth Anne knew the Valley Springs Water Company was going through a difficult financial period. Water sales were down, and maintenance costs were up. It was a constant struggle for Caleb to keep the water ditch operations in the black.

It was Ruth Anne's idea to start raising chickens, both for eggs and as broilers. Caleb agreed to build a chicken coop and fence in part of the side yard where the chickens could forage during the day.

Ruth Anne was not a cattle enthusiast. The animals were big, pooped everywhere, and trampled the wildflowers. Ruth Anne had never raised chickens. But she had been reading some books from the library and had decided that, even if she only sold eggs, the investment would pay for itself in a couple of years.

Within a couple of months, Ruth Anne had chickens running all over the place. She began to value the slow movements of cows. Except for young calves, cattle were not subject to the predation of the coyotes, bob cats and mountain lions that haunted their surroundings. Ruth Anne estimated that she had lost half her chickens to a local coyote that was now eating better than she and Caleb.

That is when Ruth Anne learned to shoot Caleb's shotgun. The first blast, under Caleb's watchful eye, knocked Ruth Anne on her butt. "I told you to put your right foot behind you for stability," Caleb said, shaking his head.

Fortunately, it was only a single shot gun.

Ruth Anne broke the gun apart as Caleb had taught her, took out the spent cartridge, and put in a new round. She steadied herself, pulled the trigger – and boom – the tin can went flying, and a cloud of dirt was kicked up by pellets.

Ruth Anne looked at Caleb for his approval. "Maybe not a dead coyote with that shot, but you scared the hell out of him enough to keep him away," laughed Caleb.

Close was good enough for Ruth Anne. She looked out over the valley on a warm autumn evening. A high, thin layer of clouds was slowly moving from the coast to cover the valley. The setting sun lit up the underside of the clouds in brilliant colors of red and orange. Ruth Anne wondered if Boyton was looking at the same sunset.

14 California Water

Caleb was in high spirits the next day, as he was not going to the office. Instead, he and several of the other Valley Springs Water Company men, along with a civil engineer, were heading up to Bretton Falls to inspect one of the wooden flumes. The flume had been partially rebuilt and strengthened several years earlier. In order to strengthen the flume, they had been forced to reduce the carrying capacity within the flume as it crossed the deep and wide New Wales Creek ravine.

The rebuilt flume had now become a pinch point for the ditch flow. Quartz Hill needed more water for the railroad, farmers, and a new prison that was slated to be built in the next year. The wooden flume over New Wales creek was over 200 yards in length and soared over 80 feet above the creek at its highest point. Built entirely of wooden timbers and milled lumber, the flume was a sight to see deep in the river canyon. It was also prone to leaks, and repairing such a structure so far off the ground was challenging.

Caleb and the work crew arrived at the flume on a cool fall afternoon. It had rained the night before. The flow in the flume had been reduced as the shorter, cooler days caused the demand for the water to drop. There was one small leak in the flume, creating a continuous stream of water that splashed down the 8-inch diameter timbers supporting the structure.

It was possible to walk across the top of the flume, as there were a series of 1" x 6" boards spaced a couple of inches apart. Caleb and the civil engineer, Lionel Simmons, walked from the earthen ditch, over the concrete transition to the flume, and across the top boards to inspect the leak. Both men dropped to their knees to examine the side boards to determine where the leak was coming from and whether it had weakened the large support timbers.

The crew below saw both men stand up as they discussed the state of the flume and if it could be enlarged or entirely rebuilt. Simmons turned and began walking back, while Caleb, standing directly in the middle of span remained focused on something he saw beneath the top boards. With no warning, a crack sounded, as one of the timbers on the river side of the flume snapped. The entire structure began to collapse, breaking mid-span.

Simmons was able to run over to the hillside and jump off the flume as it tore away from its concrete connections on either end. Caleb had nowhere to run. He dropped straight down with the flume as it crumpled into a heap of lumber. Even though the flume was only running half full, water from both ends of the long flume cascaded on top of Caleb's body as he lay soundless beneath broken timbers and boards.

The work crew raced over to Caleb, calling his name. There was no response. The wet lumber was all wedged together after the collapse, like match sticks randomly dumped into a can. Try as they might, the men were unable to lift the big timbers encasing Caleb. They brought over horses and used their strength to move some of the largest timbers.

It would take more than an hour to move enough of the lumber to get to Caleb and pull him out of the collapsed flume. He was dead. The men stood around in shock. They wrapped up his body in preparation for the long trek back to Quartz Hill.

Jonah had one of the men drive him out to Willowdale to give Ruth Anne the devastating news. She was in the kitchen canning the last of the tomatoes from the garden as the men pulled up in the wagon. She received the news from Jonah without saying a word. She sat down, and her mind simply failed to comprehend the situation. Caleb gone, Caleb dead, Caleb gone, Caleb dead, what did you say? Caleb gone, Caleb dead, Caleb gone.

Ruth Anne walked outside as Jonah watched her from the back door. She went over to the large valley oak. The trunk was so large she could not get her arms around it. She hugged the tree and began to cry, "Oh Caleb, no, you can't leave, it's not time, it's not time. I'm alone, I need you, come home, Caleb, come home." Ruth Anne slouched down to the ground, sitting underneath the spreading branches of the big valley oak, as chickens walked around her clucking and staring. Ruth Anne stared at the dirt.

Caleb's death was a tragedy Ruth Anne had never contemplated as she sat in the dirt staring across the valley. The water ditch was responsible for the two most seminal events in her life. The water ditch had brought Boyton into her life, and now it had taken away her primary reason for waking up every morning, Caleb. Water brought life into the world and cruelly took it away, she thought. She felt ambivalent about whether she would remain in California now. Her prospects for a mediocre life, let alone one filled with any sort of happiness, seemed very dim.

Alma Gosseau came up to Willowdale the next day to help Ruth Anne cope. After all, Ruth Anne had been there for her and her family when Auturo died. Now it was Alma's turn to support the one person she qualified as a friend in California.

As the days passed, Ruth Anne watched as Alma experimented with making puffy pastries with thinly rolled bread dough. Each iteration of the pastry was worse than the first, nevertheless the two women enjoyed eating the failures with tea, and sometimes over wine, a small indulgence that brought Ruth Anne some small comfort.

Father Joseph Kearney of the Episcopal Church in Quartz Hill came out several times to Willowdale to review plans for the funeral and burial service for Caleb. He also helped craft the obituary story of Caleb's life that ran in the local newspaper. The funeral at the Episcopal church was standing room only. Ruth Anne was dismayed at how many people had traveled to Quartz Hill to pay their respects to Caleb.

At the cemetery above Quartz Hill, Ruth Anne watched emotionlessly as Caleb's coffin was lowered into the ground. All she could think was that she wanted to crawl into that hole with Caleb's body and die next to him. It would take serval weeks before the headstone was ready. Ruth Anne wanted a granite headstone, as she wanted Caleb to be remembered as a man who was as strong as granite.

The monument company charged with engraving the headstone thought Ruth Anne had gotten the inscription wrong. They sent word to her and requested she review what was to be carved into the granite before they began. She stopped by the monument company, conveniently located next to the cemetery, and confirmed the text they had was correct.

Caleb Green Gibbons, Husband of Ruth Anne, Father of Boyton

Most people did not know or remember Boyton. Ruth Anne had never forgotten Boyton, and she knew Caleb had not either. She did not know if she would ever see Boyton again. If, perhaps after she was dead, Boyton returned and visited the cemetery, at least he would know that someone had considered himself his father, and that he was someone's son.

After Caleb's death, Ruth Anne kept to herself, only occasionally seeing Alma at Quartz Hill. Ruth Anne never had an active social life beyond travels with Caleb and church services. She stopped traveling to Sacramento on the train. If she could not source something for the ranch or house in Quartz Hill, she usually did without it. She was neither happy nor sad. She was just existing.

Thomas Laughlin still worked as her ranch hand at Willowdale, although she had disposed of most of the cattle by then. Her focus was on the chickens. Ruth Anne and Thomas would gather the eggs in the morning, and he would make deliveries to the American Hotel, restaurants, and homes on a route through Quartz Hill. With Caleb's savings, dividends from Caleb's Valley Springs Water Company stock, and the little income from her egg business, Ruth Anne would be able to keep the Willowdale ranch. She recoiled at the thought of having to move to Quartz Hill.

Deer season had arrived, and Thomas had gone hunting with his father up in the mountains, so she was on her own with the chores. Ruth Anne was making the egg deliveries in the carriage, which she had modified with extra springs for a smoother ride to keep the eggs from bouncing and breaking. She had just finished dropping off the eggs to Alma and was walking back to the carriage when she heard her name called, "Ruth Anne, Ruth Anne Gibbons."

Ruth Anne turned around and saw a woman who looked familiar.

"Mrs. Gibbons, I'm not sure if you remember me, I'm Miss Anna Doolittle," the woman said. "I was the schoolteacher down at Rockrose school."

Ruth Anne remembered Miss Doolittle. She remembered how Miss Doolittle had humiliated her by refusing to allow Boyton to attend the school that Caleb had helped build. Ruth Anne was not sure she wanted to engage in any conversation with Miss Doolittle.

"I'm now the head schoolteacher at Quartz Hill, and I have a situation," Anna said. "I saw you….my condolences on the death of your husband... and I thought maybe you might have an idea on how to help one of my students," said Anna.

"I'm sorry," said Ruth Anne, "I'm not a teacher, and I don't tutor students."

"It's not about tutoring," Anna interrupted. "I have a student, a young woman really, who is being abused by her father, and she needs someplace to live until she makes plans to get out of the area, away from him."

Ruth Anne was not sure whether to feel insulted or flattered. She did not know if Miss Doolittle viewed the widow Gibbons as a warehouse for neglected and orphaned children, like Boyton, or if she was seeking out Ruth Anne because she believed Ruth Anne had a maternal instinct to protect children. "Okay, continue," said Ruth Anne.

Miss Doolittle explained that Isabella Roen was the daughter of William Roen. Isabella's mother had died 10 years ago, and at a very young age Isabella began taking care of her father. Isabella cooked the meals, washed the clothes, and tried to keep the shack they inhabited in order. William was an alcoholic who spent more time drinking than working. Isabella, after her chores were done and William was asleep, would sneak off to Miss Doolittle's classroom.

Isabella liked school. William Roen thought school was a waste of time, as he had never attended school back in Spain. Miss Doolittle visited the Roen shack down by the river in an effort to convince William to allow Isabella to attend school, at least part-time.

Miss Doolittle's visit, a woman telling William how to raise his daughter, enraged him. He started to beat Isabella whenever he found out she had snuck off to school. The last beating had resulted in a black eye.

Miss Doolittle pointed to a thin young lady with pale white skin and long dark hair cowering behind her. The girl's black eye, swollen and red, had clearly been inflicted by a fist punching her face.

Ruth Anne dismissed whatever concerns she had about Anna Doolittle's intentions and walked over to Isabella. "Isabella, I'm Ruth Anne Gibbons," Ruth Anne said. "Yes, I know who you are, your husband died last year," Isabella replied.

"Correct," said Ruth Anne. "Now, climb into the carriage, and I'll take you back to the ranch and get you cleaned up and get you some supper," instructed Ruth Anne. As Ruth Anne climbed onto the bench seat beside the girl, she grabbed the reins of the horse, nodded to Miss Doolittle, and snapped the reins on the back of the horse to get him to start pulling the carriage forward.

She made for a striking image as she drove away with the girl. Boyton's old felt hat with the wide brim, while a little small, was perfect for keeping the sun out of Ruth Anne's eyes. She put her hair in a bun a little lower on her neck so the hat would fit snug. The woman who once felt so insecure over the image reflected to her in the mirror at the Eagle Hotel in Sacramento now dismissed any concerns of feminine beauty. Alma Gosseau would often needle Ruth Anne about her work clothes and how they could use some feminine touches.

Ruth Anne's daily uniform was now Boyton's old hat, gloves, loose skirt over her pantaloons, and work boots. She would flinch slightly when she considered how much she resembled the chicken-killing woman. It had taken 20 years, but she now understood that the woman, with her rough exterior and curt responses to questions, had been in survival mode. Ruth Anne's calloused hands and graying hair were her own badge of survival in a harsh environment. She was no longer a mother or wife. She had to be a survivor.

Ruth Anne drove the carriage back to Willowdale and got Isabella set up in a room at her house. Quartz Hill seemed unsafe for Isabella while her father lurked around trying to find her in Quartz Hill.

"Isabella," Ruth Anne said, "until we find you suitable accommodations, I'll work with you to continue your schooling. It is important that a young woman know how to read and write. The Bible is all scribbles unless you can read."

Isabella welcomed the attention and the warm house that did not allow the wind and rain in from the sideboards, like the shack she had lived in with her father. The two women got along splendidly. Ruth Anne welcomed the company and conversation over supper each day.

On the third day after Isabella's arrival, Ruth Anne heard a loud pounding on the front door. Concerned, she rushed to open the door, only to be greeted by a drunk and slovenly William Roen.

Isabella's father bellowed, "Give me my daughter back! You just can't take a child without permission. She is mine. She needs to be home and cook for me! Since her mother died, she is all I have."

Ruth Anne looked at the poor excuse for a man, or father, and said, "Why do you beat your daughter and not let her attend school?"

Reeking of alcohol, William steadied himself and replied, "That ain't none of your business. She's mine, do you hear me!"

Although she knew it was useless to try to calmly converse with the drunken fellow, Ruth Anne persisted. "Isabella is a young woman, 16 years of age, who can make her own decisions on where she would like to live."

"No, she can't," Roen bellowed. "She's mine. Now get her out here so I can take her back home to where she belongs."

Home sounded like quite the embellishment for Roen's shack by the river. "As you request, sir," replied Ruth Anne. "Go around to the side door, please." As Ruth Anne closed the door, she could see William stumble his way down the granite steps and walk around to the side of the house.

When Ruth Anne opened the side door from the kitchen, William could see she was holding a shotgun, pointed at his belly.

"You listen to me, Mr. Roen," Ruth Anne said grimly. "You will not ever touch this child. You will not take her from this house. She will leave here when she is good and ready, and I pray to God it is not back to you. Now, unless you would like to see how I banish the coyotes from stealing my chickens with this shotgun, I strongly suggest you leave my property. Do you understand me?"

William stumbled backward and fell on his butt, never losing eye contact with Ruth Anne. "You are a crazy lady! I'm going to get the constable and have you arrested," sputtered William. "You do that Mr. Roen. The constable knows where to find me," said Ruth Anne. William Roen broke into a trot back to the road and down to Quartz Hill.

When Ruth Anne turned around, Isabella was staring at her. "Do you think he'll come back?" asked Isabella. "Oh, he might come back, but he won't leave unless it is in a box. Now, where were we? You were practicing your penmanship. Let's see how you wrote out that last sentence."

The next day, Constable Daley of Quartz Hill arrived at Ruth Anne's door.

"Mrs. Gibbons, I've had an accusation that you pointed a shotgun at William Roen. Is that true?" asked Constable Daley. "I suppose I did, sir," answered Ruth Anne. "He further states that you threatened to shoot him," continued Constable Daley. "I suppose I did, sir," answered Ruth Anne.

"Mrs. Gibbons, you can't threaten people with guns," stated Constable Daley.

Ruth Anne began, "Let's review the facts, Constable. First, William Roen came on to my property, drunk, stinking of alcohol. Second, he was demanding that his daughter, who he beats frequently – you can see the black eye for yourself – should return to his hovel by the river. Third, this young woman is 16 years old, and unless I am mistaken, that is the age at which she can make her own decisions on where she chooses to reside."

"I will not dispute the facts, Mrs. Gibbons. All I'm requesting is that you don't threaten people with your shotgun," replied the constable.

"Fair enough. I will not threaten William Roen as long as you keep him away from me and that girl," offered Ruth Anne.

"You have a deal, Mrs. Gibbons. I know you. I know William Roen," said Constable Daly. "It is an unpleasant situation. I'd rather arrest him for public drunkenness than come up here and have to take him away in a bag. I think I can make that clear to William.

"Good day, ma'am. Oh, can you drop a couple of your broilers off at the office? The missus thinks your chickens taste the best.

"It would be my pleasure, have a good ride back to town," Ruth Anne concluded.

From that incident forward, Ruth Anne became known as a fierce matron who would take in and care for neglected children. She was not running an underground railroad like George and Caroline Bailey did. She felt too old to care for orphaned babies. But if there was a child whose parent or parents had died or were incarcerated, or who had been abused, Ruth Anne would take the child in.

Ruth Anne even became friends with the schoolteacher, Anna Doolittle. The teacher would bring her school supplies for children who could not attend the Quartz Hill school on a regular basis. Ruth Anne would tutor the children and, after their homework was finished, allowed them to run around the ranch, chase the chickens, or work in the garden. She would stand on the porch and watch the children playing in the garden, and her thoughts would return to those days in Carrolton when she was the mother to her own son.

15 The Chinese Man

A well-dressed Chinese man stepped off the train at Quartz Hill. He was wearing a narrow-brim, black felt hat, pinched on the crown, and wire rim glasses. The thin moustache above his lip made him look older than he was. The locals could tell he was not from the interior of the valley because of the wool trousers, vest and coat he wore.

The Chinese man walked to the depot and asked when the next stagecoach left for Carrolton. "Stagecoach has not run to Carrolton for years," the attendant told him. "They can rent you a horse over at the livery stable at the end of town," the attendant added. The Chinese man started walking in the direction of the stables.

Of all the skills he had learnt in California, riding a horse had not been part of the curriculum. The Chinese man inquired with the ostler about transportation out to Carrolton. A horse and buggy were settled upon. The man told him the cost would be $2 in advance, gold coin only, no greenbacks, and then directed him to sign his name on the rental register.

The Chinese man had come to the proverbial fork in the road pertaining to his identity. Did he sign his name Wen Ho, which was the name on his official documents, or Boyton Gibbons? He opted for Boyton. Wen Ho lived in San Francisco. Boyton Gibbons was from Carrolton.

Boyton had no problems with the horse and buggy, as he had learned how to successfully navigate similar four-wheeled wagons through the narrow streets of San Francisco's Chinatown. He travelled over the dirt road toward Carrolton looking at all the old landmarks and noting how they had not changed so terribly much.

What was significantly different from his memories was the lack of people. Most of the passing countryside was now either pasture or fruit trees. Cattle outnumbered people. He saw no Chinese men or women working alongside the road. He went over Saddle Gap, where he could make out the overgrown remnants of the Chinese mining maze of trenches. The Valley Springs Water ditch was still flowing, but no one was mining.

The road into Carrolton was still white from the crushed quartz of the surrounding granite hills. Boyton had forgotten how much he missed the crunching sound under foot or wagon wheel. It was a unique sound. He had always been able to tell when his Pa had returned home from the grinding sound beneath the wagon wheels.

The bright, sandy road was now the main feature of Carrolton. Most of the town's buildings had been razed or destroyed by fire years earlier. Boyton was disoriented, having been away from Carrolton for so long and with so many of the buildings missing. He did not know where his old house was.

Boyton saw a ditch tender walking along the water canal and asked him where the Gibbons' house might be located. "Gibbons? Hmmm, you mean the old Valley Springs house?" answered the ditch tender. "I suppose so," replied Boyton. "It's down the road next to the big oak tree. I wanted to move into it, but the company said it was rotten and they were going to tear it down," said the ditch tender.

Boyton located the old house and could see it needed to be torn down. The roof was sagging, and the siding was pickled with dry rot. Boyton peered through the dusty windows, but there was not much inside. He twisted the loose and floppy door handle, opened the front door, and went inside.

The cast iron stove was still in place, but the stove pipe had become disconnected from the flashing to the exterior of the house. It looked like rats had made a nest in the stove. A thick layer of dust, sand, and mouse droppings coated every surface. The only furniture that remained was a table and two chairs.

He walked into his old room, which was similarly empty of any furniture. When Boyton tried to push the old bedroom door all the way open, it hit something. Craning to look behind the door, he could see a filthy sheet, gnawed by mice, and stained by their urine, thrown over something. He pulled the filthy sheet away to reveal the old Ogee clock.

He picked up the clock and carried it to the table in the front room. Its weights were missing, the walnut veneer was peeling off, and one of its door hinges was broken. It smelled like an old barn. Boyton smiled at the project clock and carried it with him to the buggy.

Then he took the road to the wire rope suspension bridge, still in place. As his buggy pulled up to the approach to the bridge, he could see an old man, who was the toll taker, rolling a cigarette. Boyton pulled the buggy onto the landing in front of the toll booth.

The man looked up at him and, with a grin, said, "Shhh, don't tell anyone. I'm not supposed to smoke, they say I'll start a fire." The old man burst out in a high-pitched cackle of a laugh.

The man was wearing a weather-beaten old hat. His ponytail dropped over his shirt collar to the middle of his back. His dark face was thick with deep lines. The knuckles of his hands were swollen, making his fingers look like knotted tree roots. He was obviously an Indian.

"It's 10 cents if you want to walk over the bridge and two bits if you take the horse and buggy," the bridge tender informed Boyton.

"Is the Cathedral Cave still open?" inquired Boyton.

"Cathedral Cave, you mean the Creator's Cave. The white man gave it that church name before they destroyed it," replied the Indian man.

The Indian man could see that Boyton was Chinese and took the opportunity, based on his assumption that this Chinese man in front of him would hold the same perspective, to infuse his comments with his opinions on the white man in California. The Indian man told Boyton his name was Sue Crowfoot. Sue made sure that Boyton knew that he was not from the Crowfoot tribe, that was just his name. He was from the Maidu people.

"They shut the cave down to tourists years ago," explained Sue. "The limestone mine got too close, and it busted through one of the walls. They say it is unsafe to go into it now. But I know plenty of people who go in and desecrate the place. It is so sad. No respect for sacred ground."

Boyton could tell from Sue's talk and vocabulary that he must have had some modicum of education. "Are you from around here?" asked Boyton. "I was born here along the river," Sue replied. "We had our villages and way of life until the gold seekers came. I washed some of the yellow dust and nuggets for some of the first miners." Sue shook his head.

Boyton could tell Sue wanted to talk about his life experience, so he let him continue.

"The white men said we were stealing their chickens," Sue continued. "Well, you have to eat, and they would not let us fish in the river. The white man did not like us. They came with guns and horses and made us move to Tehama, a reservation they called Nome Lackee. They held us captive. We were prisoners in our own country.

"It was a lot of flat land, and the white man wanted us to push plows through the dirt. No rivers, no fish, nothing. The white man is not that smart. I watched them. I started to dress like the white man. I went to some of their classes about reading, writing, and their religion. I was there several years, watching the white man.

"Then one day, I tucked my hair - I never cut my hair like the white men – I tuck it under my hat. I looked like a white man with boots, pants, shirt, hat, and I just walked away from Nome Lackee," Sue said, bursting out with laughter. "I just walked away, no one stop me. They thought I was a white man."

After an extending period of laughing, he went over to his chair, picked up a bottle and took a swig of the amber-colored contents, then continued.

"I walked for days, weeks, months. I stay away from people, kept to the hard deer trails. Sometimes, if I was near a camp, I'd steal a little food. A man's got to eat," Sue said in defense of his thievery. "From afar, all the white people think I'm white like them.

"Finally, I get to the river canyon. I'm starving. I see the white-headed eagle flying over the river. He dives down and grabs a big salmon, huge fish. I think, that bird eats good tonight. Then the bird flies over my head and drops the big fish. It lands right at my feet. The eagle says, welcome home, Sue.

"I set up camp up in the ravine, hidden from people, except for some lions and bears. They don't bother me. Once, I'm really hungry, and I know the toll taker sometimes leaves some food in the little toll house. When the toll man walks up the hill, I go down to see if there is any food.

"I come around the corner of the toll house, and there is big wagon there, and the man shouts, 'Where you been? Here, take the money and open the gate so I can pass.'

"I seen how the toll man let the crossing arm go up in the air. So, I do it. Then before I can leave, another wagon comes along. Again, I take the toll, open the gate.

"I do this all day long. Then a carriage pulls up and shouts, 'Where's Billy?' I don't know, I tell the man. Then he says, 'Who are you?'" Sue began laughing and coughing so hard Boyton thought he might die.

"So, this dumb old Indian says, 'I'm Sue, who are you?' It was the owner of the bridge," said Sue, gasping in laughter at his own joke and the irony of the situation. "Then I think, I'm a dead Indian. So, I run over to the man in the carriage and give him all the money I had collected. 'What's this?' he says. I tell him it was the toll money.

"Then the white man with the funny round hat says, 'Billy is gone, you are here, so I guess you have a job if you want it.' I think to myself, it is one of those Christian miracles.

"I don't understand," asked Boyton. "How was that a miracle?"

"It was the first and only honest white man I ever met," exclaimed Sue, as he laughed and repeated the phrase 'honest white man' over and over again.

After a final fit of laughter, Sue was able to compose himself and asked,

"You going up to Coleville or one of the mines?" "No, I think I'll turn around and head back to Quartz Hill before dark," replied Boyton. "You be careful," Sue said. Then Sue added, "Lions and bears won't hurt you, but those white men, they are snakes, and they will bite you as sure as the sun shines."

Up until Sue's last admonition, Boyton had generally agreed with Sue's point of view toward California. But it was two white people who had saved him, fed him, raised him, and then saved him again. Not all white people were bad, Boyton thought, just like not all Chinese people are evil.

Boyton arrived back in Quartz Hill and returned the horse and buggy to the livery stable. As he walked through town, he noted how it had not changed much since he last saw it. There were a few new brick buildings, but most of the weather-beaten wood structures remained. Most of the people he encountered seemed old. There were a few children roaming around.

While Sacramento continued to grow and expand, Quartz Hill was locked in the past. The big Pacific Railroad shot from Sacramento to Flagston and over the Sierra Nevada Mountain range. The new railroad had bypassed Quartz Hill and snubbed its growth quickly. Now, it was a sad little town, Boyton thought, but at least it had not suffered the same fate as Carrolton.

Boyton passed a storefront window that was stenciled with cracked and peeling painted words: Valley Springs Water Co. He stepped through the door to see a drowsy old man sitting at a desk. "What can I do you for?" asked the man.

"Well, I'm looking for Caleb and Ruth Anne Gibbons," replied Boyton. "Well, you can visit Caleb over at the cemetery, been dead, oh, five years now, I reckon," said the man.

Boyton looked down. He was crushed. Caleb was dead, and no one had ever told him.

"Widow Gibbons is over at the Willowdale Ranch. Who are you?" quizzed the man. "Oh, I'm Boyton, Boyton Gibbons," was the muted reply.

"Boyton?! You don't say. I found you! I'm Jonah. Oh damn, I watched you grow up until those Highbinders tore you away from Ruth Anne and Caleb," Jonah said excitedly. "That broke Ruth Anne's spirit. She was never the same after you left. We all figured you were dead or something. But look at you, all dressed up, come back to the old town to see your Ma."

Boyton wondered if Jonah had always been this annoying in tone. "Well, it's a little late to travel out to, where did you say she lived, Willow…?" asked Boyton.

"Willowdale Ranch, you're gonna take the road out of town, but instead of taking the road up Saddle Gap, veer right, the Deer Valley Road, they call it, a couple of miles, and the big ranch house will be on your right," explained Jonah.

"Thank you, Jonah, I'm sure we'll bump into one another again," Boyton said. "Right now, I'm going to find a room for the night."

"Give my best to the widow, she's a fine lady. Good seeing you, Boyton, good night," offered Jonah, as Boyton closed the door and debated on whether to head to the cemetery or find a room. The sun had already set, so he decided his best option was to sleep and process all that he had learned.

In the morning, Boyton secured a seat on a stagecoach travelling to Lake Tahoe. Boyton asked the driver if he knew where the Willowdale Ranch was on Deer Valley Road. "Oh sure, the Gibbon's place, right next to the road." Boyton asked if the driver could stop there because that was his destination. "Yes, I can stop and let you off. Just know that the widow Gibbons don't take to strangers on her property," the driver said. The young stagecoach driver added, "She ran the last guy off her land by pointing a shotgun at him."

It seemed improbable to Boyton that his mother, a timid soul, would point a gun at anything. She did not even know how to shoot a gun, to the best of his knowledge. Nonetheless, Boyton was still a little apprehensive as he left the stagecoach with his large trunk and started walking up to the Willowdale house. With a slight hesitation, Boyton gently knocked on the front door of a large house that did not resemble the Carrolton cabin he grew up in.

As the front door opened, Boyton was hit with the smell of baking bread, cinnamon, and honey. Surprised, he assumed he had the wrong house, as his mother never would have cooked with such spices and sweetness. In front of him was a woman in a striped dress of white and deep blue -- another indication he had the wrong house, as his mother had always worn solid gray, black, or blue dresses.

"Could it be Boyton?" the woman said. "Ma," replied Boyton.

Then a river of tears flowed, the volume of which could fill the Valley Springs water ditch. "Oh, son, you are back, you are alive, praise the good Lord!" Ruth Anne cried. "I knew you were safe, but I never knew if you would return.

"Oh, son, I'm sorry I have to tell you, your Pa died," sighed Ruth Anne. "I know, Jonah told me," Boyton replied.

Boyton stepped into the hallway with his big trunk and looked around in amazement at the fine home with polished hardwood floors and carpeted staircase to the second level. "What is that wonderful smell?" he asked. "Oh, that is Katherine experimenting with bread. She wants to be a baker," Ruth Anne replied.

"Katherine? You and Pa had more children?" asked Boyton. "Well, not exactly. It's a long story that I'll explain after we catch up. First, tell me about you, my handsome boy in this excellent suit," replied Ruth Anne.

Boyton and Ruth Anne stepped into the parlor, where Boyton immediately spotted the tall case clock in the corner. The distinctive feature of the Ansonia clock with its dark walnut case was the pendulum. Instead of the usual circular brass disc, the Ansonia featured three glass tubes filled with mercury attached to the 3-foot-long pendulum.

The room contained various items with Chinese motifs. There were a few vases, a painting, and figurine set of a Chinese family carved out of jade sitting on the mantel over the fireplace. Boyton felt surprisingly comfortable in the parlor, surrounded by objects familiar to him. Ruth Anne pressed him to tell her everything about his life in San Francisco.

"Sam took me to the Presbyterian House when we arrived," Boyton began. "I could only stay a couple of weeks because it was only for girls, no boys allowed. The woman who ran the house was able to convince Lok Choi to take me in. Lok Choi and his family lived in San Francisco's Chinatown. He had three daughters, and I supposed he thought a young boy could help with his business.

"Lok Choi and his wife were good people. He insisted I attend Chinese school when I was not at his store. He imported different Chinese goods, like furniture, plates, bowls, stuff like that. He also had a wagon that he would rent out to other Chinese people to pick up goods down at the wharf or vegetables from the farms south of the city.

"I didn't like Chinese school because I did not know any Chinese. I only spoke English, like you taught me Ma. I did learn to speak Chinese, well Cantonese, and I can read some stuff, but I could never understand how to write it properly. Anyhow, once I learned to understand and speak Chinese, Lok Choi and the other merchants in Chinatown used me as a translator.

"I would read English and translate that into Chinese, as best I could, so the Chinese store owners could understand the documents they received from the city or an order they received from an American. Sometimes they would pay me for the translations. When someone from the city came to collect taxes, or the police came about a problem, I would help make the translation, so everybody understood what was being asked.

"When I got older and could manage the mule and wagon, Lok Choi would send me down to the Chinese farmers south of the city to pick up loads of different vegetables. I would drive the wagon across Market Street, around Rincon Hill, past the old mission and then along the railroad tracks to where the farms were.

Boyton was rattling on about all the different buildings and landmarks in San Francisco with which Ruth Anne was completely unfamiliar. She did not care. She just wanted him to keep talking. She would ask questions later.

"The old mule was stubborn. Sometimes he would just stop in the middle of the road," Boyton continued. "He wouldn't move. I'd whip his hind quarters, and nothing. I just had to wait; it was so embarrassing. Then the mule would start pulling the cart again like nothing had happened!

"One time I was driving the wagon along the road, and out of this shack next to the railroad tracks two white men came out and started calling me names. Chinese people are often insulted by white men for no reason. They think it is fun. Chinese people must be careful around some of the white men.

"Anyhow, the two men came over to the wagon; it was more of a large cart. I only had a small knife, and there was no way I could fight the two old, drunk men. They started picking up the vegetables like they wanted to eat them or something. They were talking nonsense.

"I finally said, 'Stop touching the produce unless you pay for it.' Both men looked at me, and I figured I was a dead man. One man said, 'You talk like an American, where you from?' I told them I grew up in Carrolton, and my mother and father were white. 'Carrolton?' The man said, 'I mined up there along the river back in '52. Is it still there? Is old Joe McDonald still on the river?'

"We had quite a long conversation about the river towns, mining, and the water ditch that one of the men had helped build. Then they said, 'Have a good trip back to Chinatown,' and went back to their little shack. I guess they figured I was one of them or something. But they never hassled me again on my trips out to the farm.

"Lok Choi knew a man named Hans Goldfein. Hans would hire Lok Choi's wagon to haul up some of the stuff he imported from Europe to sell in his store. Mr. Goldfein said he was from Poland, and he spoke a weird language he called Yidith or Yiddish. I could never figure it out. Sometimes after I unloaded Mr. Goldfein's crates from the wagon, he would keep me on and pay me to take the stuff out of the crates or sweep the floor.

"Mr. Goldfein said he left Poland because they did not like Jews over there, and he was a Jew. Maybe that's why Mr. Goldfein and Lok Choi got along, because there were a bunch of people who didn't like them. I don't know. Anyhow, as I got older, Lok Choi's wife didn't want me around her daughters anymore. I'm not sure why, I didn't even like her daughters. Maybe I looked too American.

"I had to move out of Lok Choi's place, and Mr. Goldfein said I could stay with him if I worked at his store. Mr. Goldfein also repaired clocks and watches. He could see how fascinated I was with his work. Mr. Goldfein was getting old, and his legs didn't work so well.

"He would have me use my feet to pump the peddle of his lathe. I could get the wheel spinning really fast. He would secure a small piece of round metal in the chuck and then lightly apply a cutting tool to the metal as it spun, powered by my feet.

"Mr. Goldfein would make all sorts of clock parts to repair clocks and some watches that had worn out or were broken. He taught me how to repair all kinds of clocks and watches. When I started, it would take me two weeks to disassemble a clock for repair and put it back together again, usually the wrong way. Mr. Goldfein could do it in a couple of days.

"Oh, I thought I saw Pa one day in Chinatown, when I had walked up there from Mr. Goldfein's shop on California Street. I saw a tall man, wearing a wide brim hat, and he had blue eyes and that reddish beard, with some gray in it."

Ruth Anne sat up straight and looked at Boyton with deep interest.

"I was across the street, and I could not tell if it was Pa or not. The man looked around like he was lost."

"Did you approach him or say anything to him?" Ruth Anne asked.

"No, it's not a good idea for a Chinese man to approach a white man without being spoken to first by the white man," Boyton responded. "Sometimes the men are drunk, and they just stab or shoot you, thinking you are trying to rob them.

"The man went into one of the stores in Chinatown. He was in there for a long time, then he came out with a package and walked away."

"Oh, oh, I think...." Ruth Anne rose from her chair and went over to the fireplace mantel. "I think he bought these little carved jade figurines. Caleb went to San Francisco for a water ditch association meeting right after we moved to Quartz Hill. When he came back, he gave me this little set of a Chinese family. He thought I would like it, and it would remind me of the time we had together as a family. Oh, gosh, he was a wonderful man," Ruth Anne said as she stared at a photo of her and Caleb taken years earlier when they first arrived in California.

"Please, continue," Ruth Anne urged.

"I worked for Mr. Goldfein for over five years. Then, one day, a man brought in a gold pocket watch for repair. I remembered the watch. I don't know if it was the same one, but it had a grapevine around the outside of the cover with a big bunch of grapes in the middle.

"It looked just like the one Mr. Bailey gave me, and he said it was my ticket to freedom. When I saw the watch, I knew that I had to come back to Carrolton and tell you I was alive. I wasn't sure if you would care because I never heard from either you or Pa after I left."

Ruth Anne tried to explain the paranoia she had felt about being followed had she tried to find him in San Francisco. Her fears sounded so silly to her ears when she told him, but at the time it had been all too real. Boyton told her he understood, as he was fearful of returning to Sacramento.

The two were still talking when the tall Ansonia clock began striking midnight on its resonant wire gong. Each strike filled the room with a low humming tone. "Caleb always hated how loud the clock struck the hours. You can hear it all the way up in the attic. I think sounds beautiful," Ruth Anne said. "I think it's a beautiful sound also," Boyton added.

Next morning, the sun streamed through the windows of his room? in a brightness that Boyton thought would blind him. He had grown accustomed to the marine layer of low clouds obscuring the sun on most San Francisco mornings. Now he was back in the valley, where the sun was bright all day long. He hitched the horse to the carriage after breakfast, and then he and Ruth Anne made the journey to the Quartz Hill Cemetery.

Ruth Anne walked Boyton over to Caleb's grave site. "I can't believe he is gone and I didn't get to say goodbye," commented Boyton. "I know," Ruth Anne said. "It seems like only yesterday I saw him at the Valley Springs Water Company office and he was planning to add to the chicken coop for me." "Oh, Ma," exclaimed Boyton as he read Caleb's headstone. "'Father of

Boyton.' Thank you, Ma, that means a lot to me. He was my father, my Pa."

"Do you remember when we went to Quartz Hill to see the train and take the ride into Sacramento?" Boyton asked. "I remember it well," Ruth Anne replied. "You were so excited to see that big steam train up close. You asked so many questions, you drove your Pa and the engineer crazy."

She did not really want to remember that train trip, as it had been the beginning of the end of their family. She changed the topic.

"Oh, do you remember when you got poison oak up at the Cathedral Cave?" Ruth Anne asked. "Oh yeah, I thought Pa was killing me when he threw me the dirt. The itchy rash was the worst. It went on for weeks and weeks," replied Boyton. "We got that awful stuff from Doc Waddle, and we both vomited at the smell of it. Thank goodness for Ah Chee and his herbal remedy," Ruth Anne recalled.

"I remember when Pa let me help skin the deer, and we took some of the meat to the neighbors and to have some smoked. That was the first time Pa let me handle a knife," reminisced Boyton. "You boys were a bloody, filthy mess. I made your Pa take you down to the river for a proper cleaning," added Ruth Anne. They both stood quietly, remembering the family they had so many years ago back in Carrolton.

On the ride back to Willowdale, Ruth Anne asked Boyton whether he was going to stay or return to San Francisco. "I don't know yet. I want to stay, be here with you. I just must find a job or something. I'm not a ranch hand, if you know what I mean," replied Boyton.

"I know, son, you are too smart to work on a ranch or farm forever. What about the clock repair work? Could you do that in Quartz Hill or Sacramento?" asked Ruth Anne.

Boyton suddenly realized that he did not have to return to San Francisco. He did have skills that were in demand in many different towns. The thought of opening a store and clock repair shop was an interesting prospect to Boyton. He needed to give it more consideration.

"Hmm, I had not thought of that possibility, Ma. Let me think about it," Boyton said. "Well, if that is something you want to do, let me know. I have a little money saved to help you out," offered Ruth Anne.

The letter that Boyton wrote had two purposes. First, he had to inform Mr. Goldfein that he would not be returning to his shop anytime soon, if at all. Second, did Mr. Goldfein know where he might obtain a watch maker's lathe and the associated tools to repair clocks? Boyton wrote to Mr. Goldfein that, if the opportunity arose, he planned to open a clock repair shop in Quartz Hill.

In the evenings, Ruth Anne and Boyton would sit on the porch talking as the shadows from the big valley oaks crept across the field. When the sun was touching the coastal range, Ruth Anne would round up the kids and get them into bed. Then she and Boyton would continue to talk late into the evening about politics, religion, history, or the quality of dried fruit offered in Quartz

Hill.

Eventually, Boyton received a reply to his letter to Mr. Goldfein. It came not from Goldfein, but from his lawyers. Mr. Goldfein had died shortly after Boyton had left for Sacramento, an apparent heart attack as he was working the treadle of the lathe. The letter informed Boyton that, after the estate had passed through probate, he could purchase Mr. Goldfein's repair shop tools and inventory.

Within a couple of weeks, Boyton had the contents of Mr. Goldfein's shop sent to Quartz Hill, where he opened a little store repairing watches and clocks, as well as selling similar items. Ruth Anne could once again visit Quartz Hill on her egg delivery route and sit for a spell with Boyton as he worked on the lathe making clock parts. Ruth Anne was happy. On occasion she and Boyton would even venture down to Quartz Hill's Chinatown to see a few of the older Chinese men they knew from Carrolton.

For the next several years, Ruth Anne, Boyton, along with the children in Ruth Anne's care, would forge a non-traditional family. Boyton's clock and watch repair shop became a fixture in Quartz Hill. Ruth Anne busied herself with her egg and broiler business. Both Ruth Anne and Boyton found it rewarding to help the young children who filtered through Willowdale. While Ruth Anne could never be truly happy since the death of Caleb, she felt a sense of contentment with her family in California.

The sky was still dark when Boyton woke. He always rose before dawn, part of his natural rhythm of life ever since he was a boy in Carrolton. He did not need one of those obnoxiously loud alarm clocks he sold at his shop to wake him up in the mornings.

Boyton pulled on a heavy red wool flannel shirt, then pulled up his cotton trousers. He then buttoned the suspenders inside the front and back of the pants and slipped on his shoes. He wondered if he might be mistaken for the prospectors of 30 years ago with his rough clothing. He had commonly seen men dressed in flannel shirts and suspenders like his in the mining district, but those were white men wearing boots.

Boyton walked slowly and cautiously down the staircase and into the kitchen. He did not want to make any noise and wake the children who were still slumbering on this cold autumn morning. He lit the lantern and put some wood in the stove to get the fire roaring.

The glass pitcher on the table was nearly empty, so he picked up the lantern and went outside to fill it with water from the hand pump at the well. As Boyton walked out to the well pump, the water droplets in the heavy fog that had descended were lit up by the light of the lantern. The lantern light only penetrated 10 feet into the fog, creating a glowing cocoon around Boyton.

Back in the kitchen, Boyton filled the kettle with water and put it on the stove to heat. When he had lived in San Francisco, Lok Choi's wife would get up early to make herbal tea for Lok Choi's father, who was dying. That was his only experience, his role model, caring for a dying person.

Boyton carefully measured the herbal tea leaves into a tea pot and poured the hot water in to let the tea steep. He put tea pot, cups, biscuits, and an open jar of jam onto a tray and took it up to Ruth Anne's room. When he entered the room, Ruth Anne was sleeping. He was glad she had fallen asleep because the pain she had been experiencing made sleep elusive for her.

Quietly placing the tray on the bureau dresser, Boyton turned up the lamp. The lamplight revealed how thin and gaunt Ruth Anne had become. He remembered Ruth Anne telling him how she had gone to the Indian camp for help when he was a baby. She had described the starving Indians as being terribly thin, their bones making unnatural angles under their skin.

Ruth Anne was not starving to death. She had some kind of cancer in her abdomen. Her belly was swollen, even as the rest of her body was withering away to skin and bones. Boyton looked at her sleeping face and thought she was still a beautiful woman.

The morning light slowly filled the room. Ruth Anne opened her eyes and saw Boyton in the same chair next to her where he had sat the night before. He was always by her side. She looked out the window and said, "Snow?" "No, fog," Boyton replied. Boyton asked, "Has it ever snowed here?" "Yes, it snowed, it snowed once," Ruth Anne said in a weak voice as she struggled to sit up.

Ruth Anne made a grimacing face, as the pain had returned in her gut. "Here, I have some herbal tea. Ah Chee said he blended it just for you," offered Boyton. "Ah Chee? He was always a nice man. I liked him," replied Ruth Anne. Boyton wanted Ruth Anne to drink the tea, as he had been putting a few drops of laudanum in it to ease her pain. She always felt better after drinking the tea.

They sat together and looked out the window at the foggy morning. The most prominent features in the dense fog were the silhouettes of the arching valley oak limbs and its thick trunk. As the sun rose and the fog began to dissipate, they could see a strange blob of a shadow in the valley oak tree.

The shadow began to rise, and Boyton and Ruth Anne could see it was a hawk. The bird made a quick circle and then dropped down to the ground. For a moment, the bird disappeared within the dry grass. Then it rose, furiously flapping its wings. In its talons they could see the tail of a field mouse.

"Did you see that, Ma? what a catch," Boyton said. "Yes, that hawk has sharp eyes in this fog," Ruth Anne replied. Ruth Anne's eyes and memory were still good. Her body was failing. "You can't see Mount Diablo this morning," Boyton commented. "No devil mountain, today," pushed out Ruth Anne in a raspy, tired voice.

It was Sunday, and Boyton had let the three children under Ruth Anne's care sleep in. He could smell sausages being cooked in the frying pan, which meant that Alma was up and making breakfast. What would Boyton have done without Alma? The aroma of bacon, or sausage, pancakes and all the fixins of a frontier breakfast created good feelings for Boyton. He may have been Chinese by birth, but he was a meat and potatoes type of guy.

Boyton stood up and told Ruth Anne, "I'll get the kids up and have them do the chores, and I'll bring you up some breakfast." "Okay, I'll get up in a minute and get the chickens fed. I want to work in the garden today," replied Ruth Anne.

Boyton laughed to himself. Every morning for the last three weeks Ruth Anne had said she was going to get dressed and work outside. He admired her spirit, but the truth was, she was so weak, she could barely sit up in bed.

The last three years had been the happiest for her and Boyton, as they forged a diverse family at Willowdale. Three children now lived at Willowdale, four if you considered Boyton, which Ruth Anne did. Boyton would always be Ruth Anne's little Chinese boy.

James and Todd were 10-year-old brothers whose parents had been tragically killed in a stagecoach accident. Judith was 14 years old. Her mother had been arrested. They were all living under Ruth Anne's roof until they were adopted, or a family reunification could take place.

Judith was helping Alma make breakfast as Boyton entered the kitchen. James and Todd had gone outside to feed the chickens but had found other activities to occupy their time. Boyton went out to supervise the boys. It had taken Boyton several weeks to understand why Ruth Anne was caring for these orphaned children. Why did she never want to let go of any child unless it was into the arms of a loving parent? That was his Ma.

Boyton and the boys were working to fix a broken latch on the chicken coop when Alma suddenly appeared and said, "Boyton." The look on Alma's face told Boyton all he needed to know.

He ran into the house, up the stairs, and into Ruth Anne's room. She looked like she was sleeping, but she had stopped breathing. She had died.

Boyton buried his face in Ruth Anne's nightgown and cried, "Oh, Ma, I just wanted one more day with you, just one more day. I love you, Ma. I'll always love you. I'm here with you, Ma. I'll always be your little boy. I love you. Goodbye, Ma, goodbye. I love you."

When Boyton walked downstairs, his eyes red from crying and tears streaming down his face, Alma came up and gave him a hug. Then the other children hugged Boyton one by one, until they were all hugging and crying together.

The headstone Boyton arranged for Ruth Anne was made of granite just like Caleb's. Ruth Anne was buried next to Caleb in a family plot at the Quartz Hill cemetery. Inscribed on Ruth Anne's headstone was "Beloved Wife of Caleb, Loving Mother to Boyton."

ABOUT THE AUTHOR

Kevin Knauss lives in Granite Bay, California, where he researches and studies the history of the American River. His focus is on the Gold Rush, water projects along the forks of the American River, and the people in the region in the 19th century. *The Chinese Boy* is his first work of fiction.

Other books by Kevin Knauss include.

- Hidden History Beneath Folsom Lake
- Benjamin Norton Bugbey, Sacramento's Champagne King
- Amos P. Catlin, The Whig Who Put Sacramento on the Map

www.ingramcontent.com/pod-product-compliance
Lightning Source LLC
LaVergne TN
LVHW010620100826
845148LV00014B/3047

* 9 7 9 8 9 8 5 1 9 4 2 0 3 *